Tampa Review

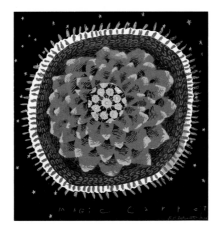

Tampa Review is published twice each year by the University of Tampa Press. Founded in 1964 as *UT Poetry Review*, *Tampa Review* is the oldest continuously published literary journal in Florida. Subscriptions in the United States are $22 per year; basic subscription is the same outside the U.S., but write for mailing cost by surface mail. Payment should be made by money order or check payable in U.S. funds. International airmail rates are available and vary; write for specific information. Subscription copies not received will be replaced without charge only if notice of nonreceipt is given by subscribers within six months following publication.

Editorial and business correspondence should be addressed to *Tampa Review*, The University of Tampa, 401 West Kennedy Boulevard, Tampa, Florida 33606-1490. Manuscripts and queries must be accompanied by a stamped, self-addressed envelope. Manuscripts are read only during September, October, November, and December. See submission guidelines at http://tampareview.ut.edu

Tampa Review is indexed by *Index of American Periodical Verse* (Metuchen, N.J.: Scarecrow Press), *Annual Bibliography of English Language and Literature* (Cambridge, England: Modern Humanities Research Association), *POEMFINDER* (CD-ROM Poetry Index), *The American Humanities Index* (Albany, N.Y.: Whitston Publishing), and the *MLA International Bibliography*. Member of the Council of Literary Magazines and Presses (CLMP), Council of Editors of Learned Journals (CELJ), and the Florida Literary Arts Coalition (FLAC).

The editors gratefully acknowledge the generous assistance of Lucie Armour of VAGA; Blair Asbury Brooks and Susannah Ash of Lisson Gallery, London; Paul Crenshaw and family; Whitney Stoepel and Kavi Gupta Gallery, Chicago and Berlin; Juliana Paciulli; Dana Greenidge, Director, Von Lintel Gallery, New York; Alan Klotz Gallery, New York; Walker Waugh and Ian Rios of Yancey Richardson Gallery, New York; Dorothy Cowden of Scarfone Hartley Gallery, University of Tampa; and Jim Lennon for their help with visual art that appears in this issue.

Typography and design by Richard Mathews

Printed on acid free paper ∞

Manufactured in the United States of America

For additional information visit *Tampa Review* at
http://tampareview.ut.edu

Editor

Richard Mathews

Fiction Editors

Audrey Colombe
Ryan Meany
Kathleen Ochshorn

Nonfiction Editor

Elizabeth Winston

Poetry Editor

Erica Dawson

Editorial Assistants

Sean Donnelly
Tony Fasciano

Staff Assistants

Alexandra Bentayou
Nicholas Eddy
Micheal Rumore

Contributing & Consulting Editor

Gregg Perkins

Published by the

University of Tampa Press

Tampa Review 43/44

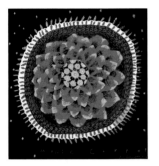

ON THE COVER: Robert Zakanitch. *Magic Carpet I.* 2012. Screen monoprint.

Robert Zakanitch evokes the intimate and the infinite in works from his *Magic Carpet* series. His carpets have a fantastical, handmade, folk art quality and a rich classical resonance. We can imagine them providing comfort and color in a rustic cabin, warming a child's playroom, or gracing a decorator-designed interior. Or like the magic carpets of fairy tales, they can transport us across infinite exterior space, as the artist suggests with backgrounds of limitless night sky, sprinkled with stars. From the flying carpets of the ancient *Arabian Nights* to pop culture embodiments in films like *The Thief of Baghdad* or Disney's *Aladdin*, magic carpets have been images in which woven patterns offer points of departure and transformation. The carpet is a fascinating icon, at once familiar and grounded, yet transporting or transformative. While a carpet is a mundane creation, practical and useful, the carpet in Persia is truly a work of art, a hand-crafted weaving that embodies the creative work of the human hand, and partakes as all weaving does, of a sense of the interconnected nature of the universe, and of the ability to discern and render these beautiful connections. As Zakanitch has written, "Beauty is. It is as natural as breathing. Its allure is transforming and I never thought art was about anything else."

Tampa Review 43/44

Contents (continued)

This issue is dedicated to

Anita Claire Scharf
1928-2010

Founding Editorial Assistant
of *Tampa Review*

Scott Treleaven. *Exit*. 2009. Ink on paper. 23.5 x 16.5 inches. Courtesy of Kavi Gupta Gallery, Chicago and Berlin.

Chris Gavaler

Talk to the Dead

Her uncle, a magician, used to cut her in half. While his sequin suit and dull-toothed saw blazed under middle school auditorium lights, Wendy lay in her half of the trick box, her knees crushed to her chest, and beamed upward at nothing, only her pretty little head and neck out there for anyone to see. Her younger, less attractive cousin bent double in the lower compartment, wriggling her toes at their uncle's command. The uncle replaced both of them after high school growth spurts, but Wendy remembered all of the routines and, despite a vow of secrecy, had demonstrated them to me on her freshman dorm bed while I watched on the rug in my underwear, sipping a beer.

The coffin must have made me think of the trick box. It was huge, and though Wendy had put on a few pounds since marrying Eric, all that meaningless interior cushioning could have concealed another cousin or two. I whispered the idea to my wife, Pam, in a corner of the funeral home, out of range of bereaved relatives, but she grimaced and blew her nose, her eyes bloodshot from allergies. The air conditioning vent hummed above her head, but the pollen still hung like smoke.

Pam didn't accompany me and the guys to the bar with Eric after the service. It was a Wednesday, a poker night, so if Wendy hadn't died of an aneurysm over the weekend, we would have gone off anyway. Eric kept reintroducing his brother-in-law, so we made a joke of it, each new greeting bellowed with back slaps and pumped elbows. I'd met the brother before, years before, at a party at my house, when Eric, one of my best friends, and Wendy, one of my best ex-girlfriends, hooked up the first time. My parents were visiting Florida and a dying aunt, so Eric and Wendy used the master bedroom, even asked first, between giggles, her bra strap at her elbow. After a fling our senior year, Wendy and I had called it quits but vowed to stay close. She liked the term "Platonic," which was probably accurate except that once when I was manic with wedding jitters and Eric had slapped her because of something she'd said about her mother-in-law. Never again, we swore it.

I was tracing beer streaks in the wood, trying to remember the way to the motel we'd found off some derelict exit ramp way across town—when Eric's laugh arced from the other end of the bar: "Hey, Travis! This guy's girlfriend reads minds!"

Eric was drunk. I'd found him bawling in the alley ten minutes before. He'd gone to take a piss and hadn't come back. The men's room empty, the toilet backed up, he was outside hanging onto a dumpster, making a noise worse than dry heaves, his face strung with snot. I wiped him down with his shirt sleeves and stuck my own mug in his hand after shoving him back toward the pitchers. Eric is no good at hiding things, consistently our worst Wednesday player. He lost more money than everyone else combined, but never griped, never made excuses like the rest of them.

The bartender exchanged glances with me while Eric kept yelling and waving me over. We'd gotten rowdier in the last half hour, and the regulars had thinned out. Wendy's brother was mid-story, going on about the swimming trophies lining the shelf in his sister's old bedroom, but I shrugged an apology and dragged the pretzels with me.

"What's all this now?"

Eric swayed behind a stranger's stool as the guy looked off sheepishly, neatening a pack of worn cards on the bar top. He'd been playing solitaire when we came in. Eric, quieter now, articulated as though to a deaf man: "His girl is a mind reader."

The guy bristled. "Hey, I'm not saying that, I just, she, I don't know. She knows things."

"Like what you're thinking, right?" Eric jostled the fella's shoulders, one hand on each, like a boxing coach between rounds.

"No, not exactly. She just guesses stuff."

A couple of the others were listening in, watching me as much as the little balding guy in the middle. "Like what?" I combed my fingers through my hair because I wanted him to flip the strands from his forehead. He fingered the cards instead and turned one up at random. A jack.

"Like if I pick this, she can tell me what it is. With her eyes closed." He exhaled a weak laugh and put the card back without raising his eyes higher than my chest. "I don't know. It's a trick or something. It's got to be."

"Ever think your deck's marked?"

Eric nodded, his whole body bobbing with the motion. "Or she's got mirrors all over the place, I bet."

"She doesn't even have to be in the room. She does it through doors, on the phone even, to anybody."

"No way!"

Allan, our second-ranking Wednesday night winner, rapped the man's elbow. "What else can she do?"

"Well," he said and paused with a grin too big for his face, "I kissed her cousin once, and she knew about that fast enough." His chuckle was dry and high-pitched, but it drew them in, Eric tilting wide-mouthed at the ceiling.

"But nothing else?" I asked. "She can't tell fortunes or talk to dead people or something?"

His fingers stopped working the deck. "She's not a freak, buddy."

"Just cards then. She's like an idiot savant of psychics."

"Hey, I didn't bring this up. You don't believe me, fine. But you don't call me a liar." He started pawing at his suit jacket for something, his car keys, I figured. "I'll put twenty bucks against anybody who says she can't do it." Instead of a wallet, he brandished a cell phone, waving it closer to my face than was wise. "Call her right now, if you don't believe me."

The muscles in Eric's forehead converged at a point at the bridge of his nose. "You're on!"

The stranger pulled his twenty and waited for Eric's two tens before setting his empty tumbler over the bills. "Anybody else?" He was looking me in the eyes now.

"You say she can read any mind, not just yours."

His phone chirped when he flipped it open, numbers glowing by my hip. "Call yourself. I won't say a word."

The rest of the poker gang matched twenties after me, and then a few others in the bar threw in, too, including some jerk who tried to double the ante. The tumbler tilted on top of a crinkled stack, almost four hundred dollars, half of it the little guy's. Wendy's brother stayed out.

I herded them over to the pay phones because Allan thought the cell was rigged, which didn't really make sense, but I made sure I had the girlfriend's number scribbled on a cocktail napkin before we drew the card from a new deck. I said Eric should do it, and he beamed like a kid called onto stage, his hand trembling as he shuffled the deck on the window ledge, dust motes frantic in the column of light. His breath caught when he saw the black ace, but it was only clubs, so it didn't mean anything, just a high card. Someone patted his shoulder, said, "Good job."

I kept my eye on the stranger as I dialed. He slouched behind everyone, shoulder against a booth. "Ask for Carrie," he said. "She lives with some friends."

I hit the last digit and stretched my arm along the window sill, one boot tip crossed in front of the other. My wife said I shouldn't have worn them to the funeral, that they clashed with the suit, but they are my best boots, my favorites. Everyone, even the last regulars too timid to open their wallets, was watching me. The bartender had switched off the TV, so the whine of the light fixtures was as loud as the hum in my other ear. A girl answered on the third ring.

"Hey," I said, my voice rumbling the way Wendy used to like, "my name's Travis. You don't know me, but your boyfriend here gave me your number."

"Is that a fact?" She sounded cute, a little peeved, but cute.

"He says you can read minds."

"Imagine that."

I snapped my fingers and wiggled one at Eric until he handed me the ace. "Well I'm holding a card in my hand right now and we got two hundred bucks that says you can't—"

"Hey," she said, "slow down there, pal. I want to talk to Randy."

"He said you can read anybody's mind."

"What am I, his performing dog? Put him on."

"Can't do that, miss. I need to hear your guess first."

She got a little snippy then, and I let her go on a bit before dropping my arm. "She's making excuses, Randy."

The boyfriend had moved in closer, nudging past Wendy's brother. He shouted, "It's okay, Carrie, just take a guess," but I'd made sure my palm was cupped over the receiver so she couldn't hear, and then I raised it slowly to my mouth. My eyes stayed on Randy.

"Listen, Mary," I said.

Randy flinched, opened his mouth to correct me, then grimaced.

I said to the phone, "If you can't do it, Mary, just say so. It's not your fault he—"

"It's the three of hearts, asshole. Now put him on."

"Three," I announced to the room. "Three of what? Hearts? Can you say that louder?"

The metal cord stretched to its length, the girl's voice like an insect's. Maybe Allan and one other guy in front could hear. Randy wasn't trying. He accepted the phone when I waved it at him, and then he stuck a finger in his other ear and turned his back. I thought Allan or somebody else might take a punch at him once they figured the scam—his girlfriend's name changed according to the card—but they either didn't notice or didn't care, too worked up about their winnings.

The bartender, the keeper of the pot, lifted the tumbler and slid the bills to me to divvy up. I would have paid Eric first, but other hands beat him to it. He kept by the window, talking to Wendy's brother, his back to me even when I nudged him with his pair of twenties in my fist.

"I don't want it," he said.

I laughed and punched him in the shoulder, harder when he didn't turn. "Don't be a punk."

"He doesn't want it, Travis." Wendy's brother touched my arm, not threateningly, but I would have slapped his hand off if I hadn't noticed that Travis's face was wet again. So I crumpled the bills into his front pocket and went outside to piss.

It was evening now, but sunlight still smoldered in the alley, a half moon overhead, faint, like a projection, a trick. I almost lost my balance staring up at it, thinking about that stupid

magic kit my mother gave me on some birthday or other, the fake rings and collapsible cans and one of those dorky hats with the secret compartment. I played with them maybe once, before trading everything for a one-armed G.I. Joe and a cap gun. My dad said I got taken and made me trade back after his shouting match on the phone with the other kid's father. I told Wendy that story, staring up at her on her dormitory bed, imagining her crammed into her uncle's box. It was so obvious. People have to want to be fooled, they have to be in on it, everybody, all together, like at church, all wanting the same stupid thing. When I tugged off Wendy's sweatshirt in that motel room five years later, I don't know, it wasn't like I was expecting saw marks or some other new kind of revelation. Her waist was still good and all, still almost perfect, her whole body basically.

I was jiggling the last drops into my puddle when the metal door creaked beside me. The Randy guy paused on the step as I zipped up.

"So," I said, "you got fifty-two girlfriends, huh?"

He made a noise, what someone else might call a laugh.

I'd sprayed my hand some and had to wipe it on my hip. "Any of them named Wendy?"

The door swung shut behind him. "Five of diamonds," he said. I pictured the typed list he must have made for the girl, probably taped it next to her land phone himself. His hands sunk into his pockets as he leaned back, one shoulder on the bricks, the other on the door frame. He wasn't all that little, and the balding was premature. He hadn't come out to piss.

"I'd like my twenty back now," he said. "And whatever else you still got on you."

The suit jacket was thin, a little frayed, and with a wallet and cell phone he didn't have room for much else, a knife maybe, not a gun. I rolled an empty beer bottle with my boot tip. "Imagine that," I said.

I hadn't been in a fight for years, not since high school, when kids steered clear of me, including Eric, whom I'd roughed up once behind the bleachers during gym. That was middle school. He grew into a decent lineman by senior year.

"Randy, Randy, Randy," I said. That's how I used to start it up.

He spoke again, but I missed the words. There was a rustle behind me, and then something struck the side of my head, something way harder than a fist. My shoulder ricocheted against the dumpster before I skidded over gravel, limbs and spine contracting around my head and groin, reflexively, like an animal, an insect, as a heel stamped my ribs. I recognized the guy when I squinted up, had thought he was one of the regulars, flicked two twenties into his palm minutes before. If Eric hadn't fallen for Randy's loner act, his partner would have stepped up, probably playing my part, the skeptic. He kicked me maybe ten times, twelve at the most. I want to say he was wearing construction boots, the kind with the reinforced toe, but what the hell do I know?

Randy peeled my arm back to feel inside my suit jacket and then chucked my wallet by my head when he was done with it. I wasn't carrying much, nowhere near what he'd lost, but it's never just about the money. He didn't say anything else. I lay there, swallowing metallic saliva, staring at an empty beer bottle while their steps faded. My fingers shone red where I touched my cheek, my ear, the matted hair. I thought my skull was split in half, air blowing embers across exposed tissue. Pam says I'm a wimp about pain, but she was the one terrified of childbirth after the hell Wendy went through, ripped all the way down to her asshole after six hours of pushing, and now the brat wouldn't even remember her.

Standing was out of the question, but I managed to inch against the dumpster, despite the row of ribs I imagined spearing through my shirt. Maybe they weren't broken. I had no idea, hadn't broken a bone since skiing in college. My breathing had almost steadied when Wendy's brother wandered out. I startled him, his leg seizing mid-step, as though above a dog turd, which made me laugh, once, which was both painful and stupid.

"Casey," I said. That was his name. "Casey."

He looked me over while unfastening his fly and walked around the other edge of the dumpster. He never said anything, just looked at me, rolled his eyes maybe. It wasn't news he didn't like me. I groaned something about the two guys, the deception, but I couldn't hear my voice over the trickle of urine against hollow metal. The dumpster must have been empty. That's all there is to most tricks, the empty space, all the room in the world for a girl to cram her knees up along the top of a box. Anybody could figure it out, if they wanted to, if they want to stop the show. If they want to kill all the fun.

Casey zipped before rounding the dumpster again. He didn't glance in my direction, and I was done talking. I had a bar full of buddies just inside anyway, their bladders getting fuller. Somebody would be out to help me soon enough. I didn't even watch the back of Casey's jacket as he climbed the step. I had half of a moon to blink up at, the way it gets brighter the longer you stare. I reached for that empty beer bottle, and let the dregs dribble onto my tongue, same way as I did on Wendy's dorm rug, looking up at her, at that body of hers, waiting for her to reveal the next trick.

❖ ❖ ❖

From the Dark

Radiator Building, Night, New York, 1927

Streetlights glow like spirits, like planets
hovering. In the distance, a solitary star
pulses. Rising from behind the building,
the beams of spotlights are as massive
as girders, illuminate a genie of steam.
Each window is a white tile shining
against black. In a playful gesture,
Alfred Stieglitz shimmers in crimson neon
like a movie marquee, like an epaulette
tacked to the shoulder of the building.

Beck Strand has become a postscript.

Some points in our lives are lived inside
parenthesis, are stretches of space and time
when we cozy against our partner's flaws,
when happiness becomes anesthetic.
We ignore the future's murkiness, clutch
a vivid postcard on which we write
Wish you were here over and over
in every language we know.

Sleeping Beauty

The alarm clocks circle around her
as if she is prey in a trap. Out
the window, night or day whistles
a nonchalant tune on the tip

of her tongue. If she could only
remember, though she has never
stopped honing the senses through
her skin—the cut edges of salt

when the seasons change, the blank
abrasions of the curious, a broth
of broken syllables when the priests
are brought in to pray over her.

She turns in her sleep, and the palace
gossips about it for days. She groans
in the middle of a sensuous dream,
and the royal guards start yet another

search for a prince born in the dark
eaves of the forest or the deep grass
across the countryside. The last
artist to paint her dies suddenly

in his sleep, perhaps the sign they
have been waiting for, perhaps he
will replace her. They reset all
the alarms, and she begins to age.

Lorna Knowles Blake

Persephone in Manhattan

Checks that mother is asleep
       on a sofa garden of chintz,
book still open, tea cold—
sneaks out of the apartment,
      streaks past doorman, dog-
        walker, corner panhandler.
        Rushing to dim the glare
of her green, sunlit potential
she crosses against the light
to a forbidden entrance
      leading down to places
        night-blooming, fluorescent.
        Danger holds the door for her,
      sweet escort to that nether city
of dark caverns: smoke-filled
bars, clubs where she, greedy,
      samples the shiny garnet seeds,
        seeds of the world's pulpy fruit.
      How can she now return to you,
to your yellow fields and flowers,
      to your blooming, tangled love?

Valerie Jaudon. *Translation*. 2011. 48 x 48 inches. Oil on linen. Courtesy of the artist and Von Lintel Gallery, New York. Art © Valerie Jaudon/Licensed by VAGA, New York, N.Y.

Jen Fawkes

A Moment on the Lips

Until the day that wily Achaean invaded my cave, I thought misery was an inevitable condition of existence. It was all I could do to haul myself vertical and roll the boulder out of the way every morning. The sunlight that drenched the rocky meadow where my flocks grazed seemed to me unnecessarily bright and oppressive. I wasted countless hours sitting with my chin in my hand and my eye on the ground. I rarely bathed, shaved, or changed my tunic. I yearned, but I couldn't put that yearning into words. I didn't even realize I was yearning.

"Polyphemus?"

I looked up from the boulder on which I slumped to find Loticleus standing in front of me. My sheep surrounded us, grazing on sparse tufts of grass. My goats wandered at a greater distance.

"Afternoon, Loticleus." I resumed staring at the ground, hoping he would clear off. He did not.

"What are you doing?"

"Tending my flocks," I said. "What does it look like?"

I guess I should point out that most Cyclopes aren't terribly bright. I don't mean to speak ill of my brethren, but it's just true. And Loticleus was the dullest of us. It wasn't that he couldn't put two and two together and come up with four, it was more like he just couldn't put two and two together. Loticleus's eye was the color of sheep shit, and it was always watering. He tore out clumps of his own hair for no reason, and his beard was full of brambles. He was, by far, the fattest Cyclopes on our island, a craggy patch of land off the Sicilian coast. This was due primarily to his inability to stop eating his own sheep and goats, which he devoured at an absurd rate. Loticleus couldn't get the hang of pacing himself, and he never seemed to grasp that his animals needed time to reproduce. I'd heard that he'd eaten himself down to a handful of goats and two ewes, and saliva glistened on his slack lips as his eye roved over my flocks.

"I'm hungry, Polyphemus."

"No, you're not. You just think you are."

"Guess what I ate yesterday."

"I can't imagine."

The lid descended over his eye, and one of his grimy hands rubbed the gut pushing out the front of his tunic. "A man."

"Bullshit."

"It's true!" Loticleus shouted, his lid flying up.

"You're lying." Even as I said it, I knew he wasn't. Loticleus wasn't really capable of deception.

"NOOO!" he howled, stomping his filth-blackened feet. The ground trembled, and my startled sheep herded away from him.

"All right," I said. "Keep your tunic on."

"He washed up on shore clinging to a piece of driftwood," he said. "I bashed his head into the ground and ate him right there. I couldn't help myself. He was so tasty."

Unlike most Cyclopes, I had never partaken of man. Generally, we subsist on a diet of sheep, goats, sheep and goat by-products, and any other warm-blooded creatures that stray into our paths. Local men avoid our island at all costs, but strangers sometimes land on its beaches, and shipwrecked men or those who've been put off sailing vessels are occasionally washed ashore. My brethren claimed that man tasted far more pleasing than sheep or goat, but the thought of devouring a being that shares my shape—two legs, two arms, a torso, a head—and walks upright, even one with an eye on either side of its face, did not sit right with me. It made my heart convulse in a way I wasn't able to identify. I'd never been face to face with a man, but I was certain that if I were, eating him would be the furthest thing from my mind.

"What we need," Loticleus was saying, "is a great storm to drive all the ships within a thousand miles aground on the island. Then we could feast on men for days!"

I silently begged him to go away.

"What about your father?" he said.

"What about him?"

"Why don't you ask him to call up such a storm?"

I should probably point out that I was born of Poseidon and a Nereid named Thoosa, but the God of the Sea and I had always had a strained relationship. Whenever he stopped by my cave with his entourage of Naiads and Nereids, I would roll the rock in place and sit there holding my breath, pretending I wasn't home.

I stood. "Don't you think Poseidon has better things to do? Would he call up a storm just to fill your fat belly? Besides, when was the last time any of us paid attention to him? Made him a sacrifice or offering? You know how gods are —they aren't apt to do anything for anybody without something in return."

As Loticleus stood absorbing my words, I patted his shoulder and took my leave. I herded my flocks into the fenced yard and through the laurels that screened my cave. Once the most stubborn of my goats was inside, I used the boulder to seal off the harshly-lit outside world, welcoming the rank gloom of my home. Amid stony protrusions and hanging rock formations, I had constructed pens for my flocks. Milking pails crowded the dirt floor, some stacked into teetering towers, some half-full of sheep's and goat's milk. Cheese, stored in baskets, overflowed the cave. The floor was littered with bones, hooves, and tufts of wool. In places the sheep and goat shit was ankle-deep. Dried brown blood splattered the walls like abstract cave art; here and there red streaks from the sheep I'd breakfasted on that morning glistened.

My ewes and does bleated, so I sat on a stool to milk them. My flocks were abundant, and the task took me the better part of three hours. Once I'd deflated every udder in the cave, I sat in near darkness surrounded by full pails of milk. The round, dully glowing white disks put me in mind of the moon. I suffered from terrible insomnia, waking most nights with a start, struggling up through thick dread, my heart a-hammer. It always took me some time to realize there was nothing to fear. I was alone in my home surrounded by the warm, wool-covered bodies of animals who knew a contentment that hovered outside my reach.

Once awake, I was unable to quiet my mind. I would rise and make my way to the shore, relishing the sharp stones that perforated the soles of my bare feet. I studied the moon until its image dissolved in my monstrous tears. There was inside me a darkness far deeper than that of the firmament, and it grew unchecked, like a cancer. My fellow Cyclopes seemed content with their solitary lives, but the lonely days of uncivilized brutality that stretched before me made me want to sleep the eternal sleep.

Sitting on the milking stool in my cave, I wept like one suffering a grievous injury. High-pitched whines. Freely-flowing fluids. Choking sobs. The sort of display that should never be witnessed. Afterward, I sat limp, feeling like a sheep's udder out of which I'd squeezed every last drop. I rose, collected sticks from a pile in a corner, and briskly rubbed two together. Igniting a small flame, I blew upon it until the twigs I'd mounded caught fire. I tried to focus on the fire's benefits—its light and heat—but as usual, my gaze was drawn to shadows the flames threw over the walls—menacing, unknowable. I chanced to drop my eye from the shadows to the cluttered cave floor, and it was then that I caught sight of the men.

I'd only seen men from afar and suspected that their minuteness had to do with perspective, but no—these men were far smaller than I'd imagined. Rejected by Galatea, a Nereid with whom I'd once become violently infatuated, I'd killed her lover, a man named Acis, by flinging a rock at him from a great distance. When my anger subsided, I was flooded with a shame that now resurfaced as I realized how miniscule the men crouching behind milking pails and baskets of cheese and bloody piles of sheep and goat bones truly were.

"How dare you?" This wasn't what I wanted to say at all, but the words erupted from me, shaking the cave walls. I was shocked and taken aback, especially as I considered the great blubbering display I'd just put on, one the small strangers had no doubt observed. I wasn't angered by their presence, however. They seemed to me tender, miniature, two-eyed Cyclopes, and at the sight of them, I was filled not with rage but with something unfamiliar and equally warm. I longed to wish them welcome.

I tried again, but my tongue continued to betray me. "Who are you? How did you come here?"

A man whose muscles filled out his tunic and whose golden hair and beard curled lyrically, a man I now know to have been Odysseus, stepped forth. Placing his hands on his hips, he squared his shoulders with a tiny show of bravado. "If you please, we are weary soldiers, followers of Agamemnon, blown off course on our way home from the sack of Troy. We ask in the name of great Zeus, who guards strangers and suppliants, that you give us food and shelter."

"Zeus be damned!" I thundered, meaning, I would offer you food and shelter even if Zeus didn't look after strangers and suppliants. Seeing what a terrifying impact my voice had, when I next spoke I did so as softly and calmly as I could. "What I mean to say is, I don't give a damn about Zeus."

I could tell they still weren't taking my meaning, and I was about to explain how lucky they were to have wandered into my cave rather than the cave of the man-hungry Loticleus, when out of the corner of my eye I noticed two of them sitting in a basket of cheese, cramming their faces full of the white stuff. I was warmed by the sight of them enjoying something I'd made with my own hands—something I'd never before had the opportunity to share—and I reached out, plucking them from the basket. Still chewing, they struggled and kicked in my grasp. Their companions shouted, pleading with me to release their friends. Dangling the men in front of my eye, I realized that, although essentially structured like Cyclopes, they were, in truth, much more comely. Their bodily proportions seemed more harmonious. Also, their eyes were almond-shaped, like the eyes of beasts.

"I order you to release my comrades!" Golden-haired, muscular Odysseus stomped his little foot as he commanded me so. I was going to obey, but instead, I did something that, at the time, I could neither explain nor understand: I slapped the two men against the cave floor. Their heads split open, and their brains soaked the ground. Tearing them limb from limb, I devoured them—organs, flesh, and marrowy bones—then washed them down with several pails of sheep's milk.

The ten remaining strangers fell to their knees or prostrated themselves on the shit-covered ground. They wept and screamed and tore their beards and flailed around in grief and horror. I licked traces of their fellows from my fingers, trying to determine what had compelled me to do such a thing. I had not been angry—far from it. In fact, from the moment I touched the men, I was flooded with a feeling more tender than any I ever felt for the Nereid Galatea. I had for a split second imagined holding them forever, yet I was compelled to beat them into the floor and devour every last part of them.

Ashamed, unable to look the men in their tiny animal eyes, I withdrew to the far side of the cave. I stretched myself out among my sheep and goats, where I pretended to sleep. Sometime in the night, one of them, Odysseus I am sure, stole across the cave. I felt the tip of his sword poke my sternum, but so miserable was I over what I'd done, I did not brush it away. A short time later, I heard him sob and curse softly, and the sword was removed.

After dozing fitfully for an hour or two, I arose, determined to make a fresh start with the men. I'd spent the night trying to reconcile my vicious behavior with the warm tingle that moved through me whenever I thought of the petite, perfectly-formed beings imprisoned in my cave, but I could not. Disgusted by what I had done, I only knew that I would never, under any circumstances, eat a man again. As I milked my ewes and does, I felt the small strangers eyeing me, and I tried to think of something to say to put them at ease, to assure them that they had nothing more to fear.

I had a speech all planned out and had only gotten as far as "Listen, men. Should I call you men? Is there something else I should call you?" when one of my hands shot out of its own volition and snatched up two more of them. Before I realized what I was doing, I'd smashed their little skulls right into the ground and gobbled them up in their entirety. My head whirled with the speed of it. The eight survivors stared at me agape. I belched, and the flavor of their companions flooded my mouth. I wanted to be sickened by it, to detest it, but the truth of the matter was, my fellow Cyclopes were right. Man does taste far more pleasing than sheep or goat.

Odysseus and his crew once again prostrated themselves, lamenting and tearing their hair, imploring great Zeus to help them, and I considered rolling the rock aside and allowing them to escape. As I watched their heartfelt display of grief, however, I knew that I could not. Not only would Loticleus and the other Cyclopes capture and eat them, but if I let the men go, they would never get the chance to know me.

For after I'd eaten the second set of them, while their blood and juices still glistened on my chin, it occurred to me that I loved the men. They were precious and pleasing to my eye, and I loved them, and I wanted them to love me—I needed them to love me. I no longer knew if their flesh was truly sweet or if it just tasted so because of the love I bore them. Love crashed down upon me like a heavenly hammer, and it made my former infatuation with the Nereid Galatea look like a meaningless crush.

I wanted to explain all of this, but I was no good at extemporaneous speeches. If I collected my thoughts and put together the right words, I felt sure I could make them understand why I'd eaten their friends. It had nothing to do with hunger or anger or vicious brutality. I hoped that if I made this clear, they would forgive me and consent to remain in my cave as my companions forever.

So I said nothing. I rolled the rock aside and drove my flocks out through the laurel-covered cave entrance. Once the animals were without, I faced the men, who stood shin-deep in sheep and goat shit, blinking up at me in terror and anguish. I wanted to flash them a reassuring smile, one that said all would be explained when I returned, but I was afraid a bit of their comrades might be stuck in my teeth. Rolling the rock in place, I sealed them inside.

I rapidly covered the sun-soaked ground that stretched between my cave and the meadow. At one point, I started skipping. My sheep and goats eyed me askance, and though they were but dumb beasts, they seemed to be wondering what had come over their master.

"Polyphemus?" Loticleus stood slack-jawed in the meadow, scratching his crotch. Nearby, two ewes and four bony goats grazed. "Great Zeus, is that you whistling?"

Apparently I was also whistling.

"I suppose so." Closing my eye, I tilted my face up to the sun. "And how does this lovely day find you, Loticleus?"

"Hungry."

I laughed—a clear, deep sound I had no recollection of heretofore making.

"What's come over you, Polyphemus? I've never seen you in such a mood."

Shrugging, I settled on a boulder. "Have you eaten yourself down to this, then?" I asked, indicating his pitiful animals.

Loticleus nodded sadly. "I don't know what will become of me. I suppose I'll starve."

I agreed. It did seem the most likely outcome.

"What about those men?" Loticleus said.

I leapt to my feet. "What men?"

"The men on ships. Ships you could ask Poseidon to run aground on our island. If only you would, pitiful Loticleus would not starve."

As a rule, Cyclopes don't bother with compassion, and his attempt at arousing it in me was yet another mark of his idiocy. However, Loticleus had caught me on the right day. My eye roved over my abundant flocks, and I made him an offer. "If you promise to give them a chance to start reproducing before you devour them, I will give you twenty sheep and twenty goats."

"Give?" So unheard of was such generosity among our brethren that Loticleus did not understand what I was talking about.

"They will be yours. They will belong to you."

His shit-colored eye filled with tears, and he yanked up the hem of his tunic to dry them.

I touched his shoulder. "Soon, you will have your own abundant flocks."

Loticleus departed with his new sheep and goats, and I paced the meadow, considering what to say to the men in my cave, who were no doubt cowering in fear. I would have to explain that it had never been my intention to eat a single one of them, and that I would do so no more. After all, if I continued, they could not become my companions, and it was this above all else that I desired.

Once I'd herded my flocks inside and replaced the boulder, I positioned myself as far from the eight remaining men as I could. Their sleepless faces bore a hunted look. Fear clouded the air between us, and it made me want to weep. I started pacing nervously, and as I walked, I kicked something sharp. Buried beneath sheep and goat shit, I found a pole I intended to use as a walking stick and herding staff. One end had been sharpened to a fine point, something

I could not remember doing, but I didn't think too much about it and tossed the pole aside. I swung around to pace in the opposite direction, and as soon as I was within arm's length of the clustered men, I grabbed two of them, dashed them headfirst into the floor, and ate them.

As I sat on a stone, hiding my face in my hands, aghast, I felt a tap on my knee. I looked up, and golden-haired Odysseus stood in front of me. In his hands he held a bowl of thick, black liquid.

"Oh great Cyclops," he said, "take this wine to wash down the flesh of my comrades. It is the finest my ships carry."

I was speechless. Despite my behavior, the little man was offering me libation. Deeply touched, I took the vessel and drained it. The drink was sweet and strong. As soon as I emptied the bowl, he filled it again. And again. And again.

"Tell me," I said, my words slurring together, "what is your name?" In my foggy vision, Odysseus seemed cloaked in mist and clouds, like a bit of heavenly stuff—a miniature god. So busy was I with thoughts of picking him up and cradling him to my chest, of placing him on my shoulder and letting him ride there forever, that I did not hear his reply. I wanted to assure him that I would never eat him; however, the wine had tricked my tongue, and I mumbled something else entirely, something about eating him but not what I wanted to say, before darkness swept over me like a tide called up by Poseidon, and I collapsed on my back.

In vivid dreams brought on by the wine of Odysseus, the island's colors were brightened, its lithic landscape made lush. Gazing upon my reflection in a clear pool, I found that my eye had been replaced by two small, almond-shaped eyes—one situated on either side of my face. Delighted, I scoured the verdant terrain for the men, who hid from me not out of fear but for a lark. Even those I'd already devoured were there, sprung back to life. When I discovered each man, he did not scream; he congratulated me, and I placed him on my shoulders amidst his fellows. With my new eyes, I could make out each strand of hair on his precious head, every bead of sweat that stood upon his sun-darkened skin.

Agony jolted me—searing, unbearable. Awake, I leapt to my feet. My eye was open, but I could see nothing. Touching my face, I discovered a narrow object protruding from the center of my crackling, sizzling, popping eyeball. I yanked on this item and heard a sucking sound followed by the gurgling of thick liquid. Once the object was in my hands, I recognized the sharpened pole I'd found on the floor. I flailed around the cave, running hither and yon in the frightful darkness. My screams must have painted the air, hanging like a portrait of anguish for those who still possessed the power of sight.

"Polyphemus?"

Voices floated to me from outside the cave.

"Why are you screaming? What's going on?"

I lurched forward. My hands landed on the rock that covered the mouth of my cave.

"Is someone stealing your sheep, Polyphemus? Is someone harming you?"

I recognized the voices of Loticleus and others. Sounds of violence and pain are not uncommon on our island, and I realized how bloodcurdling my screams must have been to bring my brethren on the run.

"Polyphemus?"

Pain thumped and hummed through me. With an act of will worthy of an immortal, I managed to silence my screams. A metallic taste filled my mouth; blood and other fluids had been flowing to it from my punctured eyeball. I spit on the floor and steadied my voice.

"Nobody is here. Nobody is stealing my sheep. Nobody is harming me."

I heard one of my brethren suggest that great Zeus had sent a sickness upon me, one that had driven me out of my mind. Afraid of contracting it, my fellow Cyclopes departed, remarking that I should call upon my father for help.

I bumbled around, feeling my way over every inch of the cave, but now that I was blind, the men could easily avoid me. I kept grabbing bleating sheep and goats. I wanted to explain to the small strangers that I'd told my fellow Cyclopes nobody was hurting me in order to protect them, to assure them that I would let no more harm befall them, but instead I barked things like, "It's no use hiding! I can smell your fear!"

Finally, I rolled the rock aside and sat in the cave entrance with my arms outstretched. It would be impossible for the men to pass without my notice. As I sat in the chill night air, drying blood stiffening my beard and tunic, quaking with pain, I realized my fellow Cyclopes were right. Great Zeus had sent a sickness upon me. Not the literal darkness in which I now found myself set adrift, but the melancholy that had tainted all the previous moments of my life.

When my ewes and does began bleating to be milked, I knew day was dawning. The rams and male goats crowded the cave entrance, but before I let them pass, I felt the back of each for any sign of a man sitting astride him. As I ran my hands over the last ram, the best and fattest I owned, my fingertips brushed something smooth and foreign on his underside. I knew instantly that Odysseus was clinging to the ram from beneath, and that his remaining companions had been clinging to the others. I was tempted to snatch up the muscular, golden-haired man and force him to remain with me, but I knew it was no use. In the end, I would only devour him. Calling upon reserves of restraint I did not discover until I'd lost my vision, I allowed my best ram to wander from the cave.

A short time later, shouts reached my ears, and I blundered toward the sea. I stumbled, falling to my knees again and again. Rocks and stones gashed my flesh. When warm water lapped at my ankles, I stood with my head cocked, listening to Odysseus, who used a new voice—one raised in triumph from the prow of his ship.

"For eating guests in your own home, you have been punished by great Zeus, oh Cyclops, with the loss of your livestock and of your sight!"

I heard the thunderous sound of my fellow Cyclopes approaching. I felt them staring at my obliterated eye, at the blood staining my flesh and tunic. I picked up a colossal stone, heaved it wide of Odysseus's voice, and held my breath. When the little man laughed and shouted, relief flowed through me.

"If any man asks who blinded you, tell him it was Odysseus, son of Laertes, sacker of cities, who makes his home in Ithaca!"

Again I felt the weight of my brethren's stares, and I knew they were thinking of the prophecy. A Cyclops named Telemos had once foretold my blinding at the hands of one called Odysseus, but being so caught up in my

melancholy, I had all but forgotten his prediction. Its fulfillment made me acutely aware of the power of the gods and my own limitations; however, I felt no more anger toward the miniscule hero than I had before I learned his identity.

I knew my fellow Cyclopes were waiting for me to retaliate, so I lifted my arms to the heavens, and for the first time in years, I spoke to my father. I asked Poseidon to prevent Odysseus from reaching his home. If he did see Ithaca again, I asked that he be late, lose all his comrades, and find trouble in his household. Considering how strained things had been between us, I doubted my father would heed my prayer, and it was just as well, for no matter how Odysseus had abused me, I could think of him with nothing but love.

I picked up another monstrous boulder and heaved it in the direction of his ship. To my relief, my brethren told me I'd missed again. Mumbling condolences, they departed, and soon, I thought myself alone on the rocky beach.

"Polyphemus?" Loticleus's rough hand landed on my shoulder. "They took your flocks?"

"The males. I've still got the ewes and does. I'll have to use the males I gave you to rebuild."

Loticleus was silent.

"How many of the animals have you eaten?"

"Several."

"How many?"

"Quite a few."

"How many?"

"All but ten!"

I was shocked. "You ate thirty animals in one day? How is that even possible?"

"I'm sorry, Polyphemus," he sobbed. "I couldn't help myself!"

Loticleus had always seemed to me nothing more than a moronic eating machine, but I now felt that I understood his compulsion to consume. It wasn't about hunger or gluttony or even boredom—it was about love. About inviting that which you love inside. Making it a part of you. Ensuring that it remains with you forever.

We put the remaining male animals to work impregnating my does and ewes, and our shared flocks are now abundant. Loticleus has moved into my cave, and he acts as my eye. The responsibility has done wonders for him—he takes better care of himself and no longer devours animals at such an alarming rate. When I now wake in the night, I have only to reach out and touch his warm, slumbering shape to feel assured by his company. I've actually grown fond of Loticleus—something I must admit is probably easier when you can't see him—though my feelings will never match the consumptive love I still bear the tiny men who invaded my cave and took my sight, six of whom I carry around inside me—my eternal companions.

❖ ❖ ❖

Martin Rock

Minotaur Caressing a Sleeping Woman

After Picasso's etching of the same title

You think the Minotaur is touching
the woman in her sleep. He is not.

He leans over her and uses his hands
to waft her smell toward his face.

Her scent is the scent of capital
punishment. In Deuteronomy,

death is prescribed to males guilty
of profligacy, drunkenness,

and disobeying their parents.
When the white bull mounted

Pasiphaë in her wooden cow,
befuddlement washed over the earth

like the dark before an awful movie.
The bull continued with the drudgery

of copulation, and now their son
is nude, hunched over the woman

like a dog humping the leg of the divine.
His mouth is open and his eye

is dark as the anus of the first mammal.
How is the word carbuncle used

to describe an infected abscess
and also an exquisite gem, redder

than the sleeping woman's unpainted lips?
On awakening, she will be alone

on a paddock of damp sheets
and the room will stink of musk.

Juliana Gray

Suicide

A study by psychologist James Kaufman has concluded that poets—particularly female poets—are more likely than fiction writers, nonfiction writers, and playwrights to have signs of mental illness, such as suicide attempts. He has dubbed this the "Sylvia Plath effect."

Such a lovely word we mustn't use.
Already, friends are keeping an eye on us.
They call on weekends, or when they haven't heard
from us in a while, just to check in.
Our co-workers are wary. If we crack
a few too many Plath jokes, we find ourselves
in mandatory counseling. And Mom,
who never trusted poetry, sighs
and sets another roll upon our plates.

We'd like to ask each other, take a poll:
How often do you think about it? Weekly?
Every day? Every fulsome night?
We want to find out what's normal, but
we know we're not the right ones to ask.

Studies blame the solipsistic "I"—
too much introspection fucks us up.
I disagree. If poets are in love
with language, then how could we not be seduced
by *suicide*, those silky vowel glides,
the sideways glance, all sibilance and curves?
It makes me think of a slinky red dress.
That color has always looked good on me.

Steven Husby. *Untitled*. 2012. Digital photograph.

Plant Voices

The Shrieks of Mowed Lawns

Late in the summer of 1956 I read a story in a comic book about a man who creates a formula he swallows to give him the ability to hear plants speaking. For a few panels, he's ecstatic as he overhears the conversations of flowers and trees. He knows he's unique. He's self-satisfied because he's the only person who can hear plant voices.

And then a neighbor snips her roses to bring some inside, and he hears them scream. A few minutes later, someone begins to mow his lawn, and there is uninterrupted wailing. He covers his ears, but there's so much terror and pain it's unendurable, and he has no antidote. He's doomed to hear constant shrieking, something like a terrible tinnitus, for the rest of his life.

Despite his regret, I tried listening to daisies when I ripped their petals off. I heard nothing but what I imagined a flower's scream would sound like, high-pitched and girlish. A tree, I imagined, would groan like a man as it was sawed in half. The weeds that grew waist-high in the field behind our house would whimper like boys trying not to cry. When I cut our lawn, whatever horrible sounds it made were drowned out by the mower.

Suits

That summer, just before sixth grade began, the language my friends and I used would change when the dusk drifted into our blood. We tried out the obscenities we'd heard from older brothers or fathers who swore viciously when they drank. All of us imagined sex acts as we walked inside the dark, only the street's familiar dogs barking at the edge of a yard. There were no streetlights. We could have walked naked, the fingerprints of our dreams undetected.

What we saw: failure in the houses of our parents. It shrank the street until there was nothing to absorb but words. One father was dead, his suits stored in a hall closet; one father wore suits which were foolishly styled; one father worked shifts and refused Sundays because they asked for suits.

All those suits belonged to us. We wore them and made ourselves fit into the street. Walking between the six-house rows, we stopped each night at a field where none of our fathers lived. The summer began to die there. By mid-August things crackled when we rolled over. We could hear yellows and browns in the dark. Always there was an age in our imagination, coming up from underneath us like an arthritic storm warning—knees, hips, ribcage, those places where the clothes of our lives refused to fit, rising inevitably to our shoulders.

At night our voices knotted themselves when the neighbors spoke, turning into tiny, choked spirits of sound. They called out from doorways, and we saw only parts of them, the yellow light reaching feebly into the halls that were always behind them. Some of the mothers rocked on porches, fanning themselves, and they were in sections, too, like everyone we saw.

Maybe the neighborhood, parked two miles from the Spang-Chalfant steel plant, had recognized the tremor of the first furnace being banked. Others might follow, all of them together the way houses go out on a dying block, every window shattered one night by vandals.

The Best Swimmer in Etna

I had a pass for the Spang-Chalfant pool, the one the steel mill had built for its employees. My grandfather had just retired from the mill; half of the customers who came to my father's bakery, a block from the mill, worked there, too. When I jumped in, acting like I could swim, I always imagined swimming the first length underwater, serious about breath and who might be staring down like moons.

What I actually did was duck my head and hold my breath. My hair dripping, I held onto the side and went hand over hand into the deep end where I acted as if I was resting after swimming a few lengths. Nobody noticed. Three years earlier, my family had moved two miles away, and the only person who talked to me was my older sister, who spent most of her time lying in the sun. After I worked my way back to the shallow end, I'd duck my head again and count to thirty. When I surfaced, I climbed out, soaked like a swimmer.

My father never went into that pool. He slept during the afternoons and baked all night. "He can't swim," my mother said. "That's why he wasn't an Eagle Scout and you won't be either unless you learn."

The Morse Code Fear

My father was the Scoutmaster of the troop I'd been in since my eleventh birthday a few months before. For three weeks, in the church basement, every Boy Scout worked at Morse Code, beginning with the dot for e, the dash for t, common letters simple as signs for stop and go. For an hour or two, it was exciting. We imagined ourselves sending an SOS and being heroes.

Semaphore was next, waving flags to speak, but still there were boys who fumbled letters like b and g. Nearly a month, and only three of us could transform dits and dahs to sentences about the joys of school and scouts, but that last Tuesday in September every boy knew the rhythmic code for tits and ass, learning language for the future we imagined, tumbling outside to wait for rides. In the early dark, already wishing for television or magazines hidden in board game boxes, I waited for my father to put the Boy Scout equipment away, some of the other boys using flashlights to form the dits and dahs of fuck. Curt Goltz was expert with the long and short of Sharon or Sue, spelling his lust for them in code, blinking the forbidden, writing what hands and tongues could do, forming whole sentences, pinning our fear under the welcome weight of words.

March of Dimes

Though Jonas Salk had begun to work his miracle, the brochures featuring pictures of smiling iron lung children still arrived in our mail. Richard Hastings, the boy in braces, still lurched on crutches into fifth grade, his metal supports sounding like spare change fingered inside a pocket. He and Anne Wells, the fourth-grade girl in a wheelchair, left school so early they never blocked the halls when we charged outside to get in line for the bus.

Every teacher, since I'd started school, had asked us to contribute to the March of Dimes. In sixth grade, Friday meant dimes for the bright, slotted map of America, filling the spaces for states, capitals and cities whose names we knew until twenty dollars sparkled with our beautiful down payment for health. The following Friday the map was deserted, as if the country had been decimated by an attack of atomic bombs, and we began to fill it again. Nobody rushed to fill Harrisburg, our state capital, but somebody always wanted to put a dime in Pittsburgh right away, bringing the city we lived close to back to life.

Once, when we were sent to scrub our hands with hot water, Paul Funovitz, laughing, licked the dime he'd only pretended to put in the slot for Nebraska, keeping it for himself. He laid it on his tongue like a cough drop, and I expected his legs to collapse.

The Unthinkable

During dinner I announced that my sixth-grade teacher was training me and my classmates for the inevitable dropping of an A-bomb on Pittsburgh, repeating "Think of the unthinkable" each time she asked us to duck under our desks and cover our heads.

I repeated her advice that a family like ours needed a hundred cases of bottled water, several shelves of canned goods, and a stockpile of batteries for a radio when we moved underground. "For the unthinkable," I quoted her, convinced that Pittsburgh, six miles away, would vanish while I cowered and covered my eyes.

"The unthinkable," my father said, "is the steel mill closing." He put down the newspaper he read while he ate dinner and stared at me to make sure I understood why that was true.

My mother picked at the cucumber slices in her salad; my sister finished her milk. I held my fork like a pencil while he went on, describing what the closed mill would look like, a mile of buildings given up to vandals while all of us packed up the bakery and watched him close its doors. "And then what?" he asked.

"I don't know," I said, and he snapped the newspaper back open into two wings that hovered above his coffee, reading as if there was nothing on his plate he couldn't find by probing with a fork.

Germs

That fall I thought I was the only person who could see bacteria unaided. Shapes that looked like evil, transparent cells floated in front of my eyes. Some of them were linked into tiny chains; some clustered into clouds. All of them shifted and tumbled when I blinked.

I hadn't read about my gift of microscope-sight in a comic book, and like that plant-voice scientist, I didn't tell anybody, but the germs swarmed so densely I was afraid to breathe. I began to hold my breath as if I was underwater at Spang's swimming pool. For a minute sometimes. Or for as long as my father talked to me about pruning shrubbery or transplanting trees. He told me our work was encouraging growth; he told me my own cells were renewing themselves, and I would be nothing like I was in seven years. I thought that was impossible, but I cut anything that looked out of place and listened to myself turning into memory, one more fantasy I worked on, snipping every branch that looked threatening on those late September shrubs, listening to their voices as they fell.

Testimony

One October morning, instead of going to sleep after work, my father put on a coat and tie and drove into Pittsburgh to testify at a trial for Jan Hughes, who had been in his Boy Scout troop before I'd started school. Jan Hughes was nineteen now and had been arrested for rape. He'd attacked girls who were parked with their boyfriends in the county park, holding a gun on the boys until the girl was in his car.

My father was speaking as a character witness, but the only thing I could remember about Jan Hughes was how he'd looked in his uniform as a sixth-grader like I was. "It looks as if he's guilty, Bill," my mother said when he got home. There'd been an article in the Pittsburgh Press that afternoon, and she'd read it twice. There was a picture of Jan Hughes, but if there hadn't been a caption I wouldn't have recognized him.

My father glanced toward me as if he was evaluating whether I should hear him answer. "I did what I could," he said.

"Of course you did," my mother said, "but there's only so much that can be done."

My father took off his shirt and tie. He slept through dinner and went directly to work at eleven o'clock.

Contagious

Each Friday, during public health, the school nurse filled the room so there wasn't space enough for us, not unless we sat inside like desks, everybody in perfect rows marked by small spots in the wax, the ones that gave away our restlessness, that shamed us if they showed like the hem of a slip.

Contagious, she said, is made of ignorance, boys who refuse milk and eat no greens. It lives on buses and streetcars and seats at the Etna Theater because we'd never knew who'd been there and given us the itch and fester.

The contagious, she said, shout words you mustn't say. They seed their yards with bottles, cans, and tires; drip snot and never cover when they sneeze.

They wipe their noses on their sleeves where crusts collect like scabs that bleed.

The contagious borrow hats and combs. Without a ring of toilet paper, they sit on public toilets, never scrub with soap and water that's been run to scalding hot. They touch their mouths on fountains, eat food dropped to floors.

The filthy are everywhere, common as flies. The contagious spread like news, splattering stains to wash and wipe. Only precaution will keep you clean.

Citizenship

I was supposed to hang bells on door knobs. They were cut from cardboard, each of them declaring, "Voting is the American Way," and I was earning a merit badge for citizenship on a clear, cold Monday night, learning how many families owned unleashed dogs, how many people, hearing me fumble with their door knobs, could burst into the cold and curse from porches while I disappeared into the dark of election eve. I could have been a vandal or a thief to the home owners who overheard me.

A dozen houses into my quota of one hundred, I was wondering why anyone would vote because some eleven-year old looped a bell to their doorknobs. Eisenhower was running again, sure to win, four more years of him smiling benignly as he spoke to the country about Communist threats, so there were only congressmen and local officials in races whose outcome was uncertain. What, exactly, was an alderman? For that matter, what was a ward, and where did it begin and end?

I started to lay the bells on doormats or prop them against the front door, tiptoeing and holding my breath, sure that some of these neighbors would vote with their hands on my throat.

Finally, after running from one more barking dog, I pitched sixty-five bells into a storm sewer, hoping they would soak into unrecognizable sludge by the time they drifted into the creek that ran into the Allegheny River two miles from where I stood. Easy enough to do, but then I decided I needed to spend another hour freezing in the darkness before I could claim I'd hand-delivered my one hundred.

I could lie about citizenship as long as I stayed outside, as long as I didn't play pinball at the corner mom & pop store for an hour, sliding nickels into GOLD DIGGERS, where women with half-exposed breasts leaned on every bumper and smiled beside each bell that told me I had a chance with them in six or seven years, maybe sooner, if I threw more than cardboard bells down the sewer.

For nearly an hour I wandered the front street where there weren't any dogs or men standing in windows looking out at the darkness as if it was a television screen. At last, to make sure I could believe my report about citizenship was the truth, I walked up and back one side street between six blocks of houses. I saw eleven sets of headlights, two that slowed enough to bring the fear-sweat out of me. When one man, improbably, whispered, "Hello there" from a shrubbery-darkened driveway, I held my breath until I passed, listening for his footsteps as if they were a reason to believe I had just changed.

Learning the Windsor Knot

Dressing for church, I wasn't thinking about anything but simplicity on Sunday mornings until my uncle said I needed to leave my "nigger knot" behind unless I wanted to announce I wasn't able to work with my brain. He took me into the one-sink men's room in the basement of our Lutheran church and made me look at my buttoned collar until the thin knot became a birthmark. He unraveled that knot and handed me each arrowed end of the cheap paisley cloth.

"Ready?" he said. "Ready?" as if we were about to run through fire. "Over. Like this, and then under," and I followed his hands at my throat until he finished and tugged that knot up close to my collar. "Now," he said, untying that knot, "show me," and I did, hands twisting like the thoughtful.

That fall the news reported that the bodies of three girls had been found, their throats knotted by silk ties, the killer wealthy or pretending, spending before each crime. I wondered if the killer had once been a Boy Scout, but kept that to myself. When I said aloud that I'd heard one of the discovered bodies was just bones, my mother declared nobody should know such things, that the dead deserved privacy. My cheap ties dangled from my closet's hook. I practiced each day, afraid I'd forget the intricate loops. My uncle told me it takes only six weeks for a body to become bones, talking like a killer, like somebody who would return and check.

Watching the Onions

In a magazine at Dick Frankie's barber shop, I read about how some scientists had been observing onion plants, believing they possessed something called "mitogenetic rays." Their theory was that one onion plant influenced the growth of another nearby plant unless glass was placed between them. I imagined the scientists' faces, how they resembled the plant-listener in my comic book as they crouched down to measure their results.

I didn't get to finish the article, but it looked as if those men were about to learn something no one else knew. If they were smart enough, they'd figure out how the onions communicated with each other, what sort of language was spoken with mitogenetic rays.

My father, when I mentioned the article, told me those experiments had taken place years ago. "Dick Frankie must have been cleaning out his cellar." He looked out our kitchen window toward the patch of back yard where he grew onions every spring, and said you had to be an idiot to believe plants could do anything but grow and die.

Two Weeks after the Presidential Election

My father, one night, was robbed at gunpoint for sixty-seven dollars the same week I watched a boy from my class steal records, promising one of them for me, desiring nothing in return but my knowing "Love Me Tender" had come for free. "There's all those atom bombs now," he said. "No sense waiting for what you want," saying something I imagined Jan Hughes must have thought as he raped those girls.

Though he worked alone, my father told the police he didn't lock the bakery door because there were men who stopped in late to talk, and he enjoyed having some company. "All these years and no problems," he said. When he was told not to keep money in the register, he said that the money had sent the robber away. If the register had been empty, what might he have done?

Thanksgiving

My father showed me all the things the government had sent to us five years earlier, when I was about to enter first grade. There were tests being done at a place called Camp Deitrich, he said. The army was looking for antidotes to terrible diseases the Russians might send our way. They mailed us and everybody else survival rules: close windows, boil water, used sealed food or else a week after the Communists sprayed us like weevils we'd have headaches and fever, something like the flu until we couldn't breathe and turned blue, coughing up blood tainted by the pneumonic plague.

Nothing, that pamphlet said, would save us from melioidosis, what Stalin's henchmen had brought back from the tropics—ulcers, swelling, and inflammation of each membrane un-

til we died. Bacteria warfare was coming in a lethal mist; the warnings were dittoed like the directions for air-raid drills I'd practiced since first grade, diving under my desk or facing a wall in the basement.

Until sixth grade, I had always obeyed. I'd never looked up until I heard a whistle, happy that I would outlive Paul Funovitz who always talked and couldn't stand still. Because he could barely read, I thought; because he didn't recognize disease in the mail, its precaution tale.

Gift

In late November, for their fifteenth anniversary, my father decided to give my mother a gift of assorted wax fruit. "Each piece will always look the same," he said in the store, and I had to admit the blended colors looked just short of ripe, as if the next day, when the anniversary arrived, they would be perfect.

While I watched, my father arranged and rearranged the apples and pears, the peach and bunched grapes, trying to figure out what would please my mother after fifteen years. He said he'd memorized the size of the bowl he intended to fill as a morning surprise, centering it upon the kitchen table after he stacked the old newspapers and swept the sweet roll crumbs into one hand to drop inside the wastebasket, removing the stained mug, the last of a wedding set, he used for a week to spare my mother from having to wash it.

"Now," he said at last, directing me to look at the arrangement, "aren't these picture perfect. Can't you see them looking beautiful forever?

We took the long way home, driving through Etna until we passed Spang-Chalfant. "It's all been decided," my father said. "The mill's shutting down for good next year. Etna might as well fall into the earth then."

I thought of the earthquake in the comic book he'd given me money for as a sort of bribe to ride along with him to the shopping center. The earth opened in huge cracks that sucked tumbling, screaming bodies into fire. The streets we were riding on seemed ready to split and heave. In the altered evening, I felt as if we were struggling to stay afloat.

❖ ❖ ❖

Alex MacLean. *Wheat Strips Run Perpendicular to the Prevailing Wind*. Chromogenic print. Courtesy of the artist and Yancey Richardson Gallery, New York.

Buried

Land had occupied him as long as I'd known him. When we started dating I'd sit down at my computer and there'd be an e-mail:

From: Tom Wright <tom.wri6ht@gmail.com>
To: Carol Jones <caJones@yahoo.com>

Subject: LAND

check this out…
http://sfbay.craigslist.org/eby/reb/848429166.html

And In the Piedmont. The Piedmont!!!

The link would take me to a page titled, "*****Nice CHEAP Lot*****," offering me an eighth of an acre for about a hundred grand. I thought it was cute, this little obsession. And I even considered that it was his financial-mindedness, hard at work, keeping an eye out for good investments. I thought this indicated marriage material. My counselor, Gil, agreed.

When the topic finally came up, Tom down on one knee in one of his fancy suits and a stone shining in my eye, what was a girl to do? I said, "Yes."

❖ ❖ ❖

"Why land?" I ask.

"It's a sure investment, Carol. Markets crash. The value of any given currency operates with inflation—"

"Housing markets fluctuate."

"—True, but when the resale value of your property goes down. You don't have any less property. If the dollar tanks compared to the Euro, my bank account has dollars of lesser value. And I can't live on a pile of dollars. Try growing beans out of dollars."

"You want to grow beans?"

"I'm just saying I can do that with land. Worst-case scenario. I know how. My father was a farmer."

My father is a deadbeat, I think; does that mean I should grow distant?

❖ ❖ ❖

On Saturdays we like to take bike rides. It's something we've done from the time we were dating. Rural routes are our favorite. We'll bike up Mt. Diablo, laughing at the retirees slogging as we pass on a climb. We'll head around the reservoir in Lafayette, over the Oakland Hills, through the farmland past Pittsburgh/Bay Point. There is a rush that comes with the speed and the pistons of our legs.

Of course, Tom is faster than me. Longer legs and lungs five years younger (I robbed the cradle, and am proud). So part of the deal is he'll wear a backpack with our picnic lunch in it. The dual purpose: to slow him down (which it never does really) and when he reaches a scenic, secluded place around noon he will get the meal ready. When I arrive a half-hour later, hauling an empty CamelBak, nothing else can look this good. Thick-sliced Brie, honey ham, and cranberry-walnut bread, a Gundlach-Bundschu rosé wine, all of this lying on the checkered blanket next to Tom. His shirt drying in a sunny spot on the grass, his black hair slick and disarrayed, mussed by his helmet. With his hands behind his head, squinting, taking in the midday sun. He smiles a white crescent moon. I climb off my bike and walk over to him, my legs weak from the ride. Tom sits up. I see him grow in his spandex as he reaches for me.

❖ ❖ ❖

"What do you think is the cause of this hesitation with Tom?" Gil says.

With a long pause I say, "Hmmmm," and look out the window at the bamboo deer chaser fountain, turning my head to the side to watch it bonk a rock, spilling water. "His dad was a farmer. He tells me this every time I question the wisdom of his 'investment strategy.' Recently I've been getting the same story out of him. A memory from his youth. It's an excuse."

"Can you tell me the memory?"

"Tom is sitting on the floor in his childhood home and he hears the screen door slam. His father walks in with dirt under his fingernails and a hiss that they might lose the farm. Tom is like eight and doesn't understand. They move to San Leandro and live poor for a while, then blue collar."

"I don't imagine that's how Tom would tell the story."

"Tom would speak slower, say *soil* instead of *dirt*, and he'd add the smell of a plum orchard, men in suits asking them to move, and a bulldozer taking the house apart for dramatic flair."

"You don't find him to be in the least bit touching?"

I can't wait to go home, I think.

❖ ❖ ❖

The wedding was amazing. Tom had been saving for a while, and he really went all out. I had always wanted something a little smaller, but the idea of having finally found The One excited Tom. He had just bought a house in the Oakland Hills. Two thousand square feet on a half-acre yard. Everyone was impressed. We married on a golf course as the sun set with over five hundred people in attendance. Then there was the live band, toasting, dinner, drinks, dancing. Around midnight the limo took us back to his house in the hills. I moved in.

Moving in might not be the right term. We had been sharing houses for the last seven months. Staying over whenever we pleased. But let me tell you, things are definitely different once you share a primary residence. Negotiations have to happen. Space needs to be made. Tom was not the best at conflict. One night in particular I remember us arguing about where my new popcorn popper would go. All the cabinet space was full of his pots and pans, and the kitchen felt like a head cold: all stuffed up. He told me we didn't need the popper. I added it to the list of things he said we didn't need: my washer and dryer, my fan, my wall art, my orchid. Then I took the list and I forgot about it. It's just stuff, I told myself.

❖ ❖ ❖

My mom calls me, "And how are things? Tell me about your week, Caroline. I want every juicy detail." She calls me Caroline.

"I got a ticket."

"That doesn't sound important or deep. That's not why a mother calls."

It was very emotional when it happened. So I say, "It was very emotional."

"You never did do well with authority. Speeding ticket?"

"Parking." I correct myself: "Stopping in a bus zone. I was dropping Tom off at the BART station and there were two cars in front of me, so even though it was a red curb, I had to stop, because I couldn't get around them that easily. Tom jumped out, since I was stopped anyway, when this fucking cop stepped out and asked for my registration. Tom was standing there. Stunned. Not knowing what to do since he knew if he stayed he'd miss his train. I was comatose with rage in the car, since this was my second ticket this week. The tears were streaming down my face and I knew I should be playing the cute little helpless woman on this jerk, but my pride made me snappy with him. Tom started walking away, like he'd decided to make his train after all. I thought, who could blame him? It wasn't like he could have helped the situation. He walked over to the entrance of the BART and then he came back and got in."

"You see, Honey, he came back to be with you."

"I asked him what he was doing over there. He said he had some trash to throw away." This last made me feel worst of all. A lack of proper priorities, my counselor says.

"Tom has good sense," she says. "Now, let's talk about Thanksgiving." And I tune out.

❖ ❖ ❖

One week's good vacation at Pismo Beach—it's Tom's idea. One week's good vacation at Pismo Beach, and I've missed my period. I check my calendar. I am fairly regular, and I put a little red sharpie dot on the day when it comes. I'm five days off. We have the money. It's not money; it's the fact that we haven't decided one way or the other on this. This is not in our five-year plans. When Tom gets home from work, I don't tell him. Instead, I tell him I went shopping and the price of cubed sweet potatoes is up by five cents. He mumbles something about gas prices affecting shipping costs. I tell him about the squeaky wheel on the BMW, and about the pre-paid dance lessons we have, which are about to expire, and about a new television series where the parents swap children for a year at birth only to find out after the first year that the switch was never made and the baby you have raised is actually your baby after all. He asks if I'm feeling OK, and I set dinner on the table with a broad smile. Ribs and beer, Tom's favorite.

The next day, as soon as I hear Tom close the garage door, I go to the pharmacy. I buy a test to take home. I make sure it's the one with the + and the – on it rather than the one-line two-line bullshit. I drink three glasses of water and one of coffee until I have to go, and then I let it rip all over the little strip. Two minutes later I imagine the addition to my life, to our lives. I try not to think about popcorn. Room will have to be made.

I wait a few weeks, and then I see the doctor. He tells me it's a sure thing. Later he tells me it's twins. My mother will be delighted.

❖ ❖ ❖

"Yes, Tom. Twins." I tell him while he's away on business. This gives him both the time to process the news on his own, and a feeling like I can handle myself in this situation. At least that's my hope.

The other line is empty space.

"I hope your pitch goes well. Go get 'em," I say cheerfully. "Love you, talk to you later." I hang up. I sit by the phone. Forty-eight seconds later it rings. "Hello?"

"Carol. I love you. I was just shocked."

"You and me both, Bud." I resist tears.

"It's just." He flounders. "This wasn't in our financial plan. And two of them. Not one, but *two*, for God's sake."

Resistance is futile. I cry.

❖ ❖ ❖

When I start to show I quit my job and stay home. Tom thinks it is important to nest. He's all for women in the workplace, equal rights. This is an opportunity, not a punishment, he says. I paint the room for the babies a blue color with a mural of frogs and lilies and a pond on one wall. This room has been our guest room. The beds have gone up on Craigslist and are

now sitting in the garage, waiting for a reasonable offer. I stand up from putting the final daubs of blue onto the bottom corner and step back to observe the room. It feels like a blanket fort that I used to make out of my mom's king-sized comforter, two chairs, and some pillows when I was a child. I guess that's fitting. I go to the kitchen to get a glass of water.

These years of marriage have changed us. The house now seems to have spheres of influence rather than one omnipresent ruler. We two haven't become one in some mystical way, but this is now a house we share. There are spaces where I get to reign and spaces where Tom's word is law. It feels like a peace. Or at worst a cold war. The kitchen and our bedroom are mine. The garage and home office are his. I think the living room and dining room are still being contested in our subtle domestic battles.

I test my theory of spheres by performing absurdities to see if Tom will question me. I start keeping my bras in the freezer. I decide, if he asks, that I will explain how nice the frosty underwire feels in the heat of summer.

Tom comes home. He drops his briefcase at the door and goes to the fridge. He opens the freezer, grabs some ice cream, and closes it. All without blinking an eye. He notices I'm watching and walks over to kiss me on the cheek. Asking me how my day was.

Good, I tell him, and I begin to wonder what is in his spheres that I should probably question.

❖ ❖ ❖

When the boys are born, we have fun timing ourselves to see who is quicker with a diaper. We have different strategies. I do one at a time. First Taylor and then Ryan. Tom does them at the same time. Switching from one boy to the next and leaving piles of wipes like mud-capped, snow-covered hills. He wins, beating me by thirty seconds. Luckily, we didn't bet on it.

Tom's job gives him three weeks paternity leave. We spend most of the time getting acclimated and eating casseroles that our friends have brought for us. The boys are a blessing. Doctors can predict gender, but they can't tell you about blessings. Tom tells me that he will buy some land for their future. We can sell it when they graduate from high school to pay for college, he says. I say OK. The money seems to be his sphere, and I know he's good with it.

For the first few months I am inseparable from the boys. Tom might be good with them, but they need me and I know it. Their greedy brown eyes let me know it. Their tiny hands grab for anything and stretch to understand what this place is, and I know a desire, instinctual, to be here and interpret. *Carpet*, I say, as I place the squirming bodies on the floor, *Carpet*.

❖ ❖ ❖

"You need to get out," my mom says, "be with your husband."

"I'm with my husband every night." When he's in town.

"I can look after the kids. You two go on one of those bike rides you used to be so fond of."

"It would be nice to get out." I look at myself in the mirror. I am still not in my pre-twins jeans. "But it hasn't been that long. They've never had a bottle."

"Get out, get air." She is loving this. "Let Grandma have a chance." She won't take no.

"Let me talk to Tom and get back to you. Sound good?"

❖ ❖ ❖

As we leave, my mother is kneeling on the floor of her living room repeating the words, "Can you say 'Grand-ma'," over and over, while she dances one hand on each child's abdomen.

My spandex was too tight, so I bought this new outfit. It's not spandex, but it's better than biking in sweats. Though out here in Tracy, where my mom lives, it probably doesn't matter much what I look like. Tom thanks her as we walk out the door and climb on the bikes. It amazes me how much labor can hurt. How could I endure that pain and find biking to be so difficult afterwards? Tom streaks past me, a blaze of yellow and shiny black, the colors of his jersey. His body is as tight as ever in spite of his eating habits.

Where to, he yells back. I shrug as I pump my legs. How about Cochrane, and he turns down West Eleventh.

❖ ❖ ❖

This is not the ideal bike ride I envisioned. My CamelBak is dry in the first hour and I haven't seen Tom since we turned south on Bird Road. I keep my head down and watch the asphalt just ahead of me for cracks or debris. The countryside out here is flat and there are few trees, besides the orchards, to block the sun, and there isn't much to look at anyway. I am glad I am wearing UV protective glasses. I can feel my neck getting warm and I think about the death rates of skin cancer and about my babies growing up motherless. The wind whips me and I lean in, balancing the forces and pedaling on as dust gets in my mouth, nose, and eyes. I taste dirt and I smell dirt, but all I see are the staccato strobe-lit images of plum trees on the right side of the road as I turn my head away from the forceful gusts and blink the dirt out. Damn farmland, I think. Cars float past me on this frontage road effortlessly, and I inhale their exhaust. I reach up and touch the back of my neck. It is radiating heat. I stop and tie my jacket tight around my neck by the sleeves to block the sun and pant as I continue biking. Faster. Hoping that Tom will find the one tree in this valley large enough to shade both of us and stop there. Hoping that stop is just around the corner. I look up ahead. It is one flat, permanent road.

There are no corners.

❖ ❖ ❖

I bike halfway over a bridge and stop. There is water below flowing rapidly and trees line either side. I look on both sides of the road on each side of the bridge. I see a sandy beach with a half-dozen empty beer bottles that have green turtles on them strewn around haphazardly. On another side I see a still water pool and a rope swing from a grassy patch. A handful of people in black inner tubes floating the river who raise their bottles to me and whistle. I am flattered, but I don't see Tom. I remount my bike and continue.

❖ ❖ ❖

Just past where the thirty-three meets the five, I find his bike. It is not by a shady tree, or by a bench, or a faucet. It lies on top of our backpack in a patch of cow melons and burrs by the side of an empty lot of farmland. I clench my brakes and can barely hold my weight on my legs as I dismount. My knees are jelly, and I think I might collapse, so I lean on my bike with my forearms and walk it like a cane with wheels. *TOM*, I shout as I look at the sapling orchard on one side of the road, then turn to the empty dirt furrows on the other. I don't see him, so I opt for the side with the orchard, the side his bike is on.

The orchard is large. I can't see the end of it. There is a layer of water between the trees, which, I assume, is slowly seeping into the ground and feeding the young roots. He couldn't be in there, I think, when I see the yellow jersey he wears draped over one of the young trees just inside the orchard. I am debating removing my shoes to wade into the muck when I hear a noise behind me. I turn to see Tom huffing and puffing across the road.

"What were you doing over there?" I ask.

"Checking out the area." He looks around with poorly feigned nonchalance. "You know."

Tom is sweating hard. It is hot. He has his shoes in his hands, and his feet trace a small trail of blood. His upper shoulders are badly sunburned, and as my eyes move down his arms what I first mistook for a tan is a thick dust coating his whole body, ending in raw black dirt on his hands, knees, and feet. He seems to be dazed, and I wonder if this might be sunstroke, or something even worse.

"No, I don't know." I wait for him to continue his explanation. But at this point I almost don't care. I am wondering where my lunch is. I am wondering why we didn't stop earlier by the beautiful river as so many partygoers clearly had before us. But all I say is, "Were you digging?" And I wait for him to answer. Tom has bent over, searching the backpack for something. He comes out with a pencil and a scrap of paper and begins scribbling.

"Yes." He admits, staring lazily around at the place we are standing.

"Why?"

"No reason." He finishes his scribbling and puts the notes back in the bag, standing up and looking at me. Whatever trance he was in, he snapped out of. "Let's go back to that river huh? There's nothing out here but empty land. That place had shade."

I nod in my fatigue, and it feels like turning a corner. We bike back to the river, eat a quick lunch, and return to my mother's.

❖ ❖ ❖

One day, several months later, Tom is at work when his office phone rings. I am in there dusting, and I hesitate, then I answer. A deep, unfamiliar voice says, "Hello. Tom?" The man speaks quickly. The boys begin to cry in the other room.

"This is Carol, can I take a message?" I say. The other line goes dead. I wait until I hear a dial tone. I begin to worry as I change the boys' diapers, and then I call Tom.

❖ ❖ ❖

"Probably a prank call. Don't think too much of it," Tom says, surprisingly not snapping over my invasion of his office, his sphere.

I do think of it though. I think about how prank callers don't usually ask for the resident by name. Usually they pull a joke, or make obscene noises in the phone. I have experienced prank calls. This man wanted to talk to Tom.

❖ ❖ ❖

"What makes you suspicious?" Gil thinks I'm worried about nothing.

"I checked the phone and wrote down the number he had called from. Then as I was cleaning Tom's office the other day, I came across a piece of paper with an address and the same phone number."

"Cleaning?"

"Fine. I was snooping. But I am getting nervous, and I have every right to be. I wake up in the middle of the night and Tom is not in our bed. I call him at work and he never has time to talk. And now this man called and Tom lied to me."

"Don't you think Tom will see this as an invasion of his personal space?"

"Damn him and damn personal space."

I leave the session early, return home, feed the babies and copy down the address and phone number from the scrap of paper in Tom's office. I need to keep a record.

❖ ❖ ❖

Tom is away on a business trip. I look up the address on Google maps. I click on the button for satellite imaging and look at it zoomed in as I scroll over the surrounding areas. There are sapling trees on one side and an empty lot on the other. I scroll north and I see a river with a little beach. I imagine I can even see beer bottles with little green turtles on them in the sand.

❖ ❖ ❖

On Sundays Tom spends his morning in his home office making calls, handling our investments and, when in season, doing our taxes. This is a part of his sphere, and I have come to understand that I am not to interfere.

I am sitting on the couch reading a magazine about what not to feed my babies when Tom comes into the living room and sits down next to me. He looks tired, and the veins of his eyes are bright. He takes my hand and begins:

"Honey, I need to talk to you about something." His voice is slow and I can feel his pulse through my hand. "I am about to make the investment of a lifetime. Something we can't pass up." I am confused. This is not how our house works. I don't feel a need to be consulted on this.

"Great, what is it?" I am trying to be supportive.

"Remember the bike ride we took? The one where I was covered in dirt?" I nod, trying not to show how clearly I remember. "The land that I was walking around on is for sale. Honey, it's for sale." His voice is quickening now and a grin creeps across his face.

"Have you been sleeping well?" I put my hand to his forehead to see if he's feverish. "If it's for sale and you think it's a good investment, then go ahead. Buy away." I smile faintly and squeeze his hand.

"This one isn't that easy. It's a bit high risk. And I'll have to move a lot of money. But I have faith that it will pay off."

"If you're sure then—" he cuts me off.

"It's investing. Nothing is sure."

❖ ❖ ❖

"Apparently it's a plot of land that's all connected." I'm trying to explain an obsession I don't understand to a mother who doesn't care. "Two and a half square miles of it, and the seller is not going to split the lot up."

My mother lets out a low whistle over the phone and says, "That's a lot of land." Deep, Mom, I think. "How much is it selling for?"

"That's the thing. It's selling for top dollar. Over twice what the farms around it are going for. Tom says the guy who owns it doesn't want to part with it. It has been in their family forever."

"Then why does the guy have it on the market?" And this gets my wheels turning. "More

importantly, when do I get to see the boys again?"

❖ ❖ ❖

I have a college friend who went into real estate. She looks into the history of this piece of land and comes up with some startling results. Apparently, every time an offer comes in that matches the asking price, the old man who owns it ups the asking price. No one has made an offer in three years, and the man has kept the price up. Way up. So that no one would think of putting money on it. My friend says that the price this old guy is asking is higher than a real estate developer's net profit on a plot of land in a more prime location. I decide not to ask her what I'm thinking. Why does Tom want to buy it?

❖ ❖ ❖

"Tom gets stranger and stranger." I am beginning to loathe these visits to Gil. I feel like the more I listen to myself talk about my life, the worse it seems to be.

"How so?"

"For one thing, we haven't had sex in over two months. That wouldn't have been uncommon when he was traveling for a month and a half at a time. But he requested more day trips, and now he's home almost every night."

"But he's not with you."

"No. Not at all. He's in his office working figures, or God knows what. He hardly plays with the boys. And all I hear him talk about is this land. Which, by the way, we can't afford. I did some calculations. Even if he sold off all the other properties we own, which were good investments, we would still be a ways away from the minimum down payment that they are asking for." I take a deep breath before I continue. "I might be a housewife, but I'm not an idiot."

"Have you expressed these feelings to Tom?"

"No."

"You don't sound happy." For some reason I think of this as a strange question, though I suppose it isn't a question. Happy has never been something I thought I was supposed to be. I close my eyes and try to recall the last time I was happy, as hot tears roll down my cheek.

❖ ❖ ❖

When I realize that Tom has sold off most of our assets to actually go through with this crazy plan, I pack a bag, bundle the kids in the car and head to my mother's. I call him on the phone and leave a message that begins, "Tom, I love you. But I can't be with you if you're doing this. Think about it, for God's sake. Even if you got a loan that size, we would have to work our whole lives just to pay it off. We'd be in servitude. Let me be clear: *it is not worth it.* I'm leaving you, Tom . . ." and I talk on and on. The message ends, and I call him back to leave another one. Gil told me to stay away from vague language. But by the end of the second message I am asking how he could do this, how could he? And I mean it not so much in what he is doing to us, Tom and me, but rather what he is doing to the boys. Some of those investments were supposed to be for them. This obsession of his with this farmland. What is that going to bring us? Am I supposed to be a farmwife and make butter from a milk cow all day? I don't tell him where I'm going, but I know he'll figure it out. Where else does a woman run to with her kids?

Gil told me I need to "hold onto myself," which I think means drawing an ultimatum in the sand. From a strictly economic perspective, if Tom wants to go through with this, I will divorce him just to save half our assets. I am thinking of the boys' future.

❖ ❖ ❖

It is sunrise when he is pounding on the front door of my mother's house.

I imagined, a week ago when I left, that he'd show up sooner, repentant and desiring to see his sons. But here I see, through the peephole, him in an old T-shirt and jeans. He is unshaven and unshowered. He looks skinnier, too, as if he hasn't been eating. For the first time in our life together, I am scared of him. He is someone I no longer know.

I don't open the door, but I listen from inside. He is yelling:

"I sold it all, Carol. The market was so sweet, I sold the house the day after you left. The furniture went with it, and I took all our clothes to the Exchange. I've moved all our assets, and look here." He whips a piece of paper from his pocket and waves it around madly, like a drunk with a stolen credit card. "Look at this. It's the deed, Carol. It's all finished now. I've got the deed."

For the second time this week, I cry, and I slide down the locked door to curl up into a ball. My head is pressed against my knees, and my face feels flushed from the stark-raving embarrassment on the front porch of my mother's house.

"Come and see, Carol." He is yelling and pounding the wall next to the door with every word. "Get the boys to come and see."

❖ ❖ ❖

Jessica Cuello

Quilting Frame

My mother's hand rises
above the frame, then pulls

the thread back through.
I lie beneath it when school lets out.

A sheet covers it when she is gone.
My eyes trace patterns:

a triangle with crooked sides
forms the stilled

body of a goose. I try the needle
and even the bright blood

is part of a design,
though I am careful

to tilt my hand away
from the taut flying geese.

Ellen Sullins

Pitch

for BHK

If you shot the movie of your life out of sequence,
it could open with the scene where a part of your psyche
breaks away and runs screaming to its cave,

while the other parts roll their eyes, line up behind
the charismatic leading man, and wait to plunge
like those Acapulco divers from the great Quebrada Cliffs

to the vast seductive Sea of What the Hell.
I would call it *Portrait of the Artist as a Lemming*.

But more likely you would call it *Tapestry*
and open with a wide soaring shot panning down
on the hot pink convertible that speeds heroically

along its vector through Mojave desolation,
where wind lifts your hair in a raven's wing as you
sing along with Carole King's "Where You Lead"

unaware of the score that swells to a haunting theme
to alert the audience that something beautiful
and tragic waits for you and nothing can be done

but watch it all unfold, the only question being
if you survive or die – either way, you will insist
on some modicum of promise. Perhaps a lone

flower on a cactus, blooming in the afterglow
of conflagration. Yes, that's the perfect backdrop
to roll the credits for all your weeping fans.

Back-Yard New Housing Project, Staten Island, New York, n.y. Dan Graham 1978

Dan Graham. *Back-Yard New Housing Project, Staten Island*. 1978. C-Print. Courtesy the artist and Lisson Gallery, London.

Julie Iromuanya

Only in America

On the whole, the boy, Victor, is cheerful. However, he has come to appreciate the fact that his mother's sole purpose in life is to deny him the delights of the world. His father agrees. When he bursts upon a mirthless room roaring at the top of his lungs in imitation of the famed X-men hero, Wolverine, forks and butter knives attached to each hand, his mother lifts him by his shoulders, holds him to her eye level, and threatens to beat him. His father intervenes. "Let the boy play." Everyone agrees with his father. For Victor's fifth birthday, the house is filled with strangers, mostly Nigerian. When he somersaults into laps, marches through the room tasting the food on their plates, when he bangs pots and pans during Dan Rather, the guests join in and agree with his mother:

"The boy is wild."

"The boy is uncontrollable."

"The boy needs to be spanked."

"America is spoiling the boy."

Still, there is an air of secret pleasure in their tone.

Victor's father sweeps Victor's gifts aside and presents him with a Big Wheel wrapped in a shiny red bow. At first, admittedly, Victor isn't particularly drawn to the contraption. He doesn't even bother to mount it, suspicious of its look. It doesn't have arms and legs, monster eyes, or claws like his other gifts. It doesn't have bright lights that swirl around or a horn that blares like his fire truck. His father heaves the Big Wheel in his direction and it spins and spirals as if unraveling. Victor heaves it back. This excites him; they shove the Big Wheel back and forth until he grows restless. He does not grow to love the Big Wheel until months later.

An ugly old man with trembling lips presides over the celebration. His voice warbles as he makes one pronouncement after another during the passing of the kola nut. Victor is supposed to call the man Uncle. Adults fill the room in long gowns of bright prints, swallowing balls of foo foo, akra, and garri, drinking palm wine. They boast of their newly purchased homes, computers, SUVs, and their second and third degrees. They disagree about politics. Most of the women are in the kitchen. Victor's mother is among them. She has banished Victor from the kitchen. Days before his birthday party, she had found Victor in the kitchen, peering into the frozen, lifeless face of the goat that had been butchered for the celebration. Victor's cheek lay flat against the counter, his tongue waggled out like that of the goat.

Victor is well aware that his mother has wanted no part in the festivities, yet there she is, bent over a pot of soup, flipping through ingredients in the cabinet like swatches. His mother had wanted to feed Victor ice cream and cake and hot dogs, purchased at the grocery. She wanted balloons and streamers and to invite one or two other boys from Victor's school to join in. She had intended to take them to the children's museum or a movie afterward. His parents fought over this as they fight over everything.

To Victor, adulthood is equated with displeasure and disagreeableness. Instead of being frightened during the fights, Victor is merely annoyed that the attention is drawn away from him. Although nearly every one of his parents' fights begins with *the boy*, he suspects that they are fighting about something that has nothing to do with him. He thinks this unfair and rivals for the due attention. He bangs louder on pots and pans. He cuts holes into the living room couches and doesn't bother to flip them over to disguise his artistry. He marks up the walls with his crayons. He pushes the food around on his plate, chews it up, and spits it out. Each time, without fail, his mother will race around the table, grasping him in her fingers, holding him to her eye level. She threatens, "I will break your head." Or "I will send you to Nigeria."

When the threats are issued, he is freshly wounded. He wails as loud as he can. His father always emerges from the wings. "Are you raising a girl?" he will ask his mother. With this, his mother cannot argue. After more threats, she sets him down and turns her fury on his father.

Of all the threats his mother has issued, the most perplexing of all is the threat to send Victor to Nigeria. He has mixed feelings. On the one hand, his father speaks so joyously of his days there as a child, running as freely as he wanted, climbing trees, playing with goats and chickens, swimming in rivers, amassed by adoring adults and children. His father shares these delights with him as they nibble moi moi or when his father secrets him a sip of palm wine, which he sucks down so quickly he comes up choking and gasping for air. No one in Nigeria will make him put away his toys. After all, there are house boys and house girls.

On the other hand, his mother tells him that in Nigeria there will be no pizza or chicken nuggets. There will be foo foo and jollof rice, which he likes well enough, but nothing can take the place of pizza. The children will make fun of the way he speaks. He will have to leave his Big Wheel behind. Worst of all, he will be beaten if he misbehaves.

Of one thing, Victor is certain. Anything that evokes any pleasure in the world is considered naughty. Because of this, he will be beaten by neighbors, family friends, school teachers. In his mind, Victor imagines a long line of men and women with his mother's arms and fingers grasping him by the shoulders, flipping him upside down, beating him with the soles of their slippers, beating him with switches from trees, beating him with belts, beating him with whatever they can grasp.

❖ ❖ ❖

When he is six, Victor's mother runs away with him. It is night, and he wakes with her face so close to his that he can smell stockfish on her breath. Victor is too groggy to put up any fight. She must know this, because she wraps him in her arms and hugs him to her chest. She pushes her lips to his forehead in a dry kiss. He is completely defenseless. They are in the cab before he realizes that he is in his shoes. Over his pajamas, he is wearing his winter coat, mittens, and hat. The pajamas are cotton and too thick to comfortably wear underneath the coat. Sweat dampens his arms, legs, and throat. He

begins to itch. In a futile attempt to free himself, Victor kicks and beats his arms. His mother has anticipated this, buttoned and zipped him in so securely that his efforts are fruitless. In frustration, Victor cries and wails. In his despair, he wants his favorite item in the universe, his Big Wheel. "Big Wheel," he shrieks.

She hasn't thought of that.

At first, the cab driver glances at him in the rearview mirror again and again. When the crying becomes a choking, spitting fury, the driver says, "Make him stop."

"I am paying," his mother says. But something about her tone tells Victor that the driver is winning. "I will buy you candy if you are good," she says to Victor.

When the car finally stops, they are in front of a brick, two-story building. A pink light flickers outside. The cab driver drops them off in front without even bothering to bring their luggage, three fat suitcases, to the door. His mother grudgingly pays the tip anyway. Victor flings himself on the sidewalk screaming, kicking, punching.

"There is a swimming pool," she says to him. "You will eat pizza and ice cream for breakfast."

Eventually, they are surrounded by a crowd. His mother shields her eyes. She attempts to collect their luggage, to collect him, to smile, to speak to him in hushed Igbo, which she rarely speaks. They look at his mother as if she is stealing him. He feels taken.

"Your Big Wheel is inside," she says to him. Victor gazes at his mother suspiciously through the tears. If she has his Big Wheel, she will not let him play with it while he cries. Is it hidden somewhere as a surprise? He decides to believe her and sucks back his tears, his cries diminished to a whimper.

By morning, Victor's father arrives. Striped under the slanted rays of light that spread through the blinded window, he hugs Victor to his chest. Victor feels the inhale of his father's staggered breaths. He tastes his father's sweat through the suit and tie he wears to work. His father heads to the car, leaving his mother to collect the unopened suitcases and store them in the car's trunk. Victor sits alongside his father in the front seat. The whole way home, his mother weeps. Her cries are a steady, uninterrupted moan wet with her tears.

❖ ❖ ❖

The boy inadvertently becomes Job and Ifi's battlefield. Nearly two years ago, when Victor first enrolled in kindergarten, his parents battled over whether to place him in the local public school or to send him to private school. Although they are not Catholic, his father insisted that Victor should attend the Catholic school where the fitted and ironed uniforms reminded him of the refined boys academies in Nigeria. Most importantly, the boy would be away from the influences of hoodlums, namely the black Americans and Mexican Americans whom he nightly sees on television. Ifi had insisted that Victor should attend the neighborhood public school. After all, it was free and just a few short blocks from their newly purchased home. She wouldn't have to worry with washing and mending uniforms. This freedom from restriction that she has observed over her few years in America is what she considers quintessentially American.

Job had nearly won the battle when a local Nigerian teenager was on the news for attempted murder. Job blamed it on the influence of black Americans. Ifi's arguments were entirely useless. In defeat, she starched and ironed his clothes, lotioned his face, and wiped his nose so that the three could visit a Catholic school. They sat along a long, noisy corridor and watched as boys and girls of various sizes tramped up and down the stairs to their classrooms. The first surprise was that the school was coed; however, Job dismissed the disappointment. Eventually, they would have a daughter. It would just be easier to have them take the same bus to school each morning. The second surprise was that the children were loud and rambunctious, not at all disciplined and scholastic like the boys on the glossy sheets of the school catalogue. But the final and most damning surprise was the cost. Even Ifi had counted on an installment or good-faith plan. Surely, good Christians couldn't turn potential parishioners away. They had already agreed to join the Catholic Church for the promised discount. But at the end of the afternoon, they drove home, the sound of the car's engine knocking. The next morning, Victor was enrolled in the neighborhood public school. As a compromise, whenever Victor went out to play, Job stood out on the porch eyeing the neighborhood boys if they approached, until they knew to leave Victor unharmed.

The house is the first purchase that Ifi and Job make together. Like the boy, the action further solidifies them as a unit, not the two strangers who met the day of their arranged honeymoon. For weeks, Job had scoured neighborhoods looking at homes until he found one they could afford, tall and willowy, but with a sound structural frame. He acquired a loan and signed the deed on the house, certain that Ifi would be pleased. When they drove up to the house, Ifi burst into tears. It was nothing like what she expected her first home to be like. She had expected a garage, a picket fence, a porch overlooking the neighborhood, pristine white siding with bright red outline. She had expected, by then, to be an accountant, a lawyer, something important. What she got was a haunted aberration with peeling siding, cracked walkways, windows agape like cavernous mouths.

Hadn't she been in America long enough to realize that anything was possible, but things took time? she asked herself later that day. Hadn't she discovered that real estate was a financial investment that would make them millionaires like Ed McMahon?

In her own way, Ifi grows to love the house. Like the boy, the house gives her a sense of use. Although she continues to send money home to her uncle and cousins, now that a new woman replaces her Aunty, it is not the same. Although Job began to build their retirement home in Nigeria almost as soon as they were married, the house in America becomes the focus of her dreams. It is her claim to America and all that is American. She can fill her kitchen with shiny appliances, watch *The Jerry Springer Show*, and order hamburgers and French fries.

Like any new homeowner, Ifi throws herself into its repairs. Some of the first repairs in order are a result of Victor's roughness. He has shoved objects in open drains, pried at loose tiling in the kitchen, burrowed his little fingers into the gaping holes in the walls. At first, Ifi attempts the repairs on her own, plastering open holes, resealing lifting tiles, plunging drains. She looks on in satisfaction after the tasks are completed one afternoon. And looks on in dissatisfaction when sealed holes sink, when tiles begin to curl once again, when ankle-deep water rises in the shower.

She flips through the pages of classified ads looking for plumbers, electricians, and carpenters to hire. But when she calls, the men who answer the phone are confused by her accent. They ask, again and again, "Excuse me? Come again?" They convince themselves and Ifi that she surely cannot afford their services until she finally gives up.

One night, she is complaining to Carmela about the misdeeds. As an American, Carmela is sure to have an answer. And she does. Her brother, Jamal, has always been skilled at fixing things. He has worked construction since he was a teenage boy. "He does all of my repairs," she says to Ifi over the phone. "I'll give him a call."

When Jamal doesn't arrive for several weeks, Ifi gives up hope. Then one afternoon, a tall, skinny man with a taut jaw on a prickly face arrives. He carries a steel box with his tools. His jeans are baggy at the waist. His hair is neatly braided in rows. He looks to be about thirty.

Job answers the door. In the background, Victor hollers and slams his toys in imitation of the wrestlers on TV. Ifi slices fresh okra into her palm.

"Hey," the man says, "I got another job at three, so we have to see what I can do till then."

Job frowns. "You have the wrong house."

The man has a slip of paper in his pocket. He retrieves it and matches it with the numbers over the porch.

"You have made a mistake," Job says. The heat rises. He begins to perspire. "Sorry," he says to the man, "I will help you find your friends."

When Ifi sees Job standing stock still in the doorway, she crowds into the door next to him. "Hello?" she asks the man in the doorway.

"Listen, I'm supposed to be here until three, but then I have to get going," he says again.

Ifi smiles at him. She says the words that Job has been searching for during the entire exchange. "We don't want any trouble."

"Carmela said," he begins, but then stops himself.

Immediately, the dour expression on Ifi's face relaxes. "Jamal," she exclaims.

He nods slowly.

Ifi turns to Job. "Jamal is here to fix our house."

Job's face deepens into a smile "Oh, I see," he says. "Thank you for coming, but we have found someone else." He reaches into his pocket and produces a twenty dollar bill. "Here, for your trouble."

Jamal shrugs, takes the twenty, and drives away. Ifi does not stop him.

"What were you thinking," Job asks Ifi, "bringing akatta into our home?"

"His sister said he would fix our house for cheap," she says back.

"Do you know," Job says to her, "if I had not paid him for no work at all, that man would come with his friends at night and rob us?"

Ifi calls him a racist. She tells him she does not see color. In America, everyone is equal. She says all the things she has heard on television and read in newspapers. She adds, "How can you discriminate a man who is your same color?"

But then, inevitably, the fight turns to the boy. In the first place, the boy was responsible for all the repairs the house needed. He rode that clunky red thing his father insisted on buying him, in the house. Because his mother was not watchful, he banged into walls. He overturned trashcans. He circled the kitchen leaving skid marks and curling tile afoot.

To prove such a point, Victor comes pedaling into the entryway, his voice loud like a fire siren, and strikes the wooden front door with such force that from the outside, passersby witness a great tremble.

❖ ❖ ❖

Just after two, on Saturdays, while his mother buys the groceries, Victor and his father drive through town stopping at one garage sale after another. They begin their afternoons with a stop at a gas station. His father gives him money to purchase the candy of his choice. Then his father leans back and scans through the classifieds, circling each destination with a felt tip pen. Victor takes the Laffy Taffy, Jujubes, or Skittles and the bill to the cashier and grins wickedly when the cashier not only gives him his candy, but some money in return. Each time, he presents the change to his father in astonishment. His father chuckles and tells him he is a clever boy.

The neighborhoods they visit are unlike their own. While the houses in Victor's neighborhood are tall and willowy with missing siding and cracked walkways, the houses in the garage sale neighborhoods are larger, pristine, with undisturbed yards, garages, wooden fences, and flowery gardens. To be perfectly honest, these neighborhoods bore Victor. At the end of every trip, he gladly returns to broken holes under porches that lead to crawl spaces, to poking sticks at beasts behind chain-link fences, to the misshapen shrubbery that shields him in hide-and-seek, to tearing through the streets on his red Big Wheel.

In the summer, the yards of each garage sale are identical. Hand-painted signs are hung on trees, sometimes with airless balloons collected in a wilted bouquet. Row upon row of tables are positioned with tennis rackets, dog-eared dime novels, scratched records, and worn shoes. They stop at garage sale after garage sale, overturning different objects in their hands, flipping switches, poking, and prodding. It is on one such journey, Victor suspects, that his father purchased his Big Wheel.

Victor enjoys these retreats. No one tells him to put his hands in his pockets. No one tells him that he cannot try on the roller skates if they are three sizes too big. No one tells him he is too small to fling the beads of the abacus or too big to taste the cool, smooth surface of a snow globe. In fact, the sellers seem to encourage it, following them with over-solicitous smiles, instructing him to step this way, push that way, in order to get the full effect. His father seems to enjoy these outings as much as he does, standing importantly in his suit and tie, in spite of the heat, in spite of the sweat that dampens the length of his arms. His father picks up one object after another and inquires, in crisp, over-pronounced English, "Tell me about this."

On one trip, Victor's suspicions about the Big Wheel are confirmed. They are met by a red-haired woman with high-waisted jeans and a baseball cap. Victor doesn't notice her at first. Nor does his father, it seems. But suddenly, abruptly, she is standing at his side. She pats the top of his head. "Victor, do you like your Big Wheel?" she asks.

Although it doesn't occur to Victor to wonder why she knows his name—surely everyone knows Victor Ogbonnaya—Victor is struck dumb. He doesn't like the way she looks at him. He doesn't like the way his father stands stiffly at his side.

"Victor, answer," his father says.

Only then does he reply. "Yeah," he says, "I like it."

"Victor," she says, "you're a big boy now. You look just like your father."

His father and the lady exchange a glance that he doesn't understand. She picks up a stuffed bear from a table and hands it to him. "You like this?" she asks. "I'll buy you this."

Just then, Victor has had enough of the woman. He wheels around and knocks the bear free from her hand. The bear is insulting. "I'm a big boy," he says to her. He thinks of his mother, just that morning, scolding him for wetting his bed, asking him if he is still a baby or if he has decided to be a big boy.

The lady's face is crimson.

"Victor, behave yourself," his father says. He jerks Victor with such force that Victor expects his arm to fall off. He has never been spoken to so sharply by anyone, including his mother. His eyes screw up and he howls. But his father doesn't relent. "Take the toy," his father says.

Victor refuses.

"Victor, behave or I will beat you," his father says in Igbo. And then, "Do not disgrace me."

Still, Victor refuses to submit. When the lady bends to pick the bear, he kicks it beyond her reach. Tears stream down his face. He wants his mother, so he says so. "Mommy!" he wails.

"Hey, Job," the lady lets out a dry laugh, "it's okay. We'll pick something else out that's just right for a big boy." When she winks at Victor, he regards her with distrust, and finally, she begins to back away. She replaces the teddy bear on the table.

It all seems like it's over. She says goodbye to his father. They hesitantly hug, bumping shoulders as they lean in to one another. She turns to Victor. Victor whips away from her.

"Victor." His father's voice is low.

"No," Victor says. His father pulls Victor's arms apart and forces them around the lady who is stock still in the captive embrace. She smells of cigarettes and strawberry shampoo.

Victor is utterly humiliated. Feeling violated, he shrinks into himself. Nothing, not even the woman's plaintive glance, not even the candy pieces she offers, can make him smile again for the rest of the outing. When they return home, his mother asks what is wrong. Victor's father tells her that Victor fell and bumped his head.

❖ ❖ ❖

After the garage sale fiasco, the outings stop, and Victor must endure long, tedious summer afternoons watching Bugs Bunny and the Road Runner, while his father snores on the couch. Inevitably, Victor stops the sound through his father's nose with his fingertips until his father wakes up sputtering and choking, looking every which way for his assailant before rousting Victor into a bear hug. It is the only thing that seems to make his mother laugh before heading to work in the late afternoons.

In early fall, the grasses of the various parks throughout town are beaten flat and browned from the scalding, dry summer heat. Nonetheless, knobby-kneed men in mesh shorts and worn polos frequent them. Caravans arrive in the early evenings during the time between an early shift's end or a late shift's beginning. The men run themselves ragged after soccer balls, while dodging ground holes. Along the side of the fields, their wives are spread out on blankets spooning children curried rice, burritos, or greasy plantains from plastic Tupperware containers and bowls covered in foil.

Job has known of these games since his earliest days in America as a student at the university. Since he has never had an acumen for athletics, he avoided the humiliation of running the field when they were one man short by not coming all together. At his ripe age, as a father, he can finally join the older men rested along the benches, sharing cigarettes, sipping from sacks of beer and placing bets on games that they will never be forced to pay.

One evening, Victor announces that he will play for the Flying Eagles when he grows up. The ripple of pleasure that spreads through the crowd of Nigerians fills Job with such pride that he makes a point to purchase Victor cleats, shin guards, and a jersey. From then on, to the nods of onlookers, Victor stylishly parades the fields kicking and elbowing past the little boys in their miniature soccer game. Victor is not exactly good, but the key, he discovers, is to elbow, push, and pull the other players one way or the other, preventing them from scoring. Only the mothers complain, confirming Victor's certainty that a mother's sole purpose in life is to deny one the pleasures of the world. He is neither resentful of nor charmed by this affirmation. Unquestioningly, he acknowledges this fact as he accepts the fact that the sky is blue. At once, he becomes the most-hated child on the field by mothers and fathers alike. Mothers are straightforward in their contempt, attempting to revive their whimpering boys. To save face, fathers decline to intervene, sometimes siding on behalf of Victor, insisting that a scraped knee or a bloodied nose are the expense of a hard fought game before reluctantly shoving their trembling little boys back to battle.

Job has always felt the need to apologize to Cheryl for Victor's behavior at the garage sale. His chance comes one evening when Cheryl agrees to meet them at the soccer field, but two out of the ordinary things happen. As Cheryl looks on, Victor huffs up and down the field elbowing and knocking little boys out of his way. Although the crowd is primarily international, with representatives of India, Malaysia, Kenya, Brazil, and Nigeria, there are a few pink-faced, jeans-wearing American wives and girlfriends sprinkled in the crowd. Among them, Cheryl sits on a blanket with potato chips, slices of fruit, cold cuts, and juice boxes.

As is eventually destined to happen to all Goliaths, the Davids of the world—boys who have nightly limped home swollen, bruised, and teary—launch an attack on Victor. In a wall, they unite, breaking one way, cutting that way, forcing their bodies into steely alignment each time Victor nears, knocking him to the ground one turn after another, tripping him, elbowing. The onslaught happens from all sides and is thoroughly unexpected. In stubborn denial, Victor refuses to acknowledge their blows, offering them a dull smile. Until then, he has assumed that the object of the game is for the other boys to fall. Not him. At one point, the great giant is knocked to the ground so viciously that groans issue from the crowd. Even the adult soccer game pauses. Job doesn't interfere. How can he? This is the duty of a mother. But the mothers along the sideline, ever vigilant, are suddenly distracted by the babies in their laps, the runny noses of younger children, the articles of trash.

Cheryl charges onto the field. Victor is limp with cries. She smothers him in the embrace he earlier denied her and carries him back to her blanket where she feeds him browning apple slices coated in peanut butter and raisins, where she bursts open a juice box and encourages him to sip.

He feels tricked. But there are no friendly faces among the crowd, not even his father's, and so he allows Cheryl to embrace him, to speak to him.

"Is it true that you are a clever boy?" she asks. "Have you been playing with your Big Wheel?"

Although Job has seen Cheryl's subtle tenderness at work—tucking extra pillows behind a patient's back, styling a patient's hair—her reaction to Victor is unexpected. For days after, he lies awake in bed thinking the moment over. Somehow, it seemed strange seeing her there, with his little boy paralyzed in her arms. The picture should be a great comfort to him; frankly, it is not. He doesn't call things off exactly, but he answers the look in her eyes less and less each time they are together. Even though her brother, Luther, is mute, because they are aware that he sleeps in the downstairs room, they have taken to a silent language of gestures. Now, something is different. What, he does not know.

For the first time, as they lie awake in bed together one early morning, Cheryl lighting a cigarette, Job face down, he asks her why she has not made good on her efforts to stop smoking. "In Nigeria," he says, "smoking is for men."

Cheryl doesn't even bother to put the cigarette away. He expects her to argue with him, to tell him that in America women are equal to men or something to that effect. But she stares numbly at him. He never sees her smoke another cigarette again, yet he can smell the scent on her now, pungent as ever. That she has taken to smoking in secret, just before and after his arrivals, he is certain.

❖ ❖ ❖

The days before the new school year begins are short. Job works the night shift at the hospital and sleeps through the morning and afternoon, rising just as Ifi leaves for the evening shift at the hotel where she vacuums rooms, empties trash bins of condoms and bottles of beer, and replaces semen-stained sheets. Few nights are shared by the two. When they do share a night together, the sex is in the dark. Neither bothers to shower before or after and so their musky bodies join together in a mingling of scents: onions from dinner, vomit from the boy, urine from a patient at the hospital,

stale cigarettes from the hotel. It is over just as quickly as it begins and the two retreat to their sides of the bed and fall into heavy slumber. But one night, after the boy has gone to bed for the night, Ifi and Job are lumped on the couches in the living room watching television when they hear a scraping outside.

Ifi's eyes open in alarm. Job raises his finger to his lips and goes out the back door. Ifi follows. At night, the backyard is a frayed forest. Bushes are tangled and unkempt. Half-grown lawn grass catches at the backs of their ankles. In the distance, one can see the outline of the full-bodied moon. Ifi clings to Job. He tells her to go inside, but leans into her anyway. Then they see its eyes, large and shining. The raccoon flips into the air letting out a squeal, which incidentally is identical to the one that Job issues as well. The suddenness of the two sounds, the similarity of the two sounds, makes Ifi laugh. Then Job laughs. And when they see that the overturned trash cans and scattered refuse are not the boy's handiwork after all, in a small way they rejoice.

❖ ❖ ❖

As the new school year approaches, Victor spends his afternoons furiously pedaling through the neighborhood streets on his red Big Wheel. Only after dusk begins to settle does he traipse home, ragged and damp with sweat, his stomach hissing in hunger. By now, his parents have relented. No longer does his father stand on the porch steps eyeing the neighborhood boys, who, frankly, don't particularly like Victor. In fact, he is the neighborhood boy that parents openly eye as they water their plants, pluck their weeds, and check their mail boxes. Postal workers are in the habit of ducking, stepping aside, widening their legs so the boy can pass through. Trees retreat when he approaches. Dogs that once barked without abandon withdraw just as they hear the grinding and swishing of his tires.

One night, Victor does not return home for dinner. Ifi and Job exchange glances across the table, but slowly swallow bites of garri. After all, they both remember the Sudanese boy, just months earlier, who had disappeared. His mother had called 9-1-1 to report him missing. When he turned up playing basketball on the other side of town, the boy's mother wept openly. Not because she had found her boy. Because the authorities made the boy's single mother pay the expenses for the fire trucks, ambulance, and police cars, because they charged her for being an abusive mother—after all, what kind of mother doesn't know where her boy is?—because they raided her home, and seeing that her three small children shared one mattress at night, fined her for negligence. Job and Ifi had agreed then, as they do now, that in Nigeria there was nothing wrong with a boy being a boy, sef.

After their slow bites have digested, Victor still doesn't turn up. Ifi and Job stagger through neighborhood after neighborhood mingling Victor's name with threats:

"Victor, boy, you come home at once!"

"This is your father, Victor, I am not playing games."

"I will beat you, oh."

When the houses along the streets are nothing more than an outline, their threats are whimpers. "Victor," his mother pleads, "I will buy you candy."

On the way home, Job and Ifi turn on one another:

Job says, "You see, let the boy play in the house in peace."

Ifi says, "Why did you buy that foolish bicycle?"

They sit up in the living room. Ifi nods to Job, and he begins to dial the police. Their minds race to all of the things that could have happened to the boy. Most frightening of all is the thought of the men they have read about in the newspaper. Yes, they have heard of that sort of thing happening to girls, but a boy? they wonder. Only in America.

Job is spelling out Victor's name, describing his Big Wheel, the color of his corduroys, when there is a small tap at the door. Before Ifi has a chance to answer the door, Job is already hanging up and thanking the operator for her assistance.

In the door, there is a police officer as expected. He is speaking, but Ifi and Job are not listening. They peer around him, expecting Victor to step out from the wings, his lips turned down in protest. Eventually, the officer does step aside revealing only what remains of Victor's Big Wheel.

❖ ❖ ❖

Michael Lauchlan

Black Dog

Up late in search of calm,
I let the dog roam the pines
along the railroad. She flits
in and out of what little light
spills from the truck lot.
The faint clink of her collar dies
and she fades utterly away.
While I stare into nothing, she
moves through a cosmos of scent.

Above, where Andromeda should be,
at the edge of the visible,
the night is obscured by clouds
and glare. Some smart insomniac
at Palomar points a lens into dark
distance, chasing specks of life
a million light years off.
Our hearts keep time, wend
without cease into worlds.

Triptych without Epiphany

i.

Take up the wand that came with the bottle, hold it
                                        at arm's length, and spin,
encircling yourself with a cylinder of film. Watch
as it breaks and swiftly re-coheres into a galaxy
of soap-bubble spheres, each one bearing
                                        a face (yours)
ready to burst, or to disappear upwards
to join in the Zodiac's deterministic wheel
                                        spinning at light-speed—
an endless swirl of whose swept arc we are each
                                        one slice.

Or think of your fate as a shadow
                                        thrown down
in a game of Statues and left on the lawn
with no one who loves you enough to call you home,
and no referee to call Time but those mute,
                                        circling beasts
(see: *Zodiac*, above) and on Earth, ten-thousand
reputed Bodhisattvas, littering Enlightenment's
Construction Zones—where the fines
                                        are always doubled.
(Fine. Fine. Whatever.)

ii.

No reason, then, to stay. So you're off—
There's a washed-out daylight slipping over
the windshield, as you race against the grain
(Iowa? Kansas?), which races in reverse
down Midwestern highways, mined
with heat mirages, and pursuing…what was it?
happiness, of course, like any good American,
going for the golden, the advertised prize:
success, that tantalizing salt
                                        in thirst's throat.

And it's there for the taking, just *Take
the Next Exit to View The Motley Plenitude*,
from which we've been taught
to cut the new immortals—the Stars,
the Superstars—costumed for the chase scene,

in which we're the extras, all of us
out there on the superhighways spinning
our wheels within wheels. We're eons
deep in error, and each of us is sure
we're the fairest at the fair and we hold
the winning ticket for the orbiting, colossal,
                    killer Ferris wheel

that will spin us inexplicably forward into Fame
(or Magnificent Disaster)
and spill us out dizzy on the tenth crystal stair
where Hollywood has kept us dancing for years
through the ruins of the runes on the run-down heels
of our celluloid slippers, so thoroughly seduced
we'll scarcely miss a beat as we slip *en masse*
from the soap-slick fingers of Whoever holds
the wand (Oh, had you forgotten?) and the keys
                    to the Kingdom.

iii.

Where it seems we've arrived (despite
                    our best intentions)
luckily in time to view the famous Stain
(the Original, the one we thought
had been removed). And now,
                    for your reward:
kneel and gaze into the leaded-light above you,
where *Your Celestial Future* is foretold in glass
                    (a slow liquid, falling like
a guillotine, but at the speed of Eden),

spun from a past that has undone us all,
                    unwinding a distinctly
unpromising ending. By tonight, you'll be lying
where Time first threw you, fragmented
by longing and fated by stars to wake long after
                            the sad game has ended
and all the beautiful beasts have gone home
down the only path open, the circular one.
And it's here, in total darkness,
                    that you've been left to follow
the incomprehensible directions on the bottle.

The author's family, circa 1951.

Paul Crenshaw

Essay in Five Photographs

1.

It was after Korea.

He is dressed in his service uniform. There are insignia sewn on the shoulder, but he is facing the camera, one arm draped over my uncle, and I cannot make the insignia out. My uncle is holding my mother. She has black hair and one tiny arm is raised, her fist clenched. She is probably less than a year old.

In the picture behind them is a screen door, and the face of a brick building. The metal letters on the screen door say it is apartment 10 C. I know that this must be in Pine Bluff, Arkansas, in 1951 or '52, where, after returning home from the war, he has taken a job at a factory that manufactures nerve agents, deadly poison to unleash on the communist bloc if the Cold War, just beginning, ever mushrooms into open war.

My uncle is a young boy, his pants legs rolled up. My mother is asleep. There is the outline of what looks to be a pack of cigarettes in my grandfather's left shirt pocket. I can vaguely remember him smoking, before the doctors and a worried wife forced him to quit.

The picture was taken ten years after he was married—ten years after he woke the morning after his wedding and learned that the Japanese had attacked Pearl Harbor. Probably seven years since he landed on the beaches of Normandy sometime in July 1944. Seven years—longer than my uncle had been alive—since the bullets streaked by and the bombs fell all around during the Battle of the Bulge, when he must have knelt, twenty-eight years old then, his wife and son halfway around the world, his M-1 carbine shaking in his hands as he returned fire, hoping the bombs and bullets did not find him, hoping that he would see his wife and son again.

It would have been only a few years since he was called to Korea that, thinking his fighting days were done, his National Guard unit would be activated and he would be asked to take up arms again. This time there was a daughter he was leaving behind as well, but he did not know that then—she was only a fertilized egg forming somewhere in my grandmother's womb.

The picture does not show the wound where the bayonet stabbed his knee, the North Korean thrusting it in in some cold rice paddy somewhere near the 38th parallel. It does not show the strokes that would make it difficult for him to walk late in his life, nor does it show the lines etched into his face like memories of long ago. It does not show the fierce pain that would grip his heart late one night, taking away his speech, his movement, and, a few hours later, his life. In the picture he is young, a soldier returned home from war sitting on the steps of a rented apartment with his arm around his oldest son, who is holding a daughter he is meeting for the first time. It does show the grin on his face at seeing his daughter—my mother. That after returning from war, here was a child, one fist raised as if to welcome him home.

2.

In this picture, my father looks like me.

The resemblance is strong. But this picture was taken in 1967, five years before I was born. Right around the time he met my mother, both of them young then, still in high school. The draft was just firing up, ghostly images of Vietnam appearing on TV screens all over the country, and more and more men were being shipped to a small country many of them had never heard of, from which many of them would never return.

It sits on a shelf at my grandmother's small apartment, where she moved after my grandfather passed. Around it are pictures of aunts and uncles I rarely see anymore, cousins and nieces and nephews that I have never even met. But my eyes are drawn to my father, young, a child himself then, his hat tilted at what seems a jaunty angle. It would have been taken at Fort Polk, Louisiana, where he learned to shoot dummies with an M-16 and stab dummies with a bayonet and throw hand grenades at other dummies, or it might have been at Fort Sam Houston in Texas, where, as a battlefield medic, he learned to treat sucking chest wounds, to triage whatever damage had been done by enemies wielding rifles and bayonets and hand grenades.

His hair is cropped close, face clean-shaven. His shoulders are narrow and bony, the same as mine were at that age. His eyes are a clear blue, the same as mine, the same as both my daughters'. His ears seem too large for his head, a curse passed down to me, as are the small, almost feminine hands the picture does not show.

The picture also does not show signs of worry. It seems it would. But there are none. Just my father, a slight grin on his face, as if this is all a joke or somehow amusing, as if he did not see the nights and days before him when he would worry over the prospect of war as the numbers of men in Vietnam continued to escalate. That he would meet and marry my mother, still worrying if at any time his unit would be activated, seeing friends drafted, knowing sometimes only their names and their flag-draped coffins came back.

He tells me he joined as a way to avoid the draft. That many men like him were joining National Guard units as a way to avoid Vietnam without moving to Canada. But he was struggling then, from a poor family, and the money was welcome, so he stayed for over twenty years, long after he married my mother, long after my brother and then I came along. Long after the divorce and a long litany of military actions in other parts of the world that most people never heard of: Libya and Lebanon and Latin America, Grenada and the Philippines and Panama, Columbia and Bolivia and Peru.

When I am eighteen he will tell me that serving was good for him. I will join his National Guard unit and while I am at Basic Training I will have a picture taken in the exact same pose, almost the same uniform, the same small smile on my face, though I can see now that the smile is not one of amusement, but rather uncertainty, wondering what all this—the uniform, the rifle I will be issued later, everything I've heard about unstable forces at large in the world—might someday mean.

3.

Almost twenty years later, I'm surprised at how young I look.

This was long before I married, had children, slipped quietly into my thirties. Long before I learned the names of the various conflicts that seem to always be ongoing, or just starting up, rarely ending. I had just graduated high school. The army jacket I am wearing is not mine. I have no name tag, no dog tags. I might be an unknown soldier. The brass and insignia are generic, and at this point I do not even know what they mean.

The picture is a public relations picture, taken only a few days after I arrive at Fort Sill. They buzz our heads and dress us from the shoulders up in military regalia and snap our pictures, then send the pictures home to our parents and girlfriends with a generic note saying we are doing well, adjusting to military life, and that we will write as soon as our duties allow.

Which we do. We write every evening, sending letters to everyone we know, and, slowly at first, then with increasing volume, we get letters back. We get letters from parents telling us how proud they are of us, our fathers recalling their days in the army or else lamenting on the flat feet or bum knee that kept them out. We get letters from buddies telling us about trips to the lake, drinking beer on a Sunday afternoon, and, closed up in the barracks as night falls around us, we can almost taste the beer in the back of our throats, smell the lake, boats cutting white froths through the blue water. We get letters from girlfriends, and sometimes the letters include pictures of them in bathing suits, or bra and panties, sometimes nothing at all.

We run the letters over and over in our minds. During the few moments we have each night to read our mail we memorize the curves of girlfriends, and the words that accompany the letters, translating "I can't wait to see you" into our own fantasies, and during long days on the rifle range and the bayonet course and the hand grenade course we recall the words and images sent to us for just that purpose. During the short nights we dream of going home, re-constructing our elaborate fantasies about what will happen when we get back there, until morning comes too early and we wake red-eyed and grainy, dreading the coming day, stalking wearily through it. When night falls again we mark the day off our calendars with much ceremony and pass around the pictures our girlfriends sent us, the pictures our parents sent of our cars or our dogs or our high school football team, anything that connects us with what we have left behind.

Because we have no contact with the outside world. Only the letters, a few pictures, a phone call once a week on Sunday morning. We have no idea what forces are stirring in the Middle East. This is late summer 1990, and we are trudging through our days, firing M-16s and thinking of breasts and black panties when Saddam Hussein invades Kuwait. Within days the 82nd Airborne and the 1st Marine Expeditionary Force, along with the aircraft carriers USS Eisenhower and USS Independence, arrive in the Gulf, and just two weeks after the United Nations Security Council passes Resolution 660, condemning the invasion and demanding the immediate withdrawal of all Iraqi troops, we are scheduled to graduate. We have completed Basic Rifle Marksmanship and hand-to-hand combat. We have thrown live hand grenades and stabbed dummies with bayonets. We have fired Claymore mines and learned to splinter broken appendages and administer the antidotes to biological and chemical weapons and what actions to take in the event of a nuclear attack, and just before we graduate we take another picture, this one of the whole platoon, though we still seem, looking at it now, far too young.

4.

It was after the Gulf War.

The platoon in the picture is C Battery, 2/142nd Field Artillery, Arkansas National Guard. They wear desert camos with a razorback on the shoulder, the insignia of the University of Arkansas's sports teams. On the other shoulder is an insignia that looks exactly like a vibrator, and that is what the men in the unit call it, but it is actually a representation of the eight inch diameter shells they fire from Howitzer artillery pieces, great cannons that can launch shells over twenty miles through the desert air and rain down death on an enemy that can't even see where the fire is coming from.

Their uniforms are cleaned and pressed, their gear cleaned as well. I will later learn they were ordered to clean their gear and polish their boots and get their uniforms squared away so they would look sharp when they returned. That they were forced to undergo inspection while their wives and children waited. That one man was sent back to shave, and the rest of the platoon had to wait to be reunited with their families while he erased the stubble that had grown on the long flights from Riyadh to Germany to Maine to Little Rock, and the two hour bus ride back to their unit, where placards and signs and yellow ribbons waved as the Greyhounds pulled in and spilled them out into the Arkansas night.

My stepfather is in the back, off to the right side. If you look closely, you can see a few beer cans half-hidden by the men holding them. One or two of them look already drunk, eyes slightly glassed over. But they are smiling, and one man in the back has his beer can half-raised already, and several of the others are glancing off to the side, to somewhere you cannot see in the picture, but where I know their families are looking on as the picture is snapped.

They have been home from Iraq for less than an hour. Right after the picture is taken they will break apart and their families will take them home, and it will not be until later, when they have taken off their uniforms, that their wives will see how much weight they have lost. You cannot tell in the picture.

Nor can you tell what will happen next. If they will go silent on the ride home. Break down crying. Wake in the middle of the night with cold sweats. Or simply sleep, everything forgotten now that it is done. In a few days they will reassemble and begin checking their gear, writing lists of what needs repaired and re-ordered and re-evaluated, preparing for what happens next, and when they see this preparation many of the men in the unit, my stepfather among them, will retire, unable or unwilling to do it again.

5.

About the last pictures, I can only guess. There are thousands of dead in the war now, and hundreds of thousands going back through time, through Desert Storm and Vietnam and all the little wars and excursions and missions in between, Korea and both the World Wars and a hundred or a thousand or a million others.

Now, you can find their faces easily enough. They stare at you from newspapers, on the Internet and TV, from billboards along the highway where you are rushing to work in the morning. Their names are printed beneath them. They look young, usually, though not always. They have dark hair or light hair, blue eyes or brown. They played football in high school, had girlfriends they would marry as soon as they returned. Or perhaps they would decide to go to college and earn a degree. They might have children already, a dark-haired girl with the same color eyes as her father, or a blond child with her mother's hands, or a boy that resembled a grandfather who died in some other war long ago.

For the most part, they are stoic. Trying to be strong, to act as they believe soldiers should act, to look as they believe soldiers should look. Some of them are smiling. That seems even worse, now that they are dead. There are a few women among them, and because I have a wife and two daughters, their faces stay with me, even though I try not to remember their names. They are Marines or Army or Air Force or Navy, privates or corporals or staff sergeants or second lieutenants, though never generals, and they joined for college money or because they were poor or because they wanted to serve their country.

But this is only speculation.

As is what the pictures don't show. How they were excited or scared or anxious or proud when they first joined the military. How they suffered or excelled during training, barely qualifying or graduating with flying colors or anywhere in between. How they sat up late at night watching the twenty-four hour news when the war first began, talking quietly about what might happen, or waiting to use the phone and call home, or driving home and making love to their wife or husband, playing with their child.

How they landed in the desert. Went on patrol. Were blown up by a roadside bomb or shot through the throat by a sniper. Their dog-tags were recovered. Someone said a few words. Their flag-draped bodies were flown home and unloaded in the dead of night on some anonymous tarmac. A mother woke to a ringing phone, holding her breath as a father reached for the receiver. A few days later she flinched each of the three times the seven guns fired. The flag fell from her hands.

Later, she turned the pages in a scrapbook she'd made of her son or daughter's life. She tried to show it to a boy or a girl that would grow up without a mother or a father, or a husband who had to go on living without a wife, or a wife without a husband, a father without a son, a mother without a daughter.

In my mind, the child is too young to look at the pictures. Too young to understand what they mean. The child is smiling. One fist is raised. It will be years before the child understands, if ever.

But, as I said, all this is only speculation. I don't know. I wasn't there, like almost all of us.

❖ ❖ ❖

Windsock

It could have been the hour,
the gray of evening and night about to fall,
but the windsock by the runway
resembled nothing less than the snout of a possum

swiveling this way and that to face
the way the wind had gone,
sniffing its invisible trail,
hearkening after it but stuck to its post,

unaware that what it longed for
was the very thing that was breathing into it
the cause of its lonely rotating,
its billowing with hopeless desire.

Hanssie Trainor. *Portrait of Daniel Goddard*. 2012. Digital photograph. Courtesy of the artist.

Soap

It has been raining for five days straight in Philadelphia. The gloom has settled into Megan's bones, her DNA. She thinks one more commute to the tower she works in, and she'll jump in the Delaware. Maybe she should ask her primary care for Prozac. She's already gotten two phone calls from Aurelie, her daughter's nanny, wanting to know where Sophia's homework is. And her husband's administrative assistant has called to tell her to please pick up her husband's dry cleaning, a non-liberated request which, Megan is sure, has no ironic resonance for his administrative assistant, who is only twenty-four.

Rain continues to assault the windshield, splattering in gray dribbles that remind her of executions, orphan trains, and the short life-spans of the pioneers who settled in this area. Nothing here is good.

She parks in the underground parking garage, gets her good pumps wet walking to the elevator with her briefcase, and prepares for another day in the corporate offices of the software giant where she works, wondering, in the elevator, if she has enough time to Google "seasonal affective disorder" before her eight-thirty meeting.

That afternoon, her boss lets her off early, because he wants her to go to Chicago for him in two days, and he's assuaging his conscience by giving her the afternoon off. "I know how it is with a kid," he says. Since Megan gets a call from Sophia every day at three-thirty, and has for years, since she was in day care. And Megan often feels tormented, after these calls. As if she's doing something wrong, when Sophia doesn't want to hang up, or when Sophia pleads with her to come home, and Megan has to say, "We're going skiing in three weeks, did you forget?" or "I'll see you in four hours, honey. Mommy has to work." And then hang up feeling some mixture of dread and guilt in her stomach. Possibly anger.

This afternoon, when she gets home, Aurelie is watching a soap opera on the big TV. Megan plops down on the sofa next to Sophia and tries to pay attention, even though she's also thinking about what she has to bring to the meeting in Chicago. Suddenly her eyes lock on an actor on the screen: it's Larry, her old boyfriend. It's him! From when she lived in Los Angeles a million years ago. It's the cheekbones, the voice, the high forehead that always made her think of his Dutch ancestors getting off an East India Company brig in New Amsterdam. It's definitely Larry, and he's got a two hundred dollar haircut.

Her heart pounds in her throat. Feelings overwhelm her. He's beautiful. She sits on the beige sofa with her hand on her chest. The segment is too short; it's just a tease. He's distressed over someone's amnesia; he's chewing out a woman doctor in a lab coat. The segment ends. She is shocked. How long has he been in this soap? Is he new? She feels as if the wallpaper has just started talking.

His life must be studios, producers, agents, all the things he longed for when she knew him in LA. The screen shows a commercial for a sleeping pill. Then pre-mixed pie crust. A laundry detergent that makes a shirt, which a woman has poured wine on, come so clean that she looks like she's just had sex. The images are orgasmic. Splashes and twirling thunderbolts of desirability. Megan stares, waiting for Larry to come back on.

And he does have a short segment, on the phone with a woman he used to love, who tells him she is the mother of his love child. He doesn't believe her, as it will screw up his engagement to someone else, whom he just (Megan is piecing this together) rescued from a terrorist attack in a restaurant. Possibly he is dating his own love child, who grew up in a convent in France.

"You know what it is," Aurelie says, from

her side of the couch. "These people are all so pretty. But they don't learn nothing. They fall in bad love over and over."

"Bad romance," Sophia says. She's wearing her after-school silver glitter pop-star pants, which Megan hasn't been able to talk her out of. Larry and the brunette, Vivian, are in a deep, tonsil-sucking kiss that she thinks she should cover Sophia's eyes for, except that Sophia is probably watching worse things on the Internet. Aurelie says, "I think Sophia got hay-fever."

Megan looks at Sophia's eyes, which are red and wet. Swollen. Sophia says she doesn't feel like eating, and kicks the edge of the sofa. She says she doesn't want to go to school tomorrow, there's no point.

"Do you have a test, or what?" Megan says.

"I can read as well as anybody. It's boring."

"Tell me about it," Megan says. "But you have to go anyway. Daddy can drive you."

"Why don't you?"

"I'm going to Chicago. I told you, remember? Last week?"

"Ah, Mom." Sophia sighs.

"Come on, Mommy's got her work to do."

Sophia shrugs. The shrug bothers Megan when she's in the drugstore, a few hours later, getting Sophia's antihistamine prescription re-filled. She tries not to think about it. She finds herself reading the magazine racks near the register, and there he is. Right on the cover. Smiling straight into the camera, with his blue eyes. She dawdles in the line so long, devouring *Soap Opera Digest*, that the checkout girl, who has pierced her eyebrow with uncomfortable-looking steel balls, says, "Can I help you?"

Megan buys the magazine, and reads it in her car in the parking lot, under the yellowy lights of the store's façade. The facts of his life are all wrong. He didn't grow up in Minneapolis, and he was never a computer programmer and a Navy SEAL. (He grew up in LA, and he could barely swim.) His name is now Bo Fullerton. It says he loves driving his Porsche along the Pacific Coast Highway.

When she knew him it wasn't a Porsche, it was a battered Nissan Maxima with rusted wheel-wells. He lived in a Spanish stucco apartment building off Sunset, with grass growing through the cracks in the sidewalk, and a pool the landlord underchlorinated, so

the algae grew. Small frogs lived in it. He had a dog named Chippie, who used to howl when Larry shut him out of the bedroom, and when he let him in, Chippie would jump on the bed. He had a series of headshots he loved, from photographers who would cut a struggling actor a break. The windows of his bedroom, she remembers now, were louvred, and let in shade and sunshine in the afternoons, narcotic light, filled with the scent of bougainvillea, and birdsong. At night, mockingbirds sang. Water dappled the light off the pool, and you could lose your mind, in those times, when there was nothing to do. Stretch out on the bed with him, and make love, twisting together like snakes. Rest, and do it again. We never talked about it, she thinks. We just did it.

She shoves the *Soap Opera Digest* into her handbag, and when she gets home, her husband is eating a warmed-over casserole Aurelie left, and telling Sophia about the difference between selling short and buying on margin.

Sophia looks bored. "Hey," her husband says to her. "You got home early."

"I have to get up at four to catch the shuttle."

"Mn," he says. He offers her food, and Megan has three conversations going on in her head at once: Bill is hurt because she forgot they were supposed to go to the marriage counselor tomorrow night; she wants to get back in time to take Sophia to karate, because it's her pink belt qualification; and she's worried she may get moved to another project if the team she's meeting in Chicago don't like the emphasis she's chosen for her presentation. You don't want to be seen as a bitch. She puts her arm around Sophia's narrow shoulders and smells her sweet, almost salty hair.

❖ ❖ ❖

A week goes by. Sophia has painted her finger-nails black and purple, alternating nails. She's in the back seat of Megan's car, still too light to sit in front, and drinking Gatorade before her violin lesson. Megan has been saving pictures of Larry off the Internet and several soap maga-zines that have pictures of him. He's got a cover, where he's stretched up over a blonde, with his biceps across her breasts. Megan has been keep-ing all these stashed in her underwear drawer, under the tampons, so Bill won't find them.

Sophia is drinking Gatorade and chattering.

"You're not listening," she says finally.

"Sorry. What?"

"I said I'm in a play on Wednesday. We're acting out the Declaration of Independence."

How do you do that? Megan wonders. And doesn't Gatorade ruin your teeth? "I don't think I can make it," Megan says. "I've got a really important meeting. I may be going to Texas."

"You were in Chicago."

"This is a different one. It's where all the people in my company will decide if my job will be there. Can't Aurelie go with you?"

"She's driving me." Megan stares out the side window, and then powers it down. She dumps the bottle of Gatorade onto the ground, and powers the window up. Folds her arms and stares ahead.

"You better pick that up, Soph," Megan says.

"Make me."

Her lips are tight. There doesn't seem to be any way to penetrate her rage. Somehow this is all Megan's fault. "Won't it be good with Aurelie?" she says.

"It's not the same, Mom, is it."

Megan stares at the clock on the dash, and her mobile device rings as she's about to respond to Sophia, who glares at her.

❖ ❖ ❖

She's found a secret way to record all the episodes of *All My Yesterdays* using the TiVo, and it seems to be working well, until one weekend Bill says she's erased all his golf matches.

"It was an accident," she says.

"Soap operas?"

"Aurelie likes to watch it," she says.

"You should learn how to do it right. You want me to show you again?"

She says yes, even though she knows. She's been watching them furtively in the bedroom for weeks, and it's too bad about the golf matches. She floats on the golden voices, the sexy lines between Larry and the blonde, or the brunette named Vivian, who, it turns out, did not have his love child. Sometimes she watches a segment three or four times, hoping to understand who he is, now. This Bo.

In Los Angeles, his apartment building had sixteen units, with broken door buzzers and a pot-smoking lawn guy who eventually got a good commercial. Larry made his living working parties, a rental clown. He could juggle, and sing, and make genitalia out of balloons when things got drunk or stoned enough. He wanted to be a star. One of Megan's friends said he was a fauve, and she wasn't quite sure what that was. Except her friend said, rolling his eyes, "He's very attractive. If you get tired of him." Which had made Megan nervous. As if her friend was going to take Larry off to some club and put the make on him. And she'd thought, I know what it's like to make love to him, honey, and it's too bad for you, you never will. The next time they were together, she wanted him more, held his neck in her hands, put her legs around him.

And it was easy to be in love with Larry then, because you couldn't take him seriously. An out-of-work actor, who maxed out his credit cards and drank himself stupid in front of the TV for weeks at a time, when his agent didn't call him with so much as an audition.

Sometimes Larry brought her on shoots, and she found she was consumed with jealousy, sexual and otherwise. Make-up girls flirted with him. The actors did stretches and passed around tins of Tiger Balm, and horsed around with each other, and compared themselves to each other behind each others' backs. They called up in euphoria, and said, "Love you, baby." The directors always fussed over Larry, and with all the actors, which allowed the actors, in Megan's view, to wallow in more infantile omnipotence than she'd thought humanly possible. Just so the director could get his perfect take.

Once it was a film about surfers who lose a buddy and form a club in his memory. It was written by someone at UCLA Film School, and somehow it got edited all wrong, so that most of Larry's scenes were cut. After the bewildering premiere at the student film festival, he'd sat around and watched TV for almost a month. His friends said he was fabulous anyway. "All thirty seconds," he said.

Glum, because an actor grasped at ribbons, Megan realizes now. You needed to get your face out there, and this was the beginning of that. A bad TV pilot. A pornish movie, a commercial. You did what you had to do. She hadn't realized that. His other film was a zombie movie that involved a Czech backer and a director who had a cocaine problem that eventually lost them their insurance. But a small beginning didn't mean a small career. As she can see now, by his many minutes on *All My Yesterdays*.

His face seems to be everywhere lately on supermarket magazines. She buys one, one afternoon, after turning it upside down on the conveyor belt, ignoring the disdainful stare of the neat, blonde, high-school cashier, who is probably going to Dartmouth.

She suspected, when she lived with him, that his looks were against him. He was too pretty. His career was refusing to take off. He made a commercial for a local phone carrier, a thirty-second spot where he mugged for the camera, but it never aired. He drove a car out of a used-car dealership and said, "I've got good things to say about Pete's Quality Pre-Owned Vehicles!" which he'd practiced, with varying intonations, for a week. But that was as far as it went. "What am I doing wrong?" he said once. He was like a tragic hero, she thought; he was too hungry. Go out for audition after audition, and mess it up on the call-back. You could want it too hard. Although in LA there were plenty of hungry actors waiting on tables. He tried not to sulk when people in his acting class got bit parts in series. A kid's program about a zoo. A pilot. A soap. A cable show that needed a singer.

And in truth, she was getting bored with his trips to the gym, his yoga, the acting classes that she had to loan him money for, from her dinky job as as administrative assistant for a lawyer in Century City.

One week, his agent, tenuous at best, had dropped him, or at least wasn't answering his calls. Megan suggested he get another job besides clowning at birthday parties.

"What?" he'd said angrily. "You want to see me fail?" Chippie was dancing around Larry, who was holding the leash. Larry had kicked at the dog and missed. Megan knew at that moment she would leave him. "And I'm not going to any more of your acting classes," she said. "Because it's pretentious."

"You and your snobby friends," he said.

"They're perfectly fine!"

"They're snobs. They're asleep from the neck down. They don't talk; they just trade facts with each other, to show how smart they are, or else they gossip. They don't really listen to each other at all!"

She'd sworn, because she was impatient. And years later, she'd realized he was right.

But that was always the way, in love affairs. You got pounded for not being something, and then when you were broken up, you took the good information and carried it forward to the next person. Another time they'd argued about something, she'd even forgotten what it was, and he shot back at her, "Because. Because! Because!" Spittle had come out of his mouth. "I don't want reasons!" Which he'd learned from his acting teacher, who made everyone stop using the word "because." "I don't want to hear 'why,'" his teacher had yelled. "I don't want REASONS!" Same drill, Megan thinks now. His teacher had been right.

Her life, it seems to her, has become a mesh of reasons.

"Mommy," Sophia says to her one day on the phone in her office, "I think I broke my finger in karate. I think Aurelie is driving me to the hospital."

Aurelie gets on the phone and says that this is so. Megan looks at the time on her cell, and it's four-thirty. The Chicago team leader will be calling. Her boss will want her to wait for the call.

❖   ❖   ❖

Sophia's hand is in a cast, which her friends at school have signed in colored markers. It looks like they won't be going skiing any time soon. Megan helps her by writing out her homework and typing on the computer for her. Sophia is soldiering on, she tells Bill when he gets home late most nights. She reads a trade journal in bed, and he kicks off his shoes and goes to take a shower. He's sweaty from the plane, he says. The shuttle flight from Detroit. Megan watches him change, his strong back and his solid, no-nonsense stride into the bathroom. He flips his undershirt over the back of the chair, and she wonders if he sleeps with other women. How could you know? He's still irritated with her for missing another appointment with the marriage counselor.

When she rests her head back against the pillows, she thinks about Larry. His character on *All My Yesterdays*, which the tabloids shorten to *AMY*, is caught between his love for his daughter, the ingénue Kari, a surgical resident, who he doesn't know is his actual daughter, and her mother, Crystal, who rejected him years before to marry an oil tycoon, who has since died and been frozen. Megan watched the last three episodes this afternoon, with Aurelie and Sophia. She wonders if Bill is faithful, and likes to think he is. But how would you know?

When he gets out of the shower, his hair is wet in little spikes, and she throws the covers back and crosses the room to him, although they are both tired, and puts her arms around his comforting sides, his neck. He is surprised. And though they are too tired to go really crazy here, and he doesn't make a lot of noise because of Sophia, they make love. Megan falls asleep against him afterwards, enjoying the fact that he's warm, and dutiful, and a good man.

A few weeks later, he finds the stash of photos torn from magazines, and the printouts of Bo's entry on Wikipedia, and he asks her what it means. He stands there in his bathrobe, with a towel around his neck, and his hand full of papers. "I was looking for a safety pin," he says. "What is this?"

"I don't know," Megan says. "Maybe it's better if you just don't ask me about it."

He stares at her, and she wishes he'd do something else. "Okay," he says finally. She has an overwhelming urge to giggle. She picks up a book, from her bedside table, and starts reading. This is a stone wall. Later, in a day or so, she will feel as if a door has slammed between them. It's a discomfort. An embarassment. She throws away the pictures unwillingly. Shreds them in the growling shredder, feeling bereft.

❖ ❖ ❖

Fifteen years before, when she and Larry were breaking up, the signs were everywhere. They, too, had gone to a couples' counselor, on La Cienega, in an old building with palm trees around the parking lot. She and Larry had had a fight about Dungeons and Dragons. He played with his friends on Friday nights, and they sat around screaming and exclaiming at each other, drinking beer, and she'd read *The Unbearable Lightness of Being* and not talked to them. He grumbled on the way home in the car, that she thought she was better than they were, just because they were enjoying themselves.

"No," she said. "I just can't relate to fantasy castles."

"It'd do you good," he said. "To stop intellectualizing, like all your snobby friends."

"They're just normal people."

"They're snobs. Don't you see? They don't have any heart. They don't even tell each other the truth. They bullshit each other." His voice fell, as they stopped at the light at Franklin. "When you're with them, you're like that. You could use some more compassion, Megan. You should learn from me."

Dragons? she thought. This is what I want to learn? He seemed hopelessly stubborn, with his friends with the crappy cars, the acting classes where they read scenes and wept and shouted. Sometimes he just seemed to eat his emotionality like food. "It's all about the here and now," he said. "That's what you don't get." As if she were an idiot. "Most people are worrying about what's going to happen, or they're thinking about what already happened. They aren't in the now."

Oh, please, she'd thought. But this was so temporary. You didn't get married to an actor who juggled tennis balls at kids' birthday parties in Laurel Canyon. After that night, she didn't want to sleep with him. They coupled, but it was boring to her. The birds continued to trill, like water, like light, in the hedge outside the window, in the fragrance of the jasmine and bougainvillea. But she was done. The light reflected up into the leaves around the swimming pool. But lying beside his sleeping form, she felt impatient and lonely.

He wasn't fooled for long. "What's the matter?" he said to her.

"Nothing."

"Come on. You're about to leave me."

She hadn't wanted him to know, because she needed to find a place to live, a friend who would be a new roommate. But she told him, yes, she was leaving. He sulked, and then disappeared in the Nissan, and didn't come back all night. She'd had to walk Chippie twice herself, and one of the neighbors in the building, a petroleum engineer who'd moved there with his wife from Texas, tried to keep her in conversation in the hallway. When Larry finally came back, after noon the next day, he brought a vase of red roses from a florist in Bev Hills, and she could only think it was money better spent on paying down his credit cards. His neediness made her feel as if she couldn't breathe.

"You can't even look me in the eye," he said.

That was when they had the emergency meeting with the therapist. But it turned out the therapist was getting a divorce, so all he could talk about was his family, and how difficult it was for his children. Afterwards Larry and Megan stood in the parking lot on La Cienega, and Megan thought how those palm trees were not really trees at all, but spongy false trees, invasive from Florida. It's like us, she thought. We're not really solid at all.

"You know what it is," Larry was saying. "He's a therapist getting a divorce, so he has to make it the most perfect divorce anyone has ever had." He leaned against his car, his long legs crossed at the ankles. "You know why he does that?"

She shook her head.

"Because he doesn't want to feel pain." She nodded impatiently. He asked did she want to get something to eat, and she said no.

He said, "You've shut me out. You're already gone."

"No I haven't. We're just not compatible."

"You just don't get it." He seemed to get teary, but she only felt uncomfortable. It was, she told one of her friends later, like slipping out of a skirt that was way too tight. Slipping out of a sleeping bag you'd been zipped up in. Later, her friends, at various times, told her they were surprised she and Larry had lasted as long as they did. But her new roommate said, "He's not so bad. He just needs a lot of support." Which made Megan depressed, for a couple of days, as if she were guilty of something. But it was a question of survival, really. And she'd packed all her things in cartons when he was at acting class, and emptied the apartment, barely stopping to say goodbye to Chippie, who was hungry, as usual.

❖ ❖ ❖

At dinner, in Philadelphia, Sophia is chewing on her steak. Megan is thinking about the difference between Bill, who is working late and not home yet, and Larry.

"Mom," Sophia says, "you're not listening."

"Sorry."

"I said, 'Did you know that Aurelie moved here from Haiti? With her family?'"

"Yes. I knew that."

"They came because they didn't have any money."

Megan nods. "It's a tropical country. That's why Aurelie is usually cold."

❖ ❖ ❖

The next afternoon, Megan is watching the soap with Aurelie and Sophia on the couch in the den. Larry's character has had a terrible car accident, and he's lying in a hospital bed. He's bandaged and has several monitors, but his handsome face is intact and highly pained, in close-up. He has flashbacks, which take up almost half the program. His mistress and his fiancée get into an argument in the hospital waiting room, but Larry is still unconscious. He has flashbacks about his previous life as a doctor, and before that as a racing-car driver, who lost his first wife when she was kidnapped by a drug cartel when they were vacationing in Mexico.

Aurelie, who is watching this and eating potato chips, finds the dream sequences disturbing and complains that they don't make sense. "Shh," Sophia says. "He's really sad about his first wife."

The cameras stay close on Larry, who yearns and twists in his drugged sleep. Suddenly he wakes up and looks at the nurse, who, being middle-aged and plain, will probably not be a permanent character. Tears stream down Larry's face. He reaches for the nurse's hand. "She understood," he says feverishly. "She was the only one who understood!"

"Now, Mr. Saint-Pierre," she says. "You must rest. You need your strength."

"No," Larry says, obviously heartbroken. He weeps for millions of people, Megan thinks, including the overseas feeds. "The first one you love," he says. "It's always the deepest. It never goes away." He weeps more. Even Sophia and Aurelie have stopped fidgeting, shocked by his manly crying on daytime television. They watch him, rapt. "It was always you, Megan. I'll always love you," he says. "Megan, my darling." He says it with all the weight of tragedy and loss. "Megan, wherever your happiness has taken you, I will always love you."

Megan, on the beige couch, feels as if he's reached right out of the wide-screen monitor and touched her. She's become an actor's material. Or maybe she's being too harsh, here. Whatever she remembers is not what he remembers at all. She watches Aurelie and Sophia go off to make peanut butter sandwiches, because Sophia is hungry. Larry has said this, she thinks. I am alive to him. The afternoon that seemed so familiar and so terrible, this room so claustrophobic in its darkness, are suddenly radiant with some large sense of love. There is a rich life, with laughter and and bright colors, that she is not part of. But it remembers her. He has said this to me, she thinks. A blessing and a secret. Even knowing I might not listen.

Sophia is chattering in the kitchen, asking for a knife from Aurelie. In her pop-star outfit she returns, with bright red lipstick on her childish mouth, holding out a yellow plate with a peanut butter sandwich on it.

"Nice lipstick," Megan says.

"It was in your bathroom."

The sandwich's crusts have been removed; its outline is irregular. "Okay, Mom. I made it for you," she says. She seems suddenly so small, so determined to be heard. Hunching the plate, to give it up. Hunching her shoulders. Waiting for Megan to take a bite.

Megan thanks her, and takes the uneven and beautiful sandwich she offers. When Bill gets home, late that night, she is awake, waiting for him. He, too, stoops, she thinks, more than she remembers. In spite of the racquetball and the visits to the personal trainer. He carries his duties like gray fat in the air surrounding his Italian suit. Like desperation. His face stolid like a soldier on a long march. A horse in harness, pulling a carriage around Central Park forever. "Come here," she says, holding her arms out for the briefcase, the laptop case she will put on the floor. "Come here."

❖ ❖ ❖

Robert Rahway Zakanitch at the University of Tampa. *Photograph by J. M. Lennon.*

Aggressive Goodness and Magic Carpets:
A Conversation with Robert Rahway Zakanitch

Robert Rahway Zakanitch has been exhibiting in New York since 1965. He has had numerous shows beginning with Elanore Wards, Stable Gallery then Reese Palley, Holly Solomon, Robert Miller, Sidney Janis, Hirschl/Adler Modern, and many group exhibitions which include the Whitney Annual (three times), the Metropolitan Museum of Art, and the Museum of Modern Art. Nationally he has had many solo exhibitions and has been included in numerous group shows. Internationally he has had one-man shows in Paris, Basel, Zurich, Köln, Berlin, Osaka, and the Venice Biennalle, American Pavillion. He received a Guggenheim Fellowship in 1995 and has been listed in *Who's Who in America*, *Who's Who in the World*, and *International Who's Who* since 1980.

Mathews: It's wonderful that Kendra and I can talk with you today here in the Scarfone-Hartley Gallery, surrounded by your beautiful art. My first glimpse of your show was a few nights ago when poet Tim Seibles visited campus and gave his reading here in the gallery. His podium faced the painting we are sitting in front of now, "Bungalow Suite I," and the first thing he did after the reading was to walk over here to stand in front of it—and just *look*. He said, "I can't believe this painting!" He was visibly overwhelmed by it—the scale, the color, the wonder of it.

Zakanitch: Wow, how great. I *love* poets. [*Laughter.*] I actually do. They are very courageous. But I have such difficulty understanding them. They understand me more than I understand them, I think. But I understand what they are doing, the distillation of words, getting things *just right*—and so personal and unflinchingly honest. But when I sit down and read poetry, well, I'm not sure if I'm getting it all . . . it's very frustrating, but I keep working at it. I think it's important.

Frorup: It's very much like the visual arts in that way. You're not sure whether or not you truly understand it, even when you admire it a great deal . . .

Zakanitch: Yes, that's right. But with visual arts, fortunately, I feel more comfortable, and I *do* think I can grasp what's being said. I'm more familiar with the visual language because it's always been with me. It's how I see the world. The poet is trying to do the same things that I'm trying to do, and I do understand that, that

sense of honesty . . . I feel all the arts are so connected: music, literature, dance, architecture, etc. They are all about optimism, civility, and compassion. It's the innate nature of the arts.

Mathews: Well, it was fun to watch Tim's response to your show, and to *see* its effect on him. Of course, the last time you were on campus, we were in the old Scarfone Gallery, much smaller and finished in rough wood, so that it had a very different feel to it. Can you say something about your own response to the presentation of your work in this new Scarfone/Hartley gallery space?

Zakanitch: It's so big and clean! I didn't know what to expect. As you say, I've never been here, so it was hard to imagine how the pieces would look. You know, that *big* painting, "Cherry Jubilee," has never been shown outside of my studio. It's never been on a wall before, because it was too difficult to hang. It is four large, heavy pieces, especially the center two parts that are done on masonite which all had to be bolted together. As a result it always sat on the floor, leaning against the wall. And I knew it was big—it's about eighteen feet by seven or eight feet— something like that. It's hard to imagine what a piece that size will feel like until it's displayed with space around it. When I first came into this big beautiful new gallery to see it, my first reaction was, "Wow! The space around it is so good." It fit perfectly. It had such good balance.

After seeing the paintings only in my studio, in the specific space they are painted in, seeing them in a gallery space or another space is often

Richard Mathews and Kendra Frorup talk with Robert Zakanitch in the Scarfone/Hartley Gallery, in front of a painting from his "Big Bungalow Suite." *Photo by Anthony Fasciano.*

like seeing them for the first time. The mystery of scale.

Mathews: Can you say a little more about scale? What does it mean to you?

Zakanitch: Scale for me is really major. It's a simple thing, and it's not understood by very many people. For example, when I did these giant thirty-foot paintings, like the one we are sitting in front of (one of five from what is called the "Big Bungalow Suite") . . . when I was doing this series, which took three years to do, at one point, I had three of them surrounding me. I have a big studio, and they filled virtually all of my wall space. It really was like being inside them. When it became time for them to be shown—of course the difficulty was to find a space large enough to show four twelve-foot by thirty-foot paintings —we, Jason McCoy, whose gallery it was, and I looked around lower Manhattan and eventually found a large, raw, unpainted space in Soho to show them. We could only show four—actually, there *were* only four finished at the time. After they were hung in this space, bigger than my studio—quite a bit bigger than my studio, with higher ceilings—I

walked in and saw them, and I remember saying, "Oh no, these look *small*! I thought they were bigger than that!" There was only about eight feet more wall space, plus the height of the ceiling, but it made a big difference to me. That's what I mean by scale. You change the context and the space, and you alter the perception of the work and the work itself. I'm really sensitive about it. I'm happy to say that this one in the gallery works beautifully here. I was worried about it, but it looks fine.

That painting over there, "A Chicken in Every Poet" from the Tureen Series [a series featuring soup tureens, first shown at the Werkstatte Gallery in New York in 2008]—they were substantial in size when I was working on them. But now that the context has been changed, look how small they become when you see them in this space, next to those two huge paintings.

Frorup: How did you decide on the pieces to be shown together here in Tampa? I know we were anxious when the works got here just to open them and see what they really look like. How did you decide on this body of work for the show? Is this all one body . . .

"Cherry Jubilee" by Robert Zakanitch. The painting had not been shown outside the artist's studio prior to the Tampa show. *Photo by Anthony Fasciano.*

Zakanitch: That's a good question, but, no, they are not one body. There are different phases here and it was hard to choose. There are some early paintings—and some recent. The Tureen Series was my last show and last Gallery I had in New York. That was just three years ago. The lace paintings are in the middle, around 2001, or right after 9/11, which is why they were painted. And the earliest piece, "Angel of Positive Rage," goes back to 1986-87. That's about a quarter-century ago now.

Mathews: I would not have been able to tell that. They don't seem time-linked or dated; and the early pieces don't seem at all out of place with the recent work. There's a strong compatibility of color—with the far end of "Cherry Jubilee" especially.

Zakanitch: Thanks. Yeah, I hope so. I think the whole nature of what I'm trying to do existed then as it does now. The subject matter changes a bit but it's always directed to civility in one form or another.

Frorup: It's hard to curate a show, especially without being in the space. You must have found it challenging.

Zakanitch: Well, I received a drawing, a layout of the gallery, with dimensions of wall. Which was a big help. I thought, well, since my work is so big, maybe seven or eight paintings would do it. I thought that seven or eight would just about fill this space. But when I started to re-read the footage, that number grew. I believe I sent about nineteen.

Frorup: And I believe we had to leave out only about three.

Mathews: Thinking about the importance you place on scale, you have been also working on a dramatically different scale. I know that you originally thought of being on campus sooner, but you have been working on a book . . .

Zakanitch: Yes. A children's book.

Mathews: And that's a very different scale from any of the actual sizes of your works here—their physical presence.

Zakanitch: That's an interesting question. Yes, they are a different scale and also completely different conceptually. One of the things I'm trying to do with this book is to extend the parameters of fine art into commercial art. There's a fine line between illustration and painting. I still wanted to keep it as fine art, but then I realized that I've seen books for kids by fine artists, and they're usually more about their paintings than about being books *for children*. It doesn't really make sense that way. I'm actually trying to do things that will cross that line and not be first so much about my paintings but also equally about being entertaining to *children* (and adults).

Mathews: What's the title.

Zakanitch: It's called, *A Garden of Ordinary Miracles: An Alphabet Book*... Rizzoli is publishing it, and it should be out in the fall and for Christmas.

Mathews: Do you work at actual size as you are creating pieces for the book? Or will your printer be reducing the scale?

Zakanitch: It will be reduced a little bit. But I try not to work much larger than the actual size of the book because it just kills me to see much reduction. That changes everything. This way there are no big surprises at the end.

Frorup: Will it be the full alphabet?

Zakanitch: Yes, it sure will. Twenty-six letters, and each a double spread.

Mathews: "Z" is for Zakanitch? [*Laughter.*]

Zakanitch: I thought about that...

Mathews: The artist's signature at the end.

Zakanitch. ... but I figured I couldn't fit that one in.... But I like it.

Frorup: I love the idea of books.

Mathews: And children's books.

Zakanitch: One last thing about working in book scale and how it almost viscerally affects me. I'm glad you are talking about this, because I do find it really interesting. As I've mentioned, I have a big studio, and I have been trying to find or to rent a *smaller* place so that I could work in a smaller space, in which I would be more comfortable with a book size. I did a couple of children's books before, and I realized I had to do something to my studio to reduce the space and make me think differently. What I ended up doing was to put some folding screens (that were part of another kind of series) around me to shut myself off from the studio. However, with this book I had a better solution. I just moved my drawing board out of the studio part and into my living space and did it there. Much more comfortable. It was nice. It felt like I was on vacation from my studio.

Frorup: Speaking again about scale, and how one thing influences the other, you said that your studio is spacious, and you have several paintings around you at the same time. Are you pushing and pulling and working on them all at the same time?

Zakanitch: Well, sometimes. I seem to move in a series, from one to another. You know, this [gesturing to the large thirty-foot canvas of "Bungalow Suite I" behind him] was the first one of the "Suite." I originally thought: I'm going to *do just one*—one really large piece. Because I was so tired at the time of going to parties or going to bars or to friends' apartments and hearing about conceptual art and how painting was dead... again. I used to be a Formalist painter, but I really rejected all that. Well, I suppose I can't really say that, because Formalism taught me a lot, and it's in this work, by the way. But the artistic buzz was that "painting is dead,"—at least it was for the Conceptualist—and how many times have we heard that? But I just said, I'm going to show you, *painting is not dead*. And I did this one big painting, and I thought, "Geez, I love this!"

Mathews: So you started the Bungalow series?

Zakanitch: Yes. It was so exciting that I wanted to do another one! I really liked the physicality of doing them, which I think transfers into the works. I worked on a scaffold, by the way. I was in very good condition doing these massive pieces. I was climbing around and moving myself physically so much as I worked.

The second one ended up being just as satisfying as the first, so I again thought, maybe I'll do a third with different coloration and atmosphere... and then a black and white one. Finally, I thought it would be wonderful to finish the series off with an all-blue one—which I did. All colors become richer around blue. It's a magic color. I thought it would be the perfect ending to this very large-scale group. It took three or four years to complete them. But while I was doing them, the pots in the works led me to doing a series of individual pot paintings—two of which are in the show ("Scarlet Scarab" and "White Bloom"). When the large paintings were shown downtown in Soho, at the same time the original Jason McCoy Gallery in the Fuller Building, on 57th Street, showed the pots that correlated to the large-scale series.

Mathews: I was thinking of this with respect to the pots, because in a sense, the scale doesn't

Robert Zakanitch discusses a print from the "Magic Carpet" series with Master Printer Carl Cowden in Studio-f. *Photo by J. M. Lennon.*

shift tremendously when you pull the pot out of the large painting and concentrate simply on that detail. The scale itself still renders the pot larger than life.

Zakanitch: Yes, actually, this is an *enormous* pot!

Frorup: It doesn't quite seem that way within the large painting, because of the scale of the overall work.

Zakanitch. That's right. I had to make them big. I have to paint them that way. I cannot paint small. It drives me crazy because people say, "Well, do you have anything smaller?" Well, *no.* I don't have anything smaller. My whole career is that way.

Frorup: But you have the little flowers.

Zakanitch: Yes, that's true. Well, I did those because I had a show with my LA. gallery, Samuel Freeman Gallery, last year, which was the first showing of these large, 8-feet x 6-feet, gouache paintings on paper which have a very, very flat and matte and dry surface. Gouache is a rarely used medium and has amazing surface. So I decided, so as to have a big contrast, to paint those very, very thick, heavy, wet-looking, and yes, small, paintings as a vivid physical contrast.

Frorup: Where are you drawing your subject matter from?

Zakanitch: The world. [*Pause.*] Listen, I could talk for hours about this, and we have to try to keep it short. But you know, up to this point. Have you heard of the Pattern and Decoration Movement? Sometimes it's referred to as "P&D." I'm supposed to be one of the originators of that . . .

Frorup: Yes, I am familiar with it . . .

Zakanitch: One of the reasons—of which there were many—it came into being, and I wasn't thinking of this at the time, only afterward—is that I was no longer interested in doing representational imagery *or* abstraction. I started out as an abstract expressionist. And then I became a Formalist, in that I became what was called a "color field painter." It came from my scientific color studies that I had in art school for years and years. And of course once I began to show them, it was labeled; they said he is doing grids, and he's doing color field. Well, I never thought of that. For me it was just what it was: beautiful changing colors moving through a canvas creat-

Robert Zakanitch at work on a monoprint in Studio-f. *Photo by J. M. Lennon.*

ing their own innate magic. But this all seemed just a beginning to me and I wanted to move on. To where I didn't know. But I felt the art scene around me dominated by Formalists had reached its end . . . because you know what Formalism is: it's the purity-of-materials concept. And it kind of has an in-grown self-destruction, in that you become so "pure" that you find yourself forced into Conceptualist thinking, saying, "We don't need paint or brushes; we just need an idea." You can't get any purer than that . . . so that's the end of painting. So back to "painting is dead" again.

I really wanted another subject matter—a third one—because abstraction and representation are the only two we artists have ever had up to that point in art history [1974], with variations of those two—and I mean sculptors as well as painters. I was no longer interested in going to galleries and museums because they only showed abstract and representational imagery. I finally decided, ok, I'm going to find a new museum and a new gallery, so my museums and galleries became flea markets, hardware stores, rug stores, linoleum stores—especially the 1940s linoleum patterns—and places like that that I was drawn to.

So I found myself finally getting into patterns and ornamentation. I did indeed find a third subject matter; there it was: pattern and ornamentation. A legitimate subject matter for mainstream painting.

Mathews: This strikes home for me, having written a dissertation on William Morris. He created wonderful patterns for fabrics, wallpapers, stained glass, carpets, and printed books. Morris was a great influence on the arts and crafts movement in the late nineteenth century.

Zakanitch: Yes, and of course, it's something that I love, because I was raised with ornamentation and patterns, from my maternal background. There was a lot of embroidery and other crafted and patterned work. What was interesting about it is that it was neither abstract nor representational, and yet it was both—and beyond either. You know ornamentation is so incredibly intense in what it does to you, as you are dealing with it, as either a pattern or as an artist. I think, for example, of Gaudí's, Güell Park in Barcelona, if you have ever seen it. I mean, you sort of evaporate into it. It gets into your soul. So *that*, I just realized, is pattern . . .

Mathews: What effect do you think it had on the Art world at that time?

Zakanitch: After the Pattern and Decoration Movement, the entire atmosphere in the art world changed. And also the world in general. I began to see patterns and ornmentation everywhere. No more "less is more" and just Norell Pillbox hats and one-color garments or "less is more" architecture. All the restricted walls of Formalism came down. Painting opened up and exploded again at the beginning of the 80s. It was wonderful. I mean it got so wild and extended that the critics here in the USA (Europe embraced it) who were still considering it a non-movement and still so negative to P&D had to come up with a new name: Pluralism. I still don't quite know what that is, but I do know I was in a few shows under that seemingly more acceptable title (actually, P&D had its effect even on that title because P&D was, for the first time, an all-inclusive movement).

Frorup: The watercolor paintings that are hung in the front give me a feeling of linoleum. The ones that include birds, blackbirds . . . they are beautiful.

Zakanitch: Thank you. There is a reason that *three* are there. They are identical watercolors, but very different because of the color. I did it as if I were looking at a book of wallpaper samples, with variations on the same patterns using different colorations. I always loved seeing those. It's such a good example of the power of color. Just by changing color, it creates a different spirit . . . different painting

Mathews: My goodness. It's Morris again—like a wallpaper pattern book for Morris & Co.

Zakanitch. Yep. It's instant art. Three ways of seeing the same thing differently. I love watercolor, I felt it was so hard to do, so I decided that I was going to get good at it. I just kept working with it for years until I started to see better results, results that I felt good enough to leave my studio. And it also kept me small—at least smaller than my other paintings. I ended up doing the four-foot watercolors. But you know, that's awfully big!

Frorup: Yes, it's big for a watercolor.

Zakanitch: But somehow it allowed me to think smaller, and I was able to work on that.

Frorup: As soon as we unpacked the pieces, I took them there.

Zakanitch: There are actually four, but I left the other one back. I didn't think you needed it to see the point.

Mathews: Maybe that's one of your next steps, then: to make these into fabrics and wallpapers.

Zakanitch: It's so funny you said that. You know, someone asked me to do wallpaper, and I thought, "that should be easy." But I couldn't. I couldn't do it. They weren't paintings, and I couldn't get into the wallpaper mode. It's a whole other set of rules.

Mathews: And of course, they must have the repeat, but you don't have the repeat in your paintings. You aren't using pattern in the same way. You suggest pattern without actually having exact repetition as part of it . . .

Zakanitch: Yes. Exactly. There is a lot of paint moving around there. It's very different from wallpaper because the intention is different.

Mathews: I would never have thought in this way about the P&D aspect of these paintings until we discussed it.

Frorup: Yes.

Zakanitch: Well, it happened early on when all of this ornamentation and this pattern hit the art world, which was solidly rejected by the New York critics.

Mathews: When was that? I think you said in '75?

Zakanitch: About 1975. I had my first show at Holly Solomon in 1978.

Mathews: How was that received?

Zakanitch: Well, a lot of artists came in, and I overheard something positive someone said: "I don't know what he's doing, but it's really painting!" It *was* painting. I was still doing paintings. But I guess it was kind of shocking at the time. Because another painter came up to me and said, "Do you call these paintings?"

Frorup: You said something earlier that the late paintings were a response to 9/11?

Zakanitch: Yeah, that's very true. They were very unconscious paintings, I would say. But I was in New York. My daughter was there in Brooklyn, right across. When this happened, *everyone* in New York could see it. You didn't realize how huge the towers were, how they were a part of everyone's life. Everyday. And then you look out and see this thing happening, you see everything coming apart. You know, you don't forget that. It's the depth of the anger into rage and violence of it all. It evoked questions such as: Does it make me irrelevant? Does art mean anything? Does anything mean anything in the face of that kind of obscene insanity and anger and rage? At first I just thought, do I know anyone in those towers? And I didn't. But they were human beings. It took a while just to grieve. Everyone was just *down* from this horror. After about a week or more I thought, you know, we have to start working. Artists have to start working. The firmament was so badly torn that we have to start to mend it; heal. We have to *balance* this world again. We have to put compassion and beauty back into it. That's one of the things art does. It is healing.

Frorup: Yes.

Zakanitch: You know, in a big way, it's emotional healing. It touches your soul. Without the arts, we wouldn't be sitting in a building. We wouldn't be wearing clothes. These fabrics are woven and built of artistry. But anyway, I actually started to get angry. I thought, I'm not going to sit here and stop doing what I'm doing because these cowardist terrorists have done this thing. I began to call people up, and I said, if you're not painting, it's time. We know it happened. It has changed everyone's life. But let's do *more.* You don't walk away from this. You create in the face of it.

So we did. I started this series of paintings—I didn't know they were going to be a series at that point—of black fields with white images on them. And I realized it was lace. I was interconnecting all these things. They grew. One was a nine-foot painting of peacocks and things. What I realized was that I was emotionally so raw from that, I realized . . . and this was something I believed before this happened . . . that we are really all interconnected. The lace was like the interconnection of all things, and it was a gesture toward weaving things back together again. It was all unconscious. It was only later that it hit me. But that's how they came about.

Mathews: It's interesting that the lace is such a delicate "fabric," particularly as set against the horrific destruction, and yet as you say, it shows the beauty in these intricate connections. A fabric that is full of holes, and yet a fabric.

Zakanitch: It is how we are linked together by these beautiful strands of living energy. I've always thought that we were all interconnected, all literally made of the same fabric. It's what Brian Greene talks about in his book *The Elegant Universe*, on the string theory.

Frorup: How many works were in the series that you did?

Zakanitch: I think there were about twelve, and they were pretty big. Arthur Danto, who is a critic in New York who wrote for *The Nation* for years, picked up on it. He saw it right away. Instead of reacting with violence, it was, "Let's heal." And then I really went crazy and changed my subject matter and did these ten or twelve large paintings of dogs . . . which to me were an anomaly, at least I thought that until I got a couple of dog commissions.

Frorup: I saw that show in New York a few years ago . . . It was great!

Zakanitch: . . . 2006. Time's flying!

Frorup: What gallery was it?

Zakanitch: The Spike Gallery. . . . But the reason for that show was pretty simple. I just wanted to remind us as human beings of our compassion and empathy. I called it "Aggressive Goodness." Actually, I subtitle all my work "Aggressive Goodness" now. It has been a quest of mine for a long time.

Mathews: It's a good quest to be on.

Zakanitch: In-your-face patterns. And what is better than dogs for showing that outreaching sympathy and connection?

Frorup: One of the things that I remember about that show was the scale. They were quite big.

Zakanitch: They were all five feet by seven feet. I loved being in that room when people came into that show. They all started jumping around. They would mimic the dogs. The good energy was just bouncing off the walls.

Mathews: You have yet another kind of motion now with the series you are doing in Studio-f, which you are calling the "Magic Carpet" series. What led you to calling it that, and to working in this mode?

Zakanitch: Desperation! I was looking for a good title.

Frorup: [*Laughing.*] That's as honest as you can get!

Mathews: [*Laughing.*] Well, it comes right out of children's books, too.

Zakanitch: I've always loved that term "Magic Carpets" and I thought, well, I do circles and patterns. Why don't you make them into carpets? You see the flowers up front? And, yes, the fact that I've been working on a children's book *did* play a role. I want to put stars on those things! And you don't *do* that. Maybe if it weren't for a children's book I wouldn't think of doing it. But

Robert Zakanitch points out details on a "Magic Carpet" monoprint to visitors in Studio-f. Photo by J. M. Lennon.

I'm going to get some stars on there somewhere. They belong with magic carpets.

Mathews: So now you are shifting again, as we follow your work into Studio-f. And you are adapting to yet another scale, both in terms of the room you are in at Studio-f, and the scale of the monoprints themselves.

Zakanitch: Yes, there is the big difference. They are prints, silk screen prints. Which changes the entire thinking process again. I'm not yet entirely sure what that result will be. But so far it feels pretty good. I find a nook somewhere, and other people can be in their own sections. It works well.

Mathews: What size will these be?

Zakanitch: They aren't very big. Something roughly 28 x 40 inches. The pieces I've done here before have been larger.

Frorup: When I look at your work, I can relate to it because I'm a collector, and your work feels like a *great* collection of things, things that I might want to collect, like pieces of linoleum or fabric that are especially appealing. Are you a collector?

Zakanitch: I have a lot of reference books, and I take photographs of things that I find especially striking, but I'm not much of a collector. There's no room! I mean there's so much stuff. But I am sort of chameleon-like in that.

Frorup: I was thinking of the lace and the pots.

Zakanitch: Oh, well . . . I do have a lot of junky little pots. Until I use them, and then I can give them away. The thing about the work is that . . . I gave a talk in Oklahoma, and I called it "Art and Civility." These words projected—white on a black screen—were shown as I was starting to talk. And I thought, that's really what art is about, and it's what my work is about. And I love that. Those two words are not only synonymous, but also redundant.

Mathews: The pairing seems similar to "Aggressive Goodness" in some ways.

Zakanitch: Yes, you're right; it is similar. But art does work this way. It's a very powerful force. It truly is. It brings all these things up—like compassion, and empathy—and when you are an artist, you are interested in everything. You try to pull everything in. You become all inclusive. There are no big rejections—or at least you only reject them when you "should," we like to think that—but you allow things to happen, which is all involved in being humane.

Mathews: We're glad you have been here on campus before, but we are particularly glad to have you here again, this time, and to see where your work will go next, how it will unfold, and whether or not stars will appear in the firmament. Thank you for talking with us.

Zakanitch: Thank you. I don't know where the work is going to go today, but it will be fun to see.

❖ ❖ ❖

Stephen Kampa

Meant to Be

Cracked acorns punctuate the ground
Like grief, their scattered caps the cups
Rain overfills with chattering drops
That are themselves what they propound.

My lapsang souchong tastes like smoke.
I watch the low, collapsing sky
Collect in pools stained brown like whisky,
And dream of endless stands of oak,

Grand emblems of entelechy,
That realm where promised primrose blooms
And brushwood fuels the brisk, hushed flames
That flicker through my achy tea.

You're back. The courtyard sidewalk pops
With raindrops' goose bumps as you call
Up to my window, *It was all
A big mistake*. You stir my hopes:

Our breaking up? *Not that. Your life.
You made your grail* a girl, *a maid
Of High Romance, a fancy played
Up version of the perfect wife,*

*One no less hokey than the virgin
Volcano-bound in jungle flicks:
Priests pour libations, white fire licks
Her feet, Sir Rescue will emerge in*

*The nick of time, and presto!—lookie
Here!—Hero sweeps the sweatless girl
Right off the sacrificial grill
And into bliss! Now, ain't she lucky?*

Well spoken. Love was never meant
To be that easy, nor that scenic—
No wide shot of the oceanic
Cruise home to "Moonlight in Vermont"—

But mostly rain and smoke and doubt.
Tea's cold, dream's scuttled. In its wake,
I hear wild drumming. Chants. I take
My flooded heart and pour it out.

In Venice Ghetto, 2006

for Shaul Bassi

If Venice changes us, it's as a thirst
that can't be quenched, a thread that tangles
etymologies, where the sea insists
on the fundamental and the *sottoportego*
tunnels to new light. In one yellow campo
shaped like a badge, walling in and walling

out are balanced on wooden pilings
a thousand years old, allegedly
immune to decay. Green shutters are closed
to eyes and afternoon, and muffle praise
the cantor utters on the highest floor
where prayers rise like heat or are scrawled

and dropped, frail boats on the boundary canal.
Across the stone pavement, soccer balls spin
between boys careful to avoid the shrine
where Auschwitz is whispered
under a marble tally of deportees.
And still the hidden Jew defies all counts.

The rabbi burnt his list of congregants
and swallowed poison, allowing time
for most to escape to new identities.
Survivors in the Hebrew Care Home toss
and turn against Adriatic swelter
as the fan intones *"Baruch, Baruch."*

In this city that passes and passes,
Vivaldi's scruffy heirs ply their bows, cases
open to coffer coins bystanders toss.
From every third shop window, masks return
our stares, forged passports at a price.
And yet we cannot bring ourselves to leave.

Here, where languages blend into babble
and babble, for an instant, rings clear,
we find haven. Along a narrow chute
called Calle del Forno, our voices mingle
with the crowd, and *impade* cakes reward
a taste for exile, a hunger for home.

Near the Capitol

From the window of our GTO,
Washington was Oz:
green square crewcuts and white façades.

While Lowell and the protesters faced helmets,
my fingers held motley Chinese vegetables
at The Inn Of The Eight Immortals.

I was three. We lived in Arlington, a bridge away,
whose lights hung red and yellow against an overcast sky.
They never took me to its cemetery.

For me, the war was over in Vietnam
when my father came home from Da Nang.
His work on K Street was up-and-coming;

he stayed out where black-suited men
drank scotch, and women sipped Pernod.
My mother dialed the bars, one by one,

while our lamb went cold.
My father's path could have crossed Lowell's,
but when I played on the Mall,

I didn't know what a protest was
or that round words in the reflecting pool
fringed by cherry tree blooms

were more than beads falling
on the wall-to-wall at home,
lost in the broadloom.

Charles Harper Webb

Post-Modernism Missed the Opry

If old George sings, "I'll love you till I die,"
he isn't kidding; call a hearse. If Dolly begs
some redhead, "Please don't take my man,"
or swears, "I will always love you"—even if

you doubt her dirigible breasts, her yellow
hair high as the Tower of Babel, you know
her love is true as water's wet, sun's hot,
and dandelions whirligig on a fall day.

You know the mockingbird that trills, *Shree!*
Shree! Shree! Shree! while bouncing
in your apple tree, was not sent by the IRS,
just as you know taxes are bad in Country.

Crawfish pie is good, and barbecue so tender
your taste buds (those friendly flowers)
wiggle their vermilion heads for joy. Irony
is what a smith beats into horseshoes;

how moms smooth their family's clothes.
Esthetic distance is the valley between
mountains full of deer, trout, bobwhites,
and the pine-shaded shack where you were born.

Post-Modern is a city boy who's never been
so lonesome he could cry—who'd never
walk the line, sigh, "Hello, walls," or waltz
across Texas—who thinks he's too smart

to place a rose from her own garden on the grave
of his wife of fifty years—who hides,
in an ice-chest that should be full of longnecks,
his really and truly cold, cold heart.

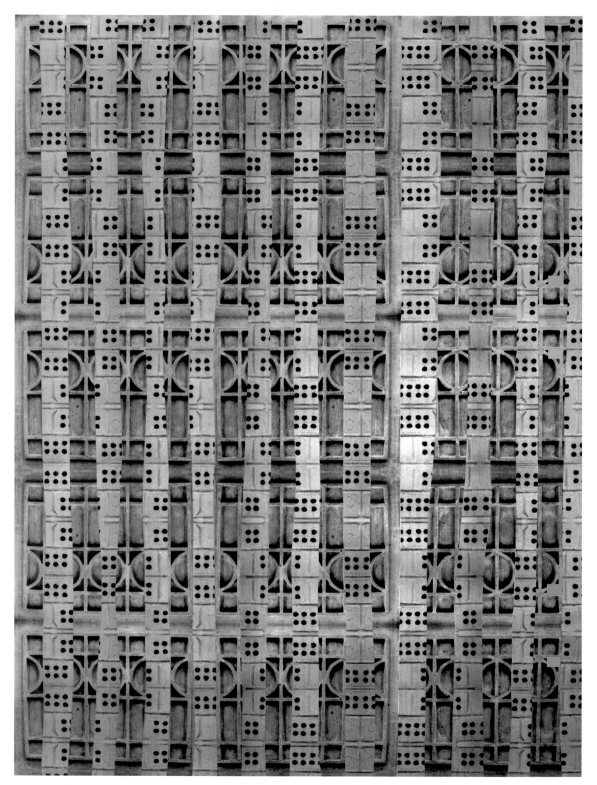

Max Warsh. *Interstate 07.* 2011. Photographs on paper. 22 x 30 inches.

This Change Not Come from Sky

Becky watched the Dalai Lama settle cross-legged into the western-style chair on the TV show set and wished she were that limber. Perfectly at ease, the holy man seemed unaware that his pose was unconventional. The national network, which had made such a show of his arrival in a black limousine, the hosts bowing like pecking chickens, instead should have provided a pillow or a couch, something more suitable to his preferred manner of sitting, but perhaps the picture would not have been as interesting. "People do weird things," her friend had said last night, and in comparison to what her aunt had done, the Lama's pose was nothing.

Becky half-watched the beginning of the morning talk show while she stood at her kitchen sink. In time, the small flat-screen TV to her left would predict Chicago's weather, but the view out the window to her right would give her the real story before her twenty-minute walk to the downtown law firm where she worked as a corporate paralegal. She was doing the dinner dishes that had been left in the sink to soak overnight. She and her friends had finished a jug of red wine with a large garbage pizza, and given everything that had happened, she felt all three aberrations—the wine, the calories, and the sloth—justified.

❖ ❖ ❖

It had been a terrible day, and she'd needed the support of her girlfriends. Her nineteen-year-old cousin had overdosed, and she'd driven up to his parents' home in a small town near the Illinois-Wisconsin border to attend his funeral. Disturbingly, his casket had remained open during the services, and she'd found herself staring at his face, pale but remarkably lifelike, the mortician's paint so delicate it was almost undetectable, his goatee thin, as if it were still growing. Over the years, at annual family reunions, he'd been alternately hyperactive or

sullen, his foot tapping incessantly while his green eyes darted from one relative to the next, or his body slumping in a lawn chair while he silently consumed a twelve-pack. At the end of the service, the mourners filed past the coffin and out of the funeral parlor, the family the last to leave. Becky had taken one obligatory final brief look and was nearly at the door when there was a flash behind her and she turned to see her aunt taking pictures of her son in his coffin.

"I think that was weird," she'd told her friends. It had been her excuse for drinking too much last night, and thus leaving the dishes unwashed.

"People do weird things," her friend Nancy had said.

"But why?" Becky persisted.

"I don't know," Nancy said. "Sometimes they don't even know themselves why they're doing something. They just do it, and then afterwards they wonder why they did it."

"Maybe, after all the drug stuff, she just wanted to remember him as finally being at peace," Ann said. Ann had recently started studying Zen, and sometimes Becky found her new-found spirituality annoying.

"Like he wasn't dead?" Becky said, putting her wine glass down.

"I'm guessing that if you took a picture of just his face, you wouldn't know the difference. He might look like he was asleep," Ann said, her voice rising a half-note in self-defense.

Becky shook her head and picked up her glass. Jean broke in, "Maybe she wanted to show other kids what can happen to you if you use." Working for trial lawyers, Jean was always coming up with alternative, even if only marginally rational, theories.

"Or maybe she just didn't know what else to do," Jean said, obviously not as intrigued with the picture-taking as Becky, and eager to move on to a discussion of their own more pressing issues: being underpaid, looking for men, worrying about layoffs at their jobs.

"Nothing she could do, really," Ann said, again serene, "except to acknowledge the reality and then go on with her life."

"With her grief, you mean," Becky said, realizing that she was in fact angry with her cousin for his reckless, or careless, or—God-forbid—perhaps deliberate, death.

"The Buddhists say suffering's optional," Ann said, and before they could get embroiled in that discussion, Jean clapped her hands. "Have some more wine," she said, and emptied the bottle for their last round.

❖ ❖ ❖

Now, Becky rubbed at the remnants of Jean's cranberry lipstick on a wine glass. "Our problems are temporary," the Dalai Lama told the TV host.

"Be gone!" Becky said to the stubborn stain, encouraged by the Dalai Lama's peaceful and nonjudgmental aura; her hangover would be cured by noon. It occurred to her the Dalai Lama was right: even her cousin's problems, whatever they were, were over.

She glanced out the window. Across the street, a man in a suit and tie—possibly one of the younger lawyers at her firm, or a banker, or someone looking for a job—stepped out on his balcony, two floors up. Becky was glad she didn't have a balcony, although many of the newer buildings in the city had them—for smokers, she guessed—but the thought of standing out on a small platform seventeen stories high made her knees buckle. The man's balcony had a small round black barbecue, one white plastic chair, and two clay pots of red geraniums. He bent down and picked a leaf, then dropped it over the side, leaning over to watch it float. Curious, Becky went to the window and saw the leaf swirling in an updraft between the buildings. When she lost sight of it, she looked back at the balcony, but the man was gone, and she returned to the sink to finish her dishes.

With impeccable timing, the Dalai Lama told the television interviewer, "This change not come from sky, but come from human experience." He added, "For the last century or two, we are not acting in true human spirit," and predicted that the twenty-first century would

be more happy and compassionate than those before it, depending on man's "positive action" and "positive vision." Becky hoped so. Her walk to work was often depressing. She passed so many homeless people begging for loose change or a dollar. On a paralegal's salary, she couldn't afford to help them all, and so she tried to avoid making eye contact. Sometimes, too, the law business felt cutthroat, the attorneys she worked with, ruthless and demanding. It encouraged her to see a man in a suit take the time to tend a plant, to gaze at a leaf on the wind.

She kept a few plants on her own window sill and a yellowing leaf on an overgrown pothos vine caught her attention. She dried her hands on a paper towel and went to the sill, where she plucked the dying leaf, and was inspecting the other plants when the man returned to his balcony. He looked up and down the street, and then stooped down to the geraniums. Instead of tending them, this time he picked up one of the clay pots and in a smooth and continuous motion dropped it over the iron railing. It smashed on the sidewalk, surprising an approaching man and woman. The woman jumped back, her hand over her mouth; the man looked skyward and raised his fist. The man on the seventeenth floor balcony stared down passively, neither delighting in his stunt nor feigning innocence. On the sidewalk, the couple put their arms around each other and crossed the street.

❖ ❖ ❖

Becky crushed the plucked leaf in her hand. The man on the balcony turned and went back inside, shutting the sliding glass doors behind him. His actions contradicted the Dalai Lama: malicious, not compassionate; negative, not positive. She could think of no gentle explanation. How tricky it was to live in a crowded city where your neighbors, even in the nice neighborhoods, did such weird and unexpected things! In the small town in southern Wisconsin where she'd grown up, if a neighbor was crazy, everybody knew it, and knew whether he or she was evil. Her aunt, for instance, might do some weird things, but everybody knew she wasn't dangerous. In the city, suspended above the ground in various layers and packed five hundred or a thousand or more to a building, who knew? How could you know? How could you walk the city streets and feel safe, with clay pots being thrown deliberately from fancy balconies? She tossed the crushed leaf in the wastebasket and went to her bedroom to finish dressing.

She stopped one last time in the kitchen and, before turning off the TV, took a final look at the balcony across the street. Her stomach flipped, and goose bumps ran up her arms. The man across the street had one leg over the railing, straddling it like a horse. Both of his hands gripped the iron railing. Before she could even think what he might be doing, he swung his other leg over the top and was hanging, his hands gripping the upper black iron cross-bar, his white cuffs stretching out from his gray suit. His head cocked back, his face to the sky. His feet dangled as if searching for a step to support his weight; a loafer slipped off his left foot and landed on the sidewalk near the shattered clay pot, its red flower like a drop of blood. She grabbed her cell phone from her purse and dialed 911.

"What is your emergency?"

"A man is hanging from a balcony on Dearborn Street," she rushed. She checked. The man was still there. How long could he last? Was there someone inside to help? Who knew he was there?

"Thank you for calling," the emergency voice said, almost bored. "We have that. Help is on the way."

In the distance she heard sirens. Turn those damn things off, she thought. Don't frighten him. As if dangling from the seventeenth floor wasn't frightening enough without that shrill keening.

The Dalai Lama was concluding his remarks about tragedies like Haiti and the tsunami in Asia. "If there is a way to overcome that, then no need to worry. If there is no way to overcome the tragedy, that suffering, then no use to worry." He giggled.

Below, a crowd was gathering, and a news truck parked at the corner. The station wouldn't broadcast his jump, would it? Or the splatter after? Who would want to see such a thing?

"The response from the rest of the world is immense," the Dalai Lama said, praising the world for its generosity to the victims of the tsunami and of the earthquakes in Haiti and Chile.

She would be late for work unless she left right away. It felt voyeuristic to stay, but also heartless to leave. She didn't know what to do. "We are getting better as a people," the Dalai Lama concluded. She saw the problem in front of her and saw that there was nothing she could do. Again, she reached for her phone, and then, her knees tingling, she pointed it out her window and snapped a picture.

❖ ❖ ❖

J. M. Lennon. *Passo Doble*. (Dancers: Kristin Glickman and Joe Adorna; Choreography: Debra Loran). 2004. Photograph. 6 x 9 inches. © 2004 by Lennon Media, Inc. All rights reserved.

Squeeze

It starts like this. Your first time dancing you're clumsy, self-conscious. All corners and no center. You try to think your way through it, like a game of chess. But it's a feeling game.

Close your eyes.

The song they're playing is in your hips, not your head. Feel the places where you're solid. There, in your pelvis. There, where your partner's one hand cups your shoulder blade and the other cradles your fingers, the rest of you disappearing into sound. Like flying.

Later you'll discover there are rules. Falling is frowned upon.

The suffocation begins.

❖ ❖ ❖

There's an order to ballroom dance competition. Arrive at the hotel. Check in. Hang your competition clothes in the closet. Put on your practice clothes—the cool, sexy ones you paid too much for and ordered from Italy but still look casual, like you threw on whatever you could find.

Locate the ballroom and practice. Look for any slick places on the floor, any crack that might catch a heel. Get comfortable with the size of the room. Re-think your choreography so you'll execute your best moves in the direction of the judges. You can test the floor any time, but it's best the night before, when the ballroom is less crowded. By morning the air is charged. Dancers on edge, more desperate as the hours before competition dissolve into minutes.

My partner Peter and I were familiar with the formula. On February 22 we checked into our hotel in Louisville, hung our competition clothes in the closet, and began our final preparations for the Latin division of the 2003 Regional Ballroom Championships. If we did well we would qualify for Nationals.

Rule Number One: Be like everyone else, only better.

Ballroom dancers have a look—tanned skin in any season, acrylic nails, hair some version of bleached or black, red or striped. Anything to stand out among competitors. There are the rock stars—young couples who move in the top echelon of professional ballroom finalists; a second tier of professional hopefuls; amateurs, some as good as the professionals; and the partnerless—some young, most not—who compete with their instructors in the Pro-Am Division. Some of the older women are elegant in spite of age, but too many try to imitate the skin-baring look of the young, packing their exposed parts into a jiggle-resistant, flesh-toned fabric called Illusion. They may work out as hard as I do—but still they jiggle. If not for Peter and a few years, I could be one of them.

At the other end of the spectrum are the children. Some pudgy and undisciplined. Others, with more ambitious parents, fierce. At age ten they've surpassed many of us in technique and rehearsal hours. And they've mastered the look—exaggerated hips, studied winks for the judges, orange tans painted on where they should be brown from playing in the sun.

The obsession of the ballroom begins long before competition. Find a Partner. Hire the Best coaches. Work out five times a week. Practice every day. Get a job that will finance the habit. Not one that matters, as long as it will cover the cost of coaches and entrance fees. It's a fantastic, all consuming addiction digested in small bites. Delicious until the day it becomes tedious. Enormous until it closes in on you. Get a haircut that will look sleek on the floor. Design a costume more wing than dress—so it will fly across the floor. Learn the culture—where to buy twenty-five millimeter Aurora Borealis rhinestones in bulk, which shoes the champions are wearing this year, how to dye them with the right mix of tea bags, coffee and chocolate. How to use eraser tips from number two pencils to secure earrings so they won't fly off during a spin. How to choose between tanning beds and creams so even a glow-in-the-dark German complexion will appear vaguely Latin. It is important to APPEAR LATIN.

Appearance matters.

Once, while daydreaming about a competition gown I was making in red velvet, a police officer pulled me over for running two stoplights. "Were there lights?" I asked.

The dress was everything. The more stones it held, the more brilliant I felt. The lighter its fabric, the higher I could fly.

The dress I brought to Louisville was new—thin Lycra the color of the Caribbean, set with heavy bands of white, twenty-five millimeter rhinestones across its one shoulder, neckline, and hem. On the hanger it held its shape without me—triple-padded bra cups pushing outward, darted fabric folding in at the waist, loosening at the hip—as if a body were already stuffed inside, more voluptuous than my own, yet oddly angular and stiff.

I was afraid to try it on. The dress had been sewn to my skin to fit perfectly at my 132-pound competitive weight. I had eaten myself to 137, the first time I hadn't been able to control my weight before a competition. Peter and our coaches worried the judges would notice.

Thin is good. Flesh is unthinkable.

Yet I was hungry. We had been working on the same ten minutes of choreography for almost a year—a perfect two minutes each of five dances: Rumba, Cha Cha, Samba, Paso Doble, and Jive. Our performances had to be flawless—every movement rehearsed, coordinated, tweaked, refined—connections seamless, passion timed to appear spontaneous.

For the ballroom I made myself neat. Compact. Like a jaguar, a Latin thing. Electric rollers and hair spray—not the regular kind but the hard stuff, like cement in a can. Eyelashes edged in tiny rhinestones. Press-on acrylic nails. Black lip liner. Body glitter. Fishnet stockings Danskin called Suntan but someone who knew better might call orange, like my skin.

I soaked in hot baths to prepare my muscles, meditated to get my mind right. I pictured the flutter of blue fabric, the curve of an arm, an elegant wrist gesturing toward First Place. I talked to myself, read out loud from Post-its taped to my bathroom mirror. "You are beautiful. You are worthy."

Outside my room hotel corridors buzzed with Everything Ballroom. Dancers whirling into character. Vendors hawking costumes, practice skirts, ballroom CDs and videos. Rhinestone studded lashes, jewelry, sunglasses, barrettes, belts, gloves. Danceshoes—Champion, Capezio, Supadance, Freed's of London. Even street wear for the chic ballroom dancer. A blue denim fitted jacket with a fluff of blue feathers around the neck caught my eye. I was certain it would be just the thing to wear to the grocery store.

Without the stuff, how would you know who you were?

The announcers introduced us as Pantelis Liatos and Rebecca Huntman. They never pronounced Peter's Greek name correctly, but Pantelis, who was Peter the rest of the time, insisted on entering the ballroom with his more exotic title. We strutted onto the dance floor, inside hands clasped and held straight in front of us, outside arms opened forty-five degrees to our sides so that together we formed the shape of a V, like Victory. We claimed it before the music began.

There would be five dances, each ninety seconds long, giving us exactly seven and a half minutes to show off our months of practice. Of those minutes, the judges would watch us for a total of fifteen or twenty seconds, depending on how many other couples competed for their attention. They would identify us by a number pinned to Peter's back. Our first dance was the Rumba.

Peter and I spun to our places on the floor, bowed before each side of the ballroom, and waited for the music to begin. On the second bar I lifted my left arm, fingers trailing the length of my torso. Each gesture unfolding exactly as we had rehearsed.

We didn't make a single mistake, and yet everything was wrong. My lashes were too heavy. My fishnets too tight. I was an eighth of an inch off center, and there was nothing I could do to bring myself back. Somewhere between the Cha Cha and the Paso Doble I realized I was no longer on the floor. The dress was still dancing. I had floated to the ceiling.

Below me a swirl of couples followed each other counter-clockwise around the floor. Red dresses. Orange. Yellow. White. Black. The blue one with the twenty-five millimeter white crystals across the shoulder. Five dances, each precisely ninety seconds in length. Judges wrote down numbers on score pads.

The blue dress curtsied and left the floor.

❖ ❖ ❖

The Dining Room Table

In 1936 my father almost went to medical school. Ten years later my mother almost became an opera singer. Together, in 1952, they almost bought a section of an unknown beach called Puerto Vallarta. In 1961 Dad put an end to almost. He sold the family funeral home and furniture store to buy land. And on the first day of his new life Grandma Antonia, who couldn't understand why the son she'd raised to be a gentleman would want to shame her by getting his hands dirty, drove to the side of the field where he was working and shot herself in the head with a revolver.

Antonia was a handsome woman who threw fantastic parties and cooked the world's most wicked German ravioli. It was weightier than its Italian inspiration, made with giant doughy ravioli squares she rolled by hand, stuffed with ground veal and spices, and topped with chicken stock, fresh parsley, and Parmesan cheese. A meal I helped my mother make for Dad's birthdays or special company. A meal we served on pink and white Lenox china against the olive green sixties-chic backdrop of our dining room.

We never spoke about Grandma. Our family's habit of avoiding the disagreeable wove itself into the almost-southern St. Louis atmosphere. It clung to magnolia branches, drifted with the aroma of honeysuckle, climbed rose bushes that grew outside our dining room windows. Sex, religion, and family insanity were not invited to the table. Neither was any practical discussion about my future. "You could be president of the United States," my father said before he sent me off to practice the piano, a skill certain to make me more marriageable. Happy. Ever After.

I hated the piano except at Christmas, when my sisters and brother came home from college and for a week filled out our home, gathering around the Steinway to sing carols, hovering over fried eggs and pecan rolls at breakfast, and dinners so large they had to be served in the dining room. When my siblings left, the dining room, living room, and extra bedrooms fell silent, vestigial remnants my parents and I claimed but didn't use.

The first hours of the day my mother stole for herself, needle-pointing pillows and footstool covers from her stuffed yellow chair. When I woke, her time became mine. She cooked me breakfast—eggs and bacon, buttered English muffins, oranges she pulled into sections and arranged on my plate like flowers. After school she made peanut butter sandwiches cut on the diagonal the way I liked them.

That was Real Mom. Real Mom helped me with my homework, took me with her to the hairdresser, sewed my clothes. Real Mom snorted a little when she laughed. She held the steering wheel close when she drove, mouth turned up nervously at the corners. She wore an apron, cooked three meals a day.

Hostess Mom was different. Hostess Mom hired people to help her cook, worried about which crystal she should use, got mad if I spilled anything on her embroidered tablecloths. Hostess Mom expected me to make an appearance at the dining table among her Hostess Mom friends, who were not the same as her Bridge friends or Girlfriend friends. These were Important People—St. Louis musicians and business owners. They packed our home with the weight of their self-measure.

My mother kept the dining room dressed and ready—linens crisp, silver polished—its formality interrupted only by quarterly tax preparation and the occasional sewing project or birthday dinner. She didn't believe in store bought cakes —they bothered her as much as the neighbors' friends who honked from their cars instead of ringing the doorbell, and vacationed in Orlando instead of Paris; my mother made German Chocolate cake for Dad and Vicki, Angel Food with chocolate frosting for Susan and me, and pecan pie for Jon, squiggling our names across the tops in neon icing and saving the pans for us to spoon clean.

The day she died I devoured a twelve pack of Ding Dongs. First edges, then middles, creamy centers last. Each individually-wrapped cake a meditation in tin foil and hydrogenated fat. A flirtation of my own with Colon Cancer.

We were eating popovers at Neiman Marcus's Tea Room when the two words first hit the air. They hung in the vapor between us, a dark, intractable pair. They followed us to the parking lot. Sat between us at the movies. Cooked with us in the kitchen, the family stepping around them, my mother's cancer added to the list of prohibited topics of table conversation. The first words to break the ban were in the past tense, first spoken from the altar and then the receiving line, the words of distinguished friends telling me how gracious and accomplished my mother had been. Real Mom was dead.

At my father's funeral we ate finger sandwiches and deviled eggs from paper plates we balanced on our laps, then gathered around the dining room table to pick over the remains of our parents' lives. My brother wanted my father's gun collection. My sisters chose my mother's diamond rings. I took the dining room table.

A young woman believes she should have certain things—a husband, a family, a house in the suburbs, the formal dining set—proof her adult self has caught up with its adolescent dreams. But the dining table's sensible Chippendale lines clashed with the Caribbean art and bright walls of my home. It was several years before I had the courage to paint over its

polished maple finish with black gloss and a burst of emerald-leafed poppies.

I never became the pianist, wife, or president my parents dreamed. I'm a dancer, an artist, a single mom. I've started a dance company, raised a son, traveled to Cuba. Other things, like winning a national dance title or meeting Oprah, I've only almost done.

The dining room table, pretty but hardly practical, Alex and I use for company or creative projects that require a large surface. For meals we prefer the intimacy of the kitchen, where we make our own rules about manners and dinner conversation, and whether hot dogs and pizza constitute a meal.

I'm not as patient as my mother. My time is not always my son's. But I try. I pull oranges into sections and arrange them into flowers on his plate, cut peanut butter sandwiches on a diagonal, toast his bagel with lightly melted cheese on top the way he likes. I don't believe in store-bought cakes, but sometimes I buy them.

I keep the recipe for Alex's great grandmother Antonia's ravioli on the top shelf of the kitchen cupboard between my mother's *Joy of Cooking* and my *Mexico Illustrated* cookbooks. Worn and stained, traces of flour and salt fading along with my grandmother's handwriting, the card gives no measurements, only ingredients to guide a bloodline of well-rehearsed cooks. Ground veal, flour, eggs, parsley, sage. I tell myself I should make the dish for Alex. The tradition may end with us if I don't. But the recipe is for six and takes an entire day to prepare. It's dining room food. We're kitchen people.

❖ ❖ ❖

J. Allyn Rosser

Sidewalk Café Closed Monday

It takes courage to loiter here alone
at one of three tables, three chairs each,
as on the high banks of a dried-up river
without something poised: cup, book,
cigarette. To idle with nothing but thought
on one's mind, to lean upon
the taut line of one's own spine.
Takes a certain obstinacy to throw off
all pretense of purpose like the pilled
pink cardigan of a solicitous aunt.
People will wonder if you're homeless,
hopeless.
             To watch as from far, far away
the steaming mops rinse the hotel steps
opposite, hotels being steps to more hotels
where other taxis than these
get the faceless passenger there,
no there, stoplights blinking
with incredulity as huge trucks
pause delicately to sniff the curb.
To loiter within sight of the park's
deserted carousel, mares impaled
on their own mane-flung gaiety
like divorced patrons of Happy Hour
waiting to be jerked back into action.
To watch men walk by fast in search
of something that will allow them
to search in greater comfort
for the rest of their years.
To sit perfectly still like an infinitive
without subject or predicate,
to let the vagaries of tossed-up
thought on thought on thought
spin like saucers on sticks
no one sees, none falling but none
exactly mattering, spinning above
and beyond the axis we live by,
so — how to put this — unthinkingly,
without extenuation or resolve.

J. Allyn Rosser

Heart's Desire

There it is, by heaven. *Look.*
No sacred star or rainbow
leads you to it. No path of crystal trees
or wise guide crouched in urchin guise.
No writing in any tongue on any wall.

At last here's proof it exists,
however unrecordably.
None of anyone's dreams did it justice.
The bonfires of expectancy
all these years had cast a chill,
and now you are warm, warmer.

But be content to look your fill.
Stand back! A closer gaze could cause alarm,
or pierce, or char, or petrify;
your sigh could be its chloroform,
your touch a corruption.

Memorize the contours of its shadow,
the notes of silence it won't break.
Hold still; try not to swoon
at the scent it slyly withholds
like night-blooming cereus
at noon.

Ernst Stadler (*Translated from the German by William Wright and Martin Sheehan*)

Dusk in the City

Nightfall flatters with saccharine words—alleys
in slumber and the sweetness of old lullabies:
Dusk has swathed itself in ample plumage—
an immense bird flown to the blue roof's peak.

Dark has ripped all sheen from the windows
that stood, still wet, like violet mirrors.
Houses sit in grayness through which first lights break—
like corpses of huge ships, hoisting night-signals at sea.

Towers dive, weightless, delicate, into the late sky
as they watch the shores, asleep in the lap of chill shadows.
Soundless, night now swims on the gazing galleys,
black-sailed, into the light-plowed harbor.

Jesse Wallis

Setting the Track Record

It's no mean feat to do the story justice when
The story is always changing, as is the reporter,
And the words that make up the story. No small
Feat either to set the record straight after the fact.

You know this if you've ever owned a clock, or
Not known where you were when you woke up.
The clock can only tell the time by the minute.
And for a minute, you could have been anywhere. . . .

In his dream, the veteran jockey bolts out of bed to
Look hard at himself in a ridiculously tall mirror.
He feels out of place in his goggles and blowsy silks.
Shocked. Indignant. He can't remember ever being

So small. . . . Inside the musty stable, it's not his dark
Horse being bridled now, but a horse of a frighteningly
Indistinct color. Blindingly bright. Beside it, he seems
Smaller still—he's late to weigh in—and that suddenly

They're headlong into the dust down the fleet, unfamiliar
Track, his nameless mount guiding them from straightaway
To turn. Its every flexed muscle mirrored in his movement.
As if, for a pale weightless moment, he wasn't there at all.

W. Scott Olsen. *Aerial View.* Digital photograph.

Tag

I remember the running.
Usually twilight, or later.
You're it.
Now run.
Chase.
Reach.
Feel that touch.
Run.
Turn.
Bank.
Dodge.
You're it.
Now run.
Just run.
Reach and run some more.
Nothing to win or lose.
Just the speed of the chase.
The adrenaline joy of running hard and turning sharp.
Your hand on someone's arm or back or shoulder or head changes everything.
Tag.
You're it.
Now run.

❖ ❖ ❖

Game on, I think. We are cleared for takeoff, and as I move the throttle forward I can feel the familiar, wonderful press of a seat against my back. We are rolling, pointed west, heading down Runway Two-Seven. The airspeed indicator moves past sixty knots, I pull back on the wheel, and somewhere in my body I can feel that moment when the airplane lifts easily into a warm and clear July morning on the northern prairie. Run, I think. Reach. We are off to Rugby, North Dakota, to tag the geographical center of North America. Just to touch it, to press a hand to the stone, to say we are here. Even though it's not really there.

The airplane is a Cessna 172. Tail-number: N6065M. Six-Five Mike. In the seat next to me, Tim Megorden, the pastor at the college where

I teach, looks out the window as the ground recedes and the horizon leaps toward the huge. He loves to fly and has been asking for a ride. Who better to take to the middle of something?

"Oh, what a beautiful morning," I sing, enthusiastically, fully off-key, not opening the microphone, but loud enough for the intercom to work.

"Did you sing for the choir?" he asks.

"Yeah, can't you tell?"

Below us, the landscape north and west of Fargo, North Dakota, quickly becomes cropland. Small grains and sugar beets. Sunflowers and canola. Section roads divide the farms into neat squares. Shelterbelts run just as straight, protection from the wind here that humbles mountaineers. Field and forest and riverbank. Every field is green, though there are a hundred variations. Yellow green. Emerald green. Neon green. First car green. Bad sweater green. Chocolate green.

"This is smooth," Tim says.

I know he's talking about the air. We are early enough in this day the thermals have yet to get going, and even though there's a wind it's coming straight at us, slowing us down a bit, it passes easily over the wings. But I agree for the other reason. We are two thousand feet above the ground, motoring through the morning, able to see a larger version of this day no one on the ground will know. Yes, I think, this is smooth.

I hand Tim a small camera.

"What do you want me to take pictures of?" he asks.

"Any kind of panorama," I say. "Anything at all."

❖ ❖ ❖

Run.
Chase.
Reach.
Three is good. Seven is better. You need a crowd for a good game of tag. You need to have that wonder—who is he really chasing? You run

and the whole world weaves away. You are the center of everything, and everyone reacts to you. You make a choice and give it your best shot, but even then another choice comes into range. You change course, surprise everyone. Your hand hits an elbow or thigh. Tag. The center shifts. Star becomes satellite. You're it. Now run.

Like all the good trips, this one began with a simple wondering. I was reading about a very young sailor, alone in the southeastern Pacific Ocean, passing what is called Point Nemo. Just a bit of math, really. Point Nemo is the spot farthest from any land, sitting in unbroken water between New Zealand and South America, a bit more than 1,600 miles in any direction from any soil. The very middle of nowhere, I thought. Unless you're an oceanographer, which would make it the very middle of everywhere. Tough to get there, I thought.

Then I was hooked. North Pole, South Pole, Equator, Everest, Marianas Trench—those are easy. Those are the edges. But where are the middles? By definition, a middle is the average farthest away from more than one edge. The middle of the earth's population is somewhere in India. Zero latitude meets zero longitude under the water of the Atlantic off the coast of Africa. The encyclopedia lists the Poles of Inaccessibility—those places that are farthest from other places. Point Nocean, in the Xinjiang region of China, is the farthest from any ocean. The island farthest away from other land is Bouvet Island in the South Atlantic.

Yet there are problems. None of this is real in the way that a peak or a valley is real. The measurements depend upon assumptions. If I am looking for the center of my house, do I count the garage? If I am looking for the center of the earth, do I go by average sea level or do I include Everest? There is no center to the universe. What we learned in school is true. The speed and position of any object depends on the speed and position of the observer, unless we're talking about the speed of light, which is constant.

To declare a middle says almost nothing about the place itself and quite a lot about the act of declaration. Tag, I thought. You're it.

❖ ❖ ❖

"What towns will we be flying over?" Tim asks.

I point to the moving map on the instrument panel, the little picture of an airplane and a line from us straight to Rugby. Town names appear on the left and right. Arthur. Page. Colegate. Galesburg. Hope. Cooperstown. Jessie. Binford. I tell him I have a paper chart, too, if he wants to follow along. But the names are enough and his eyes return to the prairie under the wings.

A large radio tower goes by on the right.

"Can you imagine building that?" I ask. "It's as high as we are now."

Fields of small grains quilt their way to every compass point. Small drainages appear in the fields, wind their way toward lower ground. Canola appears, the bright yellow crop a sharp and pretty contrast to the many shades of deep green. A windfarm appears in the distance. A semi-truck heads down a gravel road, the white plume of dust rising behind him and lingering in the air.

It's the type of day where every sight is an invitation to wondering. See that town? Who lives there? See that road? I wonder what it's like to be there. Where does this one begin? Who drives it so often the grooves are more remembered than seen, and who drives it for a first time? Look at that small lake. I wonder if there are any fish.

We cross small streams and look for the Sheyenne River and Lake Ashtabula in the distance off the left side. Tim takes pictures of the meandering courses, the thick trees on each riverbank. Water, we tell each other, is a deep-rooted fascination. Ancient and genetic. On the prairie, it's the break from the straight line section roads and crop rows. Thomas Jefferson, I say, set up the surveying that created the grids we see, but water's sense of history has nothing to do with measurement.

We are flying at three thousand feet above sea level, about eighteen-hundred feet above the ground here, at 9 on a clear Friday morning. Below us, just farmsteads and waterways, roads and windbreaks and marks on the land. Evidence of agriculture, economics, culture, settlement, transportation, politics, history, geology, hydrology, limnology, meteorology, psychology, and art. Tag, I think. Pick a target. Reach. It all could not be prettier.

I change radio frequency to hear the small airport traffic.

"The difference in color would indicate it's not as flat down there as it appears from the ground," Tim says.

"Wind is picking up," I say. "We may be in for a couple bumps."

"This is so cool, so cool," he says.

❖ ❖ ❖

The Center of North America is too good to pass, even if it's not really true. Rugby claims the title and has a monument, a stone cairn with a sign on each side that reads: "Geographical Center of North America. Rugby, N.D." People stop and have their pictures taken here. Across the parking lot, at the Cornerstone Café, people buy cups of coffee, milkshakes, and hamburgers, and marvel at the wonder of being in the very exact precise middle of North America. It doesn't matter that this version of the middle does not include Mexico, much less the rest of southern North America. It doesn't matter that the real center, even just considering the U.S. and Canada, is actually sixteen miles away, six miles west of Balta, N.D., population 73, in the middle of a large pond. There is a marker here, something people can touch and feel and see.

Tag, I think.

I send an email to two friends, extraordinary cartographers, to ask, if there is an official list of center-places, given all the problems with definitions.

Jon Kimerling writes:

Scott,
The starting point for surveying the North American Datum of 1927 is a monument at Meades Ranch, Kansas in the center of the continent. The center of population for the United States has been computed for each census and the westward and southward shift over time is shown on maps.
Jon.

Now this, I think, is a place to go see. I have to look it up, but the North American Datum of 1927 was nothing less than the exact measurement of a continent. It set the coordinates for everything. It was elegant math and dirty boots. And something called a Triangulation Station at Meades Ranch was zero zero, the beginning place for everything measured. Another monument. Another thing to touch and claim. (A quick look on line, however, tells me there is no café and thus no coffee, milkshakes or hamburgers.) But wait, I thought. Kansas is the middle of the continent? Who says?

Mark Monmonier's email comes next:

Hi Scott,
I haven't thought much of the significance of places recognized as geographic centers or extrema. It's probably human nature to try to capitalize on any point of notoriety. I'm curious in particular about the mathematical stability of some of these places, including issues of how distance is calculated (on the sphere or on an ellipsoid, and if so, which one) and how the reference space is defined (especially if there are outliers that might spin the outcome). What's included in a continent, for instance? For the US, what do we do about Alaska and Hawaii. And then there's the issue of center of population vis-à-vis center of land area. And what if we throw in maritime territory— the territorial sea, the contiguous area, the Exclusive Economic Zone. Doesn't the wide range of centers undermine the significance of center? I'd think so.
All best,
Mark

Exactly, I think. But damn, what fun is that? Grain elevators and farmsteads and power lines go by below us. The windfarm north of Valley City grows closer, nearly every blade turning. On the radio, someone says "Man it's just gorgeous out here today." We are coming up on a town called Hope.

I don't care if Rugby is the real center or not. You can't win the game of Tag. All you can do is play, run as hard and fast as you can, reach with the full length of your arm.

❖ ❖ ❖

A small church appears on Tim's side. A tall steeple, a white clapboard structure, it's small and completely alone. We count section roads away from the church and run out of line of sight before we come to any town. At least ten miles in every direction.

"I would love to land there," I say. "I would love to just plunk down on that gravel road and pull up to the church, in an airplane, and get out to see who is there."

"There probably isn't any one there," Tim says.

"I know. Part of a circuit. On Sunday morning, some pastor who has three different churches to get to. He or she could live anywhere inside fifty miles of here."

"My father," Tim says, "had seven churches."

It takes me a minute to do the math.

"How in the world did he do seven churches? First one at dawn, last one at midnight?"

"He left before the service was over."

"What?"

"That was back in the day when communion was less common. Maybe once a month. After the sermon he would go out the back and get on the road to the next one. The congregation would finish up the service."

"God love the Deacons," I say.

"Amen."

I have a vision of a flying pastor service, something like the Royal Flying Doctor Service in Australia. Small airplanes at idle outside small churches, pastors in robes ducking out from behind the sanctuaries and rushing to the co-pilot's seat. The choir and congregation's hymn joined by the thrumming of a prop-biting air and the sight of wings lifting skyward. The next church listening for a sound in the heavens, seeing the wings appear, the glint of lowered flaps in the sunshine, the appearance of a body in flowing robes. It could work. It could work really well, I think. Unless the weather was bad. Or the winds too strong.

Tim and I talk about flying. Many years ago he took lessons. Troubled eyesight keeps him from the pilot's seat now. But I cannot get the image of that church out of my head, or the image of a very small plane coming to earth in front of it. There are airplanes that can do that. Late at night, browsing airplane ads and dreaming, I have imagined flying the airplanes that specialize in short takeoff and landing. Here in Six-Five Mike, at slow cruise, we are flying faster than the top speed of most of those. It would take forever to get anywhere, but speed would not be the issue. I have imagined landing in the middle of the college campus. I have imagined landing it on the college football field, in the church parking lot next to my home, on the bike path where I walk my dog, on a thousand dirt roads I know in Minnesota, North Dakota, Kansas, Missouri, Texas. And I have imagined landing it in a thousand places I still want to visit. In Wyoming and Colorado and New Mexico. With floats attached I want to land on James Bay, Hudson Bay, Prudhoe Bay, Bay of Fundy, Lake Superior, Lake of the Ozarks, Upper Red Lake, Tablerock Lake, Lake Baikal.

To imagine an airplane is to imagine the way it lifts you into the sky and the way it places you back again. The full curved flap of an angel's wings.

❖ ❖ ❖

Devil's Lake is a problem.

We are not there yet, but the earth below us is swelling with water. Ditches and coolies. Streams. The Maple River. The Sheyenne River. Lake Coe. Johnson Lake. Stump Lake. A thousand potholes filled with rainwater and snowmelt. It all drains to the Maple or the Sheyenne. The Maple and Sheyenne drain to the Red River. The Red River flows north, into Canada, into Lake Winnipeg, eventually into Hudson Bay.

But not Devil's Lake. Devil's Lake is a terminal lake. There is no outlet, no drain, nowhere for the lake water to go. Evaporation takes a bit, but the water continues to rise. It is higher now than at any time in record keeping. In 1940 the lake level was fourteen hundred feet above sea level. This morning as Six-Five Mike heads toward it, the level is fifty feet higher. And it can rise very fast. Fish finders on boats see hay bales still in fields now under water. Corn crops planted in spring seem to march into the sea at harvest. The lake has risen more than 30 feet since 1993 and the surface area has quadrupled. State geologists claim it's overflowed at least seven times, most recently about eighteen-hundred years ago. The USGS says our current cycle of wet weather will go on for at least another decade.

When it gets high enough, Devil's Lake will flow into Stump Lake. A little bit higher and both flow into the Sheyenne. It's possible to build an outlet, to drain some of the lake. But Canada does not want Devil's Lake water. Canada is against the water in Devil's Lake. The town of Minnewaukan used to be eight miles from the western lakeshore. Today the village is partly flooded and there is talk, serious talk, of moving the entire thing. The population has diminished from 318 to 260 people as the lake fills basements and yards.

Underneath the airplane now, however, fields appear with hay cut and swathed but not yet collected into bales, long straight lines of golden feed.

"There was a slough back there," Tim says, "that actually looked like it had ripples, like someone had dredged concentric circles."

Oak and elm and ash trees line the banks of the Sheyenne River. The river turns in lazy oxbows.

"That's what I love," I say. "You see one thing and it provokes a thousand questions. It implies so many stories, all of them possible, and god you want to know which one is true. How did those ripples get there? What did this place look like 500 years ago? How long does it take a river like this to meander, to cut just one loop?"

"Does your mind always go to land history?" he asks.

"It goes to story," I say. "Everything is connected. See those new powerlines down there? Remember the blizzards of 1997 when the old ones all froze and toppled over? What I see this morning is a new tower. Push that sight just a bit and you uncover a huge story of very bad weather. Those birds we passed a bit back? We're on the edge here of something called the Central Flyway, a huge migration corridor for birds. Siberia to Mexico. Sandhill cranes and swans and geese and everything else. Look down there. See that one farmstead sitting alone in that section? That home is there because of old homesteading laws. When you got the free or cheap land, the rule was you had to live on it. It was a good idea to prevent hording and speculation. But it also went against what most of the immigrants were used to. In Europe, you lived in town and went out each morning to your fields. When you came here, you basically had to live in the fields. The whole notion of town and place-identity changed."

I should shut up, I think. But there is a pickup truck driving on a remote county road below us.

"See that guy?" I ask. "I would imagine he knows exactly where he is. And I would also imagine he's not thinking about how this place is part of a thousand stories. He probably has no idea the shape of that road began in Thomas Jefferson's brain. He is not thinking about how the land he sees is evidence of a prehistoric inland sea. He does not know that we can see him, and that this little Cessna's GPS can see satellites in outer space. All the stories are complicated and woven together. Why so much canola this year? Is the answer in some futures market in Chicago?"

"Sharon Parks," Tim says, "who has done a lot of writing in student affairs, has written about being on the dance floor but also needing to get up to the balcony. Both are needed. That's exactly the same idea. Both are needed. If you never dance you never get down on the floor. If you never get to the balcony you never see the real beauty."

"That's the blessing of altitude," I say.

"Look at this shelter belt down here," Tim

says. "It's really something."

"Take a picture."

"Ah, the thing shut off. Missed it. Missed it, sorry."

❖ ❖ ❖

Run.

Chase.

Reach.

Large homes ring a beautiful lake south of Stump Lake. There are baseball fields behind what looks like a school. Rock piles rise out the middle of some fields.

"The horizon is just forever today," I say.

"Oh man."

The instruments tell me we have a headwind of sixteen knots this morning at three thousand feet. I know the surface air is much calmer, but still there are ripples on the lake water.

"There is a blueness to this field!" Tim says.

"Look at that! I don't know what that is, but you're right. It's a kind of gunmetal gray blue."

The James River is off to the left, thin and twisting. What a rush it would be, I think, to settle this airplane just a little above the river water and bank and turn my way toward Jamestown. Devils Lake takes up the whole of the eye from in front off to the right. Two airplanes, both heading for the Devil's Lake airport and both about the same distance away, begin the dance of who gets to land first.

"The horizon gets really blue with all this water," Tim says.

Devils Lake looks absolutely calm and beautiful on a summer morning. One airplane lands, the other announces short final, the first says he has to back taxi, the second says he'll go around. Sorry about that, the first one says.

A thermal bumps us a little. We both smile.

Abandoned farmsteads sit in lonely and completely incongruous places. Tim and I point them out to each other. We both wonder what history put them there. What farmer or settler said "This is the place for the barn, this is the place for the house," and then a hundred years later it clearly is not.

"This land, this farmland," Tim asks, "would be fourth generation, would you guess? From the immigrants?"

I try to do the math, but fail. How many generation ago do we count? Just back to European settlement? What about the trappers before them? What about the Métis? The Hudson Bay company? I know a wave of New England Yankees came through before the Norwegians.

"At least," I say.

A handful of boats leave wake trails on the lake this morning. I count one, two, three, four five—maybe more.

"Got some grain bins in the water," Tim says.

"Really? How far off shore?"

"One hundred feet. Maybe more."

Section roads, nearly white with sun-bleached gravel, run into the lake and disappear into the water. We pass over a farmstead cut neatly in two by water. The house and a couple of sheds on dry land. Two large barns look like arks setting sail. We pass over Minnewauken. Water to the north and east.

❖ ❖ ❖

In the game of Tag, there is a moment you must decide. This person, you think. Billy or Craig or Suzy or Anne. You've made a choice and you reach, lunge, hope. Sometimes your hand finds their head or shoulder and you wheel hard away, laughing. Sometimes, however, you miss. Sometimes they turn in a way you did not anticipate and your hand finds nothing but empty air. You stumble. Sometimes it's just a misstep and you're fast back up to speed. Sometimes, however, the whole world is off balance and you go cartwheeling through the grass, down the hill, through the brambles and thickets.

It's time to think about landing.

Sixty-nine degrees outside the airplane. Altitude three thousand feet. Ground speed eighty-nine. Ninety-seven knots on the airspeed indicator.

Ten miles away I self-announce on the radio. Straight in for Runway 30.

"I think I see what might be the runway there," I say. "It ends in the canola field."

"Ah," Tim.

I call again at four miles out.

Tim points. "Is that it?"

"Yep, it ends in the canola field."

I pull the throttle back and set approach speeds. I call at three miles out. No one else in the pattern or on the ground in my way.

I pull the power all the way out, coasting in on a perfect glide path. Nearly silent.

Suddenly it occurs to me that this is all wrong. I have a fourteen-knot headwind and I'm about to lose it. When I do, there will be much less air moving over the wings. Less air means less lift. Less lift means I will sink, fast, right when I want to have lift the most. Without the headwind, my ground speed will also shoot up. I'll be too slow to fly and too fast to land at the very same time.

The headwind disappears just as my hand reaches to the throttle. A little power is all it takes. Increase airspeed just a bit. Our wheels hit the runway but damn we're fast. We roll, not entirely straight, toward the canola field. I pull the throttle out and gently press the brakes.

"Sorry about that," I say.

"Can't expect everything," Tim says.

The two windsocks by the runway are empty and hanging at right angles to each other.

"You didn't want that on video, did you?" Tim asks.

"Absolutely I wanted that on video," I say. "That was without a doubt the worst landing of my entire life."

"And I was the witness!" Tim laughs. "What's the old saying? On a wing and a prayer?"

"Just don't tell anyone," I say.

"Oh, there is pastoral confidentiality on this," he says.

"There is?"

"Yeah. There's stuff I just can't tell anyone!"

Tag, I think. You're it.

❖ ❖ ❖

There is no such thing as the Geographical Center of North America. Nonetheless, we park the airplane and go inside the small terminal building. The airport has a courtesy car for pilots and we drive through town to the Cornerstone Café. On the street side of the parking lot a large stone cairn marks the spot. I take a picture of Tim, smiling, his hand on the rock. He takes a picture of me, smiling, arms outstretched. Even if it's all a fantasy we are standing in a place people need to define.

The day is warm and the sunshine is bright. There is no wind at all. We walk to the café and place an order to go. An oatmeal raisin cookie for me. A cup of coffee for Tim. Both are really very good. Back at the airport I look at the pictures and it dawns on me: I never touched the thing. Stood next to it, yes. But my hand did not meet the thing itself.

Tag, I think.

Or not.

Just run, chase, reach.

Peter Meinke

The Teacher

for David Carr (1942-2009)

He'd enter more *Thin Man* than *Mr Chips*
with scotch in hand and Guna on his arm
poised for his second drink or seventh quip

a hint of edginess beneath the charm
ready for either banter or a hit
He was a medievalist and a Democrat

and well familiar with the fall of Camelot
whose towers touched undocumented heights
where courtesy was applauded like a sport

So in the latest telling of this story
David played the dashing Lancelot
whose shield was manners and whose sword was wit

and Guna was his Guinevere and glory
and they were luckier than all those knights
and damsels in King Arthur's shining court

Witching for Water, Etc.

Call us a hard, scrabbled people who trust
seared air more than grace. How could we

pretend otherwise in our fretted world of dust?
We live by axioms of the gut: we witch

year round, tender treaties with the sun, build
crooked houses that mimic crooked skies.

Who can explain a beauty so cleanly thin?
A blouse of lichen takes centuries to sew.

A magpie's hop measures the horizon's pull
better than surveyors. Wind jabbers amen.

When will the desert blossom like a rose?
The locust is our tormentor, the hummingbird

sipping nectar at dusk our longshot truth.
Patience is an argument water always wins.

Lance Larsen

To Sunlight Falling in an Old Growth Forest

Who needs a sky bright as forever when I can drown
in refracted green? Thank you, sunlight,
for waking me up to myself. Shadows speak
their gravest truths when you leak in
from above, as if a flock of angels had chewed
summer into lace. And wherever you fall,
a haunting: the good kind that lets me taste
my life without mourning it. I close my eyes.
Each tree a forest of one, each forest a prime
raised to the power of the wandering navies
in my blood. Teach me to total the world
without counting my fingers, to breathe
in *now* and zero the abacus. I lift a ripe
dandelion to my mouth and scatter the prophets.

Everglades Kite

What kyries does the kite
sing in its fall

and taking? The air parts
and lets it flow

with an edge on
purpose, a stoned

exhilaration
looking for the one

movement too slow,
one out of all

those possibilities
below,

the blown motion of trees,
beetle barrows,

cricket's crawl, scree
of snails and dry

rustle of grasshopper
wings, falling

like Moses
parting the waters,

and the tall
woods wait

the silence of
a heart's stilled beat.

Travis Mossotti

The Second Coming of Christ in the Form of a North American Alligator

Somewhere amidst the reclaimed wetlands
between Naples and Ft. Lauderdale,

a little gator tooths open his shell, crawls
out of a womb of mud and stillborn brothers

into his mother's mouth and is led directly
to water. Nearby a man in khaki shorts—

elastic sewn into the waistband, top shirt
buttons undone—remains oblivious

to everything but a rusted lug nut. Time
and again he pauses to wipe the sweat

from his neck with a kerchief, but fails
to feel the ground waxing holy beneath him,

fails to recognize this new Bethlehem
born in a bed of sweet flag and standing water,

this hatchling, sizing things up, tastes the residue
of the after and before world still in the air.

Malerie Marder. *Untitled.* 1998. Archival pigment print. 20 x 24 inches. Courtesy of the artist.

Like Flying

Carl and Janet sat on a bench across from Cosmic Ray's Starlight Café, waiting for Eric, who was in Tomorrowland with a girl he'd met while standing in line. Carl was pleased Eric was having fun, but knew Janet resented him being off with the girl instead of with them. Maybe worried was a better word. Still, Carl hoped they could take advantage of their time alone to talk.

Eric and the girl had been standing close to each other when a man with yellow boxer shorts sticking out the top of his jeans walked by humming "The Battle Hymn of the Republic." That's how it started, the two of them snickering. Later, she asked Eric if he was coming back over spring break, his baldness and six-foot-three frame fooling her into thinking he was older than he was. Carl had held his breath as he waited for Eric's answer, then for her reaction, but Eric only said, no, he wouldn't be back. She'd said her name, but Carl couldn't remember it. Loreena, Lauren, maybe Laura. She wore bright pink shorts with lettering across the seat, and Carl had caught himself staring, trying to make out the word.

The rides were off-limits for Eric, except those suitable for the very young and the very old, and he had been pleased to find someone close to his own age in line for Stitch's Great Escape. As they moved forward, he turned to his parents and suggested they meet later, say at Cosmic Ray's. Say around six.

But now he was ten minutes late and nowhere in sight. "He'll be here in a minute," Carl said.

Janet sat with her arms across her chest and stared at a Japanese couple with a young boy coming out of Auntie Gravity's Galactic Goodies. Carl was about to say that Eric had just lost track of time when she turned and said, "He's fifteen minutes late. I don't know why we agreed to this."

Carl wanted to say that Eric was sixteen, and, all things considered, he ought to be do-

ing what he wanted. Carl suspected Eric had come on the trip to Disney World not for himself, but for them, especially his mother, who had planned it. His one stipulation had been that there were to be no pictures. The camera had to be left at home.

Carl looked at his watch. He was hungry. "Want an ice cream cone?" he asked. He worried that Janet might give him that look, the one that accused him of not feeling the pain as deeply as she did.

"Something could be wrong," she said. "What if something happened? This was stupid."

By this, Carl assumed she meant leaving Eric. Disneyworld had been her idea. She wanted Eric to have experiences, but Carl thought they were wearing Eric out, making time pass too quickly. The three of them could have been at an IHOP downing a stack of blueberry pancakes or fishing with Eric's granddad. He glanced over at the Plaza Ice Cream Parlor. He sensed Janet resented that he could still get hungry when Eric was off with the girl, but she nodded. "Vanilla," she said.

Secretly, he was proud of Eric, the way he had chatted with the girl, teasing her about her oversized box of popcorn until she poured some into his hand. Carl had never been much of a talker. Words tumbled from his mouth like forks falling from the kitchen counter. Even a short conversation could cause a woman to stare over his shoulder, a squint wrinkling her forehead. And now he couldn't even talk with Janet. The first two times Eric had been through chemo and radiation, he and Janet had been like a team, always pulling in the same direction, but now she misinterpreted every word he said and a battle had developed over which one of them knew what was best for Eric.

When he returned with the cones, Mickey Mouse was standing in front of Janet, his hands on his cheeks. "Fuck off," she said.

Mickey threw his arms up in alarm and scurried away while Janet mumbled something about a fucking rat. "I wanted him to get away and have fun for a couple days," she said. "I didn't think he'd fall in love."

Carl thought falling in love would be better than sitting through Stitch's Great Escape, but he shrugged, handed her the cone. "It's her long legs," he said. He expected Janet to give him a disapproving look, but, if she heard him, she gave no sign.

❖ ❖ ❖

By the time Eric showed up, they'd finished their cones. He caught the looks, the way they studied his face, trying to spot any problems. "Sorry," he said. "We went for a walk." He nodded at his father, "You got sunburned."

During dinner Eric talked about the girl. Her name was Samantha. Sam, he called her. "She's staying at the Holiday Inn next to ours. I'm meeting her later by the pool. " He squinted at the Mickey Mouse clock on the wall.

"I thought her name was Laura," Carl said.

Janet looked at him as if he'd said something wrong.

Eric laughed.

❖ ❖ ❖

Twenty minutes after Eric left to meet the girl, Carl said he was going out to stretch his legs, that the room was too cold. He patted his pocket to make sure he had the room key and then waited at the door when Janet signaled that she was coming, too. "Let's walk by the pool," she said.

On the other side of the palmettos that separated the Holiday Inn parking lot from the Best Western, they saw Eric and the girl. She was wearing a black bikini, waving her long arms, then poking Eric in the chest.

Carl stopped, but Janet moved a few steps closer to the fence that enclosed the pool. "Let's not bother them," Carl said.

Janet ignored him for a second, then turned around. "There's no lifeguard for Christsakes."

Traffic hummed on Memorial Highway on the other side of the hotel. Carl took a step back. "Come on. They'll be okay."

Eric whispered in the girl's ear. She nodded, and they both jumped in, keeping their heads low when they surfaced, so they could barely

be seen. There was a splash as one of them kicked the water, and then her screams carried across the parking lot. Seconds later, the screams turned to laughter.

Janet stayed near the fence another minute before backing into the shadow of the camellia bushes.

Carl listened to the water lapping the edge of the pool and the girl's laughter. "I never talked with him about the birds and the bees," he said.

Janet gave a soft snort. "It's a bit late for that, don't you think?"

"I told him to keep his pants zipped. That's all. I said, 'Keep your pants zipped.'"

❖ ❖ ❖

Back in their room Janet rubbed the goosebumps on her arms and fiddled with the dials on the air conditioner. "You can see his ribs," she said.

"I know."

Carl couldn't see them from the window, but he stood there looking out. "How old you think she is?"

Janet slapped the air conditioner. "Does it matter?" She went to the bed and flipped through the channels on the television, eventually stopping at a weather station. A line of thunderstorms was moving in from the Gulf, a nasty blob of radar green and orange growing larger. By ten, she was pacing the room. "He should be back by now," she said. "They'll be closing the pool."

Carl didn't blame Janet for being angry, but he was afraid to give into it himself. He thought getting angry would poison the time they had. "He's with a girl," Carl said. "He's sixteen."

Janet pulled the corner of the curtain back and pressed her cheek against the window, trying to see the Holiday Inn pool. "Would you mind?" she said.

Carl nodded. "Back in a minute."

"And if you see him, just make sure he's okay. He doesn't have to come back yet."

Carl waved that he understood and slipped out the door.

❖ ❖ ❖

Large, white moths fluttered around the security lights as he stood in the shadows of the camellia bushes, close enough to the pool to

❖ ❖ ❖

hear the water gurgling down a drain. Eric and the girl were sitting next to each other, their feet dangling in the water. Carl figured there was no place else for them to go. As she talked, her hands waved, opened, and fluttered in front of her. From time to time she leaned against him and pressed her head into the crook of his neck.

He envied them for the way they whispered back and forth, and the casual way Eric draped his arm over her shoulder. He wanted to tell Eric that he and his mother were going to go out and wouldn't be back until midnight. He wanted to give them time alone, in private. He watched for another minute, then turned and walked back across the still warm pavement to the room.

He closed the door softly, said they were okay, that they were talking.

"You think he told her?"

"Don't know."

Janet sat on the bed looking as if she was trying to remember something. "He's never going to make love to a girl."

The statement surprised Carl, although he'd been thinking the same thing. "I don't think so," he said.

❖ ❖ ❖

After they flew home and he and Janet were in their own bed, he told her his idea. "I'm going to find a girl to sleep with Eric," he whispered.

Janet didn't answer, and Carl thought the idea had offended her, but he persisted. "It's not just the sex. It's . . . " he struggled to find the right word, decided there might not be any word for it, whatever it was.

He heard Janet breathing in the dark. "A college girl," she said. "No one cheap. She could come to the house while we're gone. Can you do that, can you find someone?"

Carl propped himself up on an elbow. He was surprised at how quickly the discussion had raced ahead of his own vague plans. "Maybe in Cleveland," he said. He was a small town cop unfamiliar with the big city. Finding someone young and attractive and willing to drive out to their place would be difficult, maybe impossible.

Janet was still thinking. "No one strung out on drugs. You have to be careful about that. No drugs. No diseases either. And Eric mustn't know. He can't know we arranged this."

Carl wasn't sure how they could do that. He wasn't sure if he could find the right girl. He tried to read Janet's face but couldn't see her in the dark. "I'll try," he said.

❖ ❖ ❖

Although he knew he was breaking several laws and there would be hell to pay if his plan was discovered, it felt good to be doing something. He first asked for help from a friend in the Cleveland police department, who gave him several names and places and didn't ask any questions, but Carl had no luck. The women were either too old, too cold, too made-up, or too skimpily dressed. On the second day he found a cabbie, who, for twenty bucks, gave him a name and pointed him in another direction. Two hours later he was sitting in the student union of Case Western Reserve University, talking with a girl who introduced herself as Lydia. Her brown eyes were clear and bright behind her dark framed glasses, and she had a wide mouth with pretty lips. She looked like a teenager in her jeans and pink flip-flops, and Carl worried that she might not even be eighteen. When he asked, she said she was in law school although Carl thought that was probably a lie, just like her name.

"This is for my son," he said, running a hand over his forehead, which was beginning to peel.

The girl cocked an eyebrow.

"I was hoping, we were hoping, my wife and I, that he wouldn't know this was. . . . " He glanced out the window behind the sofa. A groundskeeper was blowing leaves into piles next to the sidewalk.

"Arranged?"

"Yes, arranged."

She looked away and smiled at an old man, probably a professor, leaving the cafeteria.

"He's sixteen."

She began gathering herself to leave. "Sorry."

"Please," Carl said. He had planned on only saying that Eric wasn't well, but, once he started, he couldn't stop. Nearly ten minutes passed before Carl stopped, shrugged as if there was nothing more he could say.

She frowned, perhaps out of sympathy or perhaps trying to gauge whether or not his story was true.

Carl waited for a couple students to pass.

"He's not allowed to drive and he's not happy about that, but otherwise he's handling it okay, I think. He's been to Disneyworld, and my wife keeps renting movies for him to watch, mostly comedies. They're just distractions, I think." He looked away, momentarily embarrassed. "He's a teenage boy. You could . . . "

"How long?" she asked.

"A couple hours, longer if possible. It's not just sex. I want him to have . . . " He tried to find the word. "A connection. Yeah, a connection."

"No, how much time did the doctors say?"

Carl nodded rapidly to indicate he understood. The question had come up several times before with friends and family, but he was never sure how to answer. He was afraid that saying not long or before Christmas might cause it to happen sooner than later. He felt as if any answer was betraying Eric. He gave the girl his stock reply. "We don't know."

The girl stared at an abstract painting on the opposite wall. Blue triangles and a red ball. She had long fingers and unpainted nails. No rings. No watch. Carl had a horrible feeling she wasn't a student at all, that she worked for the vice squad, and as soon as he handed her the money the cops would come in and cuff him. "I'm a cop," he said. "Chesterland. This is a personal matter. I need your help."

If she was surprised he was a cop, she didn't show it. "Where would we meet?" She crossed her legs. A pink flip flop hung from her toes. Her feet were tan.

Her matter-of-fact manner caught Carl off-guard. He'd expected her to play him along, act reluctant so she could ask for more money. She sat facing him, her knees only inches from his. "Our home," he said. "I've got a map. It has my cell phone number on it. This Saturday? Would Saturday be okay? My wife and I'll be gone from ten until about five in the afternoon. I'll pay extra for you to drive to our place. It's a half-hour from here. Forty minutes at most. You can pretend you're lost."

"Lost?"

"Lost. Come to the door and ask for directions. Get him talking."

She studied the painting again, then nodded to someone in the cafeteria. Carl glanced around for plainclothes cops. She pushed her glasses higher on her nose, an act that Carl thought might be a signal. "Okay," she said.

"Five hundred. Cash. Drop it in the bag by my foot. Don't be obvious. She looked at the map he handed her. "Saturday."

"His name is Eric and—"

"I don't need any more information," she said.

❖ ❖ ❖

Janet thought he'd been tricked. "What makes you think she'll show up? How do you know you didn't hand money over to a girl we'll never see again?" She shook her head as if she couldn't believe he'd fallen for the arrangement.

"She'll be here," Carl said. "Lydia, her name is Lydia. She'll show." He was going to add that she was a law student and had pretty teeth, that of all the women he'd seen, she had the prettiest teeth. Instead, he asked, "Where's Eric?"

Janet looked out the window above the kitchen sink. "Listening to music in the garage with Darrel and Tubby." She grimaced. "I'm not sure about the hooker. This may be a bad idea. Saturday?" Janet and her best friend, who lived on the west side of Cleveland, were meeting, an outing that had been planned for weeks and was an attempt on her friend's part to give Janet a chance to "catch her breath."

Carl didn't like Janet calling the girl a hooker, and it bothered him how quickly she had changed her mind. He wanted to mention that their being gone was the plan. They couldn't very well sit downstairs while Eric and the girl were up in his bedroom.

"Everything will be fine," Carl said. "I can be home in five minutes if he needs me."

❖ ❖ ❖

Saturday morning, a few minutes after Janet pulled out of the drive, Eric woke up with a bad headache. Carl pulled the curtains, put a cold washcloth on his head and gave him a Darvocet, then went to the door and watched for the girl. But by ten Eric was up and other than feeling a little lightheaded said he was okay.

"You sure?" Carl asked. He looked pale and there were dark circles under his eyes.

Eric sat at the kitchen table with the morning paper. "Well, the headache's gone." He looked up from the sports page and sighed as if gathering himself for something important. "You know what the best thing was?" he asked.

Carl shook his head, thinking the question was in reference to Disneyworld.

Eric waited so long before answering that Carl thought something had happened, that maybe he'd had a seizure.

"Dunking a basketball." He flipped his wrist, mimicking the motion of a dunk. "It was like flying. I think the best things are like flying. That's my insight."

Carl fought the urge to tell him he'd be dunking basketballs again. Eric had made them promise two things: no phony hopes and no photographs. "You got up there," he said.

Shortly after ten Carl left for the station. He worried that Eric's two buddies, Tubby and Darnell, might stop over. He worried about Janet, how she'd gone cold on the idea of the girl coming to the house and had considered staying home. He worried that the girl wouldn't find the house or that she wouldn't come at all. Most of all, he worried about Eric. He felt guilty, angry, scared, alone, helpless and something else he couldn't identify. Time had been going crazy, speeding up and slowing down, stopping, then zooming forward so fast he felt as if he were on a merry-go-round that had spun completely out of control. He pushed the coffee cup to the corner of his desk. He sure as hell didn't need any more caffeine. He tapped the tip of a pencil on a yellow legal pad.

The clock on the wall ticked.

A little before two his cell phone rang. He grabbed it thinking it was Eric.

"I'm home," Janet said. "I got here just in time. The girl was getting out of her car. I sent her away."

"What?" Carl said.

"It would have been a mistake. Eric never needs to know." She waited. "Carl? You there?"

"I'm here," he said.

Three weeks later, Eric died.

❖ ❖ ❖

Throughout the fall and winter, Carl felt like he had the flu. He hurt all over, his knees, his elbows, his back, his neck. It took all the energy he had to go to work. Grief and guilt. It was impossible to tell where one left off and the other started.

By December, Carl and Janet were spending their nights staring at the television, unable to remember what they were watching, often going the entire evening without looking at one another. Once, after a particularly long quiet spell, Janet said, "It would have been wrong." Another time she said, "If you get terminal brain cancer and you want to fuck some girl, go ahead, but it would have been wrong for Eric."

Other arguments took place without either of them saying a word, Janet thinking that having sex with a girl he'd only known for a few minutes was morally wrong, that they wouldn't have wanted Eric to fuck a hooker had he been well, and Carl thinking that it was different for boys, that the girl should have come to the house earlier.

In bed, Janet's foot never bumped his ankle. He stopped laying his hand on her hip. It was as if any physical intimacy might remind them of Eric and the girl, what could have happened and what didn't.

Sometimes, when the phone rang, he thought it was Eric calling, asking for a ride home from basketball practice or saying he was going to stop by Tubby's. Sometimes, in the mornings after he showered, Carl stopped at the door to Eric's room to tell him it was time to get up. Sometimes, Janet pulled three plates out of the cupboard. They were unable to talk about Eric at the same time. It was as if one person's grief might overwhelm the other's. When Carl reminisced about the time Eric hooked a seagull while fishing, Janet stared at the wall, tight-lipped, like she was holding her breath beneath water. Carl walked out of the room in the middle of Janet repeating Eric's often told story about Mr. Houser, his math teacher, setting fire to the wastebasket.

They went to a counselor. Carl didn't think it would help, but Janet insisted they go, so he did.

During one of the sessions Janet brought up the incident with the girl and how she'd sent her away. "I did the right thing," she said.

The counselor looked at Carl, expecting him to respond. When he didn't, Janet answered for him. "He thinks it would have been more than a fuck. He thinks it could have been—what do you call it, Carl?"

Carl struggled to find the right word, shook his head that he couldn't remember. Sometimes it felt as if she were accusing him of wanting to sleep with the girl.

The counselor said these things take time, that it's natural to second-guess decisions made when caring for a dying child.

"Like flying," Carl blurted out, pleased he'd found the word.

The counselor and Janet exchanged a puzzled look.

But Janet had been right. He thought the girl could have given Eric more than a fuck, although it seemed to him that even a simple fuck would have been better than Disneyworld. He played Janet's version of the events that fall afternoon, the way she had come home just as the girl was arriving. Four hours. Eric had been home alone for four hours and for what? He and Eric could have gone for a walk or sat by the pond.

The following spring Janet began going out with her friends, meeting them for coffee and a bagel on Saturday morning. She planted red petunias along the side of the house and hung a hummingbird feeder near the back window. Occasionally, in the evenings before the mosquitoes came out, Carl shot baskets at the lopsided hoop on the garage, feeling in the brief time between the ball leaving his fingertips and clanging off the rim, that he was Eric.

❖ ❖ ❖

The day after Mother's Day, a day they did their best to ignore, he told Janet he had business in Cleveland and might be late. He arrived at the student union shortly after ten. The odds were against him, but he'd been sitting on the sofa only twenty minutes when he saw her walking out of the bookstore. She was wearing a pink T-shirt with "TORTS" in small, black letters across the breast, and her hair was cut short. She looked older than before, more academic. "Lydia?" he said.

She cocked her head briefly, frowned, then pushed her sunglasses up on her head.

Carl thought she might be going by another name. "Lydia?" he repeated.

She looked puzzled.

"My son. We talked last fall."

"Your son?" There was a flash of recognition. "I'm busy," she said, an edge to her voice, a warning that he should leave her alone. She turned her shoulders as if squeezing by someone in a crowded room although at that moment they were the only two in the lobby.

"He died," he said. "Eric. He died last October."

She pulled her notebook close to her chest and shook her head as if anticipating his next question. "I need to be going. I'm sorry about your son."

Carl felt like he was on a stage and had forgotten his lines. "My wife shouldn't have sent you away," he said. "It was a mistake."

"Please," she said. "Not here. It's over."

Carl dropped his voice to a whisper. "Why didn't you come earlier? He was alone. He was dying and we all left him alone."

Her cell phone played a tune he'd heard before but couldn't identify. She reached into her purse and turned it off without looking to see who was calling, then nodded at the two sofas near the steps. They went there and sat facing each other although not as close as during their first meeting. "She was angry," she said. "Your wife. I thought you said it was her idea, too."

"She changed her mind."

"I have a class. I don't understand what you want."

Carl pressed a fist against his mouth, shook his head. "I don't know."

A tall boy with a wimpy goatee walked by, glanced at the girl. A mower roared beneath the window.

Carl wanted to tell her about Eric, how he'd been able to mimic anyone's walk, that when he dunked a basketball it looked as if he was hanging in air, that he couldn't carry a tune, that he liked to tease. "He was only sixteen. Your coming to see him was the one thing I thought I could do for him." He shrugged. "I'm sorry. This was a bad idea." He shifted his weight forward, ready to stand.

"He acted much older," she said, letting the backpack slip off her shoulder and onto the floor with a thud.

"What?"

"He acted older than sixteen."

"You never saw him."

"I did. I was there."

A bubble of hope rose inside him and then broke. He'd heard his share of alibis and stories that ran contrary to the evidence. "My wife sent you home," he said.

The girl cocked one eyebrow.

"She sent you home," Carl repeated. "She sent you home before you ever got in the house."

The girl sat and waited.

Carl figured she was either a law student who had mastered the art of the dramatic pause or she was a liar thinking about how to start her story. Maybe she was both.

"I went back for my lipstick. It fell out of my purse. I was careless. That's when your wife stopped me."

Carl stared at her, waiting for her to look away or give him a tight grin, something the speeders and drunks always did. "You're making this up," he said.

She glanced out the window.

"You told him you were lost?"

"Lost? No."

"I told you to tell him you were lost, I said—"

"I had a better plan. You should include some truth when you're lying. Law school 101."

"What did you tell him?"

She pressed her lips together, raised her eyebrows, a clear signal that she wasn't telling or, Carl thought, perhaps there was nothing to tell.

"I wore a black skirt, white blouse. He had on"—she closed her eyes—"a pair of jeans. A white T-shirt, I think." She touched the spot over her heart with an open hand, a gesture liars seldom used.

Carl looked at her as Eric might have. Intelligent eyes, wide mouth, large white teeth. A girl comfortable in her body. Yes, she could have been convincing.

She bit her bottom lip as if debating whether or not to go on.

"Please," Carl said.

"There were birds outside the window."

"Birds?"

"Crows. They were squawking, I mean really squawking, and he thought it was funny. We couldn't stop laughing. A nervous thing I think."

Carl tried to remember if there had been crows around the house last fall. Maybe. They sometimes came swooping out of the cornfield behind the pond. "Crows," he said. He imagined a cool breeze coming through the bedroom window, the warm skin of the girl. But then he remembered the way liars always go on too long, adding details to their story after they should have stopped.

The girl rubbed a thin, white scar on her earlobe with her thumb and forefinger. "I was there," she said.

On the other side of the window, students walked to class, and pink blossoms fell from the cherry trees that lined the walk. In a moment he'd stand, give her a little nod, say thanks, walk to his car, and drive home in time for lunch. He rehearsed the movements in his head, so he could get them right and not make a fool of himself. She'd walk down the hall, out into the sunshine, and he'd never see her again. He'd never tell Janet that he'd talked with her. He'd say he'd given a lot of thought to her sending the girl away, and she'd done the right thing. He, too, could be convincing and a small lie could be such a comfort.

❖ ❖ ❖

Buffalo Rock

Ten miles south of Fayette, Alabama,
a rock shaped
like a Buffalo stands

somewhere in a thicket
off a dirt road.
My great-grandmother

described how it was carved
by lightning.
She remembered the ground

speaking. Before she died, I
packed a lunch,
and each weekend

for a month, I went
looking for it.
Buffalo Rock, she called it,

though, she must have been lying,
because I never found
the rock, but you and I know

the only thing that matters
is the rock,
the rock and the field

around it. We don't understand
myth: a world
inside a world inside a world

—a place so quiet, it fails
to be heard,
like you, like me.

❖ ❖ ❖

Robert Bense

December Morning from a Rural Time

He rose like the others in the four o'clock
blueback to slaughter hogs. A sky still
pricked by pinhole stars, as if to obscure
further the darkness he was in charge of.

Tall flames swathed streaming water
in cauldrons. Men moved around
in shadows. Dawn beginning to reveal
the day's guile.

Quick, close-range reports
of a neighbor's .22—squeals softening to
whistle, silence. A shame he felt like guilt.
Then thump of dead weight.

Carcasses dangling from tree limbs
over water for scalding. Plings of bell scrapers.
Bodies splayed, opened like diptychs.
At the edge dogs snapping for tossed offal.

Fat tissue peeled off like onion silk.
Two hundred pounds animal gutted
into tubs. A peritoneal stench like revenge.
Someone skimming boiled kidneys to eat.

Racks of sausage extruded from a black
cast iron press. Klumpenwurst to be eaten
quickly. Hams will take months to cure.
Snow will fall long before.

No longer squealing for their lives
the hogs have become known by their parts.
He, especially, had almost loved them
and knew them by their names.

Wayne Thiebaud. *Scoop*. 1984. Pen and ink on paper. 6 7/8 x 7 1/2 inches. Art ©
Wayne Thiebaud/Licensed by VAGA, New York, N.Y.

Rebecca McClanahan

The Soul of Brevity:
Thirteen Ways of Looking at the Brief Essay

(Served with Occasional Senryu Sorbet)

FIRST, A CAUTIONARY NOTE: Just because you can make something brief doesn't mean you should. Less isn't always more. Sometimes less is less. I admire long novels and biographies, long poems, book-length essays and massive nonfiction books. Nothing better than to lose myself in a vast read, preferably during a long soak in a large, deep tub. I recently resurfaced from a deep, nonfictional dream of a book, Isabel Wilkerson's *The Warmth of Other Suns: The Epic Story of America's Great Migration*, followed by a langorous reread of Susan Fromberg Schaeffer's overstuffed novel, *The Madness of a Seduced Woman*. I like overstuffed novels, overstuffed furniture, eighteenth-century epistolary tales. Big things have their charms: Russia, the Solar System, the twice-a-year Big Mac my internist allows, the hardback twenty-volume *Oxford English Dictionary* whose weight threatens the bookcase over my writing desk. Blue whales. Texas.

And I confess to a soft spot for long letters, long movies, long legs, long friendships, long marriages, and even—here I risk sounding like a personals ad cliché—long walks on the beach. I mourn the loss of our culture's collective attention span. I don't want to be tweeted, twittered, or texted. Write me a letter, the bigger the better. If I can make time, I'll write you back. It might be a long letter; sometimes I like to write big. I recently completed a thousand-page nonfiction saga that, in mercy for potential readers, I cut to three hundred and fifty pages. I prefer the bigger version, but I'm trying to be realistic. Plus, I'm haunted by the memory of a novel I wrote twenty-five years ago. A novel that, the more I think about it, probably should have been a haiku. Maybe even a senryu.

Sometimes less *is* more.

Which brings us to the subject of the brief essay, a varied and elastic subgenre of nonfiction sometimes referred to as the "short short" or simply "brief nonfiction," encompassing such forms as lyric essay, collage, mosaic, meditation, memoir, commentary, profile, rant, reverie, humorous sketch, journal, diary, letter, hypothesis, analysis, hybrid, language-propelled texts I call "exhalations," and any number of other forms. I admit that the term "brief essay" is insufficient for our purposes here, just as "nonfiction," a term that defines by what it is not, is insufficient to describe all the varied texts dwelling within the universe of what Gay Talese and Barbara Lounsberry name "the literature of fact."

My favorite term for the brief nonfiction text is what Lia Purpura employs in her craft essay "On Miniatures": "The miniature, a working, functioning complete world unto itself," she writes, "is not merely a 'small' or 'brief' thing or a 'shortened' form of something larger." I agree. The brief essay is not a condensation or an excerpt. It stands alone, a self-contained literary entity requiring no outside support system. The brief essay lives in a separate universe from the long essay, the two being different life forms requiring different atmospheres in which to move and breathe. Yet, despite their differences, many of the same qualities found in longer, more traditional essays—and, indeed, in some fiction and poetry—appear in brief nonfiction texts as well. In the pages that follow, I will enumerate thirteen suppositions regarding the brief essay form, with the hope that my comments may also apply to other forms of writing, both prose and poetry. Drawing on brief essays that I admire, I will suggest techniques for creating a text that is "a working, functioning complete world unto itself."

1. Close cover *after* striking.

You can't start a fire with one stick; you need at least two elements, rubbed together, to send sparks flying. In one of her many fine essays, Barbara Hurd ignites a flame almost instantly. First element: Her title, "Moon Snail." Rubbed against the second element, a quotation from Aristotle. By the time Hurd's first sentence appears (just three words) heat is rising off the page: "Surely Aristotle's wrong." This reader is engaged from the first sentence on. I sense that something matters here, something important enough to create friction—in this case, the friction of argument or discord.

How soon can you ignite the first spark of a brief essay by rubbing two or three sticks together? The sticks could be different voices, rhetorical modes, subjects, speakers, timelines, quotations, or opposing opinions.

Casual Sex

In bed again
with husband of thirty years,
wearing flip-flops.

2. "A Tiny Bead of Pure Life"

The triggering subject of a brief essay doesn't have to be large, or, on the surface, important. The smallest key can open a door into a large, sumptuous room. I think of Barbara Mallonee's intriguing "Semi-Colon," a paean of praise for what is often considered the lowliest of punctuation marks. I think of G. K. Chesterton's "A Piece of Chalk," in which a seemingly mundane occurrence—the speaker's inability to locate a piece of white chalk—grows into an exploration of, among other things, religious morality, mercy, the souls of cows, the nature of art, and the landscape of Southern England. And who has written more eloquently about the first, crisp days of autumn than A. A. Milne in his rhapsodic meditation on a stalk of celery?

The tiniest thing can yield wonders when we give it our careful attention; indeed, it may be the quality of smallness itself that invites

our keenest focus, as writers and as readers. "Miniatures encourage attention—in the way whispering requires a listener to quiet down and incline toward the speaker," suggests Lia Purpura. Decades have passed, but I still remember my first encounter with Virginia Woolf's essay "The Death of the Moth." Reading her words, my own breath quickened as I fixated on the moth "fluttering from side to side of his square of the window-pane." Had a St. Bernard trotted past the window of my mind at this moment, I doubt that his presence would have registered at all, so intent was I on the miniature scene playing out before my eyes. I would never look at a moth in the same way again, and to this day I continue to be astonished by Woolf's astonishment: "It was as if someone had taken a tiny bead of pure life and . . . had set it dancing and zigzagging to show us the true nature of life."

3. Brief essay as time travel.

Essays-in-brief can move fluidly in and out of time, dipping into the past or imagining the future while still remaining grounded in a present tense timeline. They can also incorporate timeline techniques similar to those found in book length narratives—the simultaneous narration of John Hersey's *Hiroshima*, for example, or the sequential/contrapuntal narration of Capote's *In Cold Blood*. In Anne Panning's brief essay "Remembering, I Was Not There," the partly imagined stories of her parents' early lives act as independent trains, commencing at separate stations but about to collide in the main event, their marital union and the eventual "new anti-life that is forming—one minus one equals zero."

How many time periods can you suggest in your brief essay? Can you dip back into the past to illuminate a particular moment, flash forward into an uncertain future event, or incorporate simultaneous, independent stories within the same moment in time? If you are writing a memoir-based essay, how far can you stretch the timeline of your life, or of one brief experience in that life? Reg Saner, in his long, braided essay "Pliny and the Mountain Mouse," incorporates the phrase "We are not here yet." Is there a way to create a brief essay in which you "are not here yet" as Panning does in her essay? Or write a memoir that extends beyond your life, into a future in which you are no more?

Sealed in Time Capsule:
Open One Hundred Years from Today

We danced, we lifted
goblets and skirts. Sorry
you had to miss it.

4. How many I's does it take to change an essay?

Brief essays can move seamlessly among various speakers and various points of view. In some essays, the "I" speaker is absent altogether except as an "eye" surveying the landscape, or as an unseen hand shaping the text. Sometimes the "I" is absent at first then pops in after a page or two, as in Jane Brox's "Bread" or Dinty W. Moore's "Son of Mr. Green Jeans," an essay that borrows the template of the alphabet, withholding the first person narrator until the letter "I" is introduced. In other texts, however, the "I" presents early on as multiple versions or variations of a self, each self locked within another like a Russian nesting doll: speaker as present tense author, as child or adolescent, as imagined or shadow self, as the second person "you" or even the plural "we" that emerges in Michael Datcher's "the spinners."

If you are locked into one perspective of an essay-in-progress, consider shifting from "I" into "you" or "he" or "we," or lose the "I" entirely so that the reader senses a presiding presence hovering over the text, though the identity of that presence remains unnamed.

Dairy Case

Three cows in a field:
One whole, one skim,
One two-percent.

5. Ride the train of language all the way to meaning.

In a brief essay, every single word matters. The compression of the form causes us to focus not only on individual words and phrases but also on their placement, their rhythms and sounds—in short, on the musical soundtrack that runs beneath the train of thought, event, story, or memory. Reading certain lyric essays, I can almost feel the engine of language pulling the train of meaning. Here, I quote from Judith Kitchen's lyric essay "Blue," supplying boldface type to emphasize the dominant sounds that caught my attention as I read: "My father's **eyes**, **ice** in the center. **Steel**, or something more durable than **steel**. **Still**, they could burst into laughter. Flame. **Heal**-all blue, though in the end they clouded, didn't **heal**. Blue you could **hear** . . . ."

"When I see shorter essays that fail to realize their potential," says Kim Barnes in an interview for *Brevity* magazine, "this is usually the problem: the author has seen the form as a short cut rather than an even greater challenge to balance music and meaning." In Kitchen's hands, music and meaning are inseparable. Listen to how "eyes" calls for, and to, "ice," just as "steel" calls out across the tracks to "still," which calls out to "heal," which leads us to "hear." I'm not suggesting that Kitchen was conscious of the sound echoes working themselves through the text, though it's difficult to miss the musical track playing beneath her words. No, Kitchen's essay isn't *about* sound. But the sounds and rhythms of "Blue," along with the author's surprising leaps into reverie, meditation and speculation, form a successful and memorable brief essay that challenges us to think deeply about the nature of memory.

6. Beauty is as beauty does.

Though it is true that many brief essays are propelled by musical language, it's important to remember that not all music is melodic, harmonious, pleasing to listen to, or even recognizable as music. Some music is atonal. Some hurts our ears. Sometimes, even a familiar tune sounds strange when played in a minor key. My musician brother tells me that if you take any Walt Disney song and play it in a minor key, it sounds exactly like a Russian folk dance. Move up or down a half step, and you can move from major key to minor. The slightest key shift, on the keyboard of your piano or your computer, can be significant. Change "bridal gown" to "bridal shroud" and your essay has moved into a different key, a different tonal dimension.

Just as all music doesn't have to be melodic or harmonically pleasing, the subject of a brief essay, even a lyric essay, need not be pretty, "poetic" or "lyrical" in the way those terms are often used. Sometimes, violence is called for. As readers, we need to witness, with Mary Oliver, not only the shells and clams washed up on the shore, but also the hypodermic needles, mustard bottles, and the "decomposing bodies of baitfish" she exposes to our eyes in "At Herring Cove." Our ears, too, are hungry for the world of the actual. We require the "damp splat of fur-bearing roadkill" and the "bulk and chuff of each mastodon eighteen-wheeler" to travel the road of Reg Saner's "Late July, 4:40 A.M." And in order to feel, with essayist Ann Daum, the "hundreds of different ways a heart can freeze" (from "Calving Heifers in a March Blizzard") we must first reach inside the calving heifer, place our hands "past her vulva, into the heat of her vagina" where "she clenches down . . . in a hot fist" until we can feel the calf, "catch the slick rod of a foreleg for an instant before it slips away." Pretty is as pretty does. Any subject, if handled with care and attention, can reveal the beauty hidden beneath its seemingly ugly surface.

And while we essayists are plumbing the depths of our subjects, we need to acknowledge that not every subject is deadly serious, or, as a fourth-grade boy I once taught wrote: "Poets need a sense of human." If humor is an essential part of our humanity, then why, I wonder, is humor almost never discussed in the same pedagogical room with the brief essay, particularly the lyric essay? "It's as if," essayist Kim Dana Kupperman suggested in a recent e-mail to me, "lyricism is a dark, haunted thing that can never laugh." A funny line, a wry aside, a mirthful turn of phrase administered at the right time and for the right reasons, can break a reader's heart. Or at the very least, break the expected path of the essay.

Taxidermist's Motto

Forever Yours:
The Look of Life,
Without the Trouble.

7. Take a breath.

Music, like literature, cannot exist without the silences between the sounds. "It depends on gaps," the critic Helen Vendler once wrote of the lyric poem; the same can be said of the lyric essay. Many brief essays are characterized primarily by the essayist's suggestion of silence, absence, and the white space that floats beneath and between thoughts.

Writers working in this mode attempt to say the unsayable by associating ideas or images without making overt connections. Some essayists create these associations by juxtaposing or colliding disparate or contradictory ideas; others, by using actual white space on the page. Still others borrow extra-literary templates from art, nature, or popular culture, or employ section breaks, segments, or subtitles within their essays. In "Artifacts," a segmented essay containing five different subtitles, Brenda Miller explores the relationships among several physical objects to suggest a deeper relationship, the emptied yet infinitely filling vessel of one's body within a changing world. Dinty W. Moore's "Son of Mr. Green Jeans" is a notable example of the segmented, hybrid essay, combining factual information, memoir, definition, anecdote, even a pop quiz, to create a narrative. Still, it is the spaces *between* the segments that make Moore's essay successful, the spaces where the reader supplies the connections, completing the transaction Moore has so carefully set in place.

Silent Senryu

*

*

*

8. Say it Again, Sam.

The poet Stanley Kunitz called the repetition of a writer's passions or obsessions, as seen within her work, her "constellation of images." I like to think that this constellation—of images, sounds, particular words or rhythms—can also rule a particular piece of writing. Imagine the following words scattered in various patterns across your desk, allowing for occasional repetitions: *torn, broken, graves, gone, buried, ruts, no, left, blown, litter, rubble, patina*. What pattern of meaning begins to emerge as you study these words in relation to each other? If each of these words were a star in a galaxy, what constellation might they form?

I composed this list of words from Ted Kooser's lyric essay "In Nebraska," a brief meditation in which the careful placement of particular words, some of which are repeated, forms a constellation of meaning. You could also think of Kooser's essay as a tapestry, woven with intricate loops or braids or netting, or as a web of small but elaborate design, a web that captures and holds his main subject of loss.

Road Construction Crews

Slow.
Average.
Gifted.

9. Right here, right now, or "the luminous whereabouts of horse."

Brief essays can create a sense of immediacy, the feeling that we readers are close up and personal to what's happening before our very eyes, ears, and noses. I'm not talking here about present tense narratives but rather about a reader's felt sense that a mind is discovering its subject, from the inside out, even as the words appear on the page. This journey of discovery becomes, in part, the subject of the essay. In "Night Song" by Stephen Kuusisto, the narrator asks more than once, "What else?" … "And what else?" as if ransacking memory for moments that stick, moving at one point from sight to sound to touch and smell, a movement toward intimacy that culminates in the narrator's encountering the "luminous whereabouts of horse."

In Steven Harvey's contribution to a recent AWP panel on the subject of the lyric essay, he included some thoughts about his own recent journey from writing personal essays to writing lyric essays. Harvey had become "tired," he said, of the "made up voice" of his personal essays: "My persona was having a nervous breakdown." The persona of the lyric essay, Harvey went on to say, does not come from the familiar or "the invented self" but rather from "the self coming apart," a self that becomes "absorbed by its subject." When we encounter our subject, not only in our imagination but on the page it-self, even as we compose, we are entering that intimate and present tense space of discovery that Harvey described, and that Kuusisto's essay demonstrates: the "luminous whereabouts of horse."

The First Rough Draft

Let there be
~~zebras, umbrellas, pincushions~~,
LIGHT!

10. Imagine there's a heaven (or hell).

One of the many reasons I dislike the term "creative nonfiction" is that it so often leads directly into a discussion of whether it is permissible for nonfiction writers to "make things up," a tiresome and often pointless discussion that robs us of energy to explore the myriad ways in which nonfiction writers can approach their subjects with imagination. Essayists are free to speculate, to wonder and imagine, to employ what Fran Kupfer names "the gift of perhaps" without inventing or distorting actual facts or events. In "Moon Snail," Hurd does not tell us that she painted an image of the moon snail; rather, she speculates on how she *might* paint the moon snail, moving through three imagined possibilities, still life painting to diptych and finally to triptych. Anne Panning uses the gift of perhaps, in the essay I mentioned earlier, by imagining herself into a life before she was born.

Think of all the possible ways you can imagine your way into, above, beneath, or around the subject of your essay. Employ negative space. What dress did your mother never wear? How would your life be different if you'd moved to Wyoming rather than Baltimore, or if you'd been a triplet rather than a twin? Pose questions that have no answers. Keep posing them until you discover a possible answer, or better yet, a more interesting question. Retract a statement, talk yourself out of your own argument, create a dialogue between two of your (many) selves.

Meeting My Needs

Glad to finally
make your acquaintance,
after all these years.

11. Teach me something. Change my mind.

Any writer who has ever attended a workshop, a writers' forum, or a panel of fellow practitioners, has probably been warned against "telling" the reader, well, almost anything. We are supposed to describe, to show, to enact, to intimate, to engage by the accumulation of specific and sensory detail, and to bring the reader into the scene. But never, never, to say precisely what we mean *if* what we precisely mean to say is: *Here is what I know. Here is what I've learned. And here is what this means for you.* To transgress into the reader's territory by suggesting that actual action on that reader's part might be required? How does *this* fit within the genre of the essay? Ask Vicki Hearne, whose "What's Wrong With Animal Rights" might dismantle all your notions about animal rights institutions. Ask Peter Singer, whose essay "The Singer Solution to World Poverty" I have reread many times, hoping he will let me off the hook. He won't. His case is clear; his call to arms, even clearer. Yes, Singer's essay makes me uncomfortable. I'd rather be reading about lilies. But many essayists are not only working their form but also working their forum, creating a space for public discourse. They are agents of change. And because their essays are, in many cases, brief, even the most hesitant or cynical reader will usually stay until the bitter end. Afterwards, some readers will simply close the book. Others will go directly to their desk to write a check to UNICEF, or go online to book a flight to a flood-ravaged city, or pick up the phone to volunteer at the nearest homeless shelter.

12. Go ahead, wear the crazy hat.

The brief essay, especially the lyric, the hybrid, the polemic or the rant, is forgiving of the odd and idiosyncratic. It's a perfect form in which to experiment with a different pose, a rakish angle, or an uncommon structure like the use of the second person, for example, a point of view that is hard to sustain and might feel forced or mannered if employed in a longer work. Weird, outlandish ideas and obsessions, too, often play out well in the brief essay form. Design your own modest proposal, Swiftian style. Thomas Lynch did just that in a portion of his essay "The Golfatorium"; in briefer form, Charlotte Perkins Gilman essayed her way into "On Advertising for Marriage," an essay whose subject, given its time period (more than a century before match.com) must have seemed shocking and preposterous to readers. When you write briefly, your chances for holding a reader's attention—even a reader who judges your essay the most crack-brained he's ever read—are much stronger than they would be if you were writing a longer piece. So go ahead, wear the crazy hat. Granted, the hat probably won't be enough, on its own, to guarantee success. But it might get you into a great club where things are really happening, and where you meet the object of your affection: your true subject.

Irate Response to My Phone Call to Pest Control (True Story)

> *"I'm not the cockroach secretary, I'm the <u>termite</u> secretary!"*

13. Get out while the getting's good.

I am not a fan of "wrapping up," in life or in literature. Many years ago, I stopped using the word "endings" to characterize those last few gestures in successful texts; I started calling them "openings." In a successful brief essay, the reader completes the transaction that has been set in motion very carefully, though not always consciously, by the writer. The most satisfying works of literature are those in which the reader, not the writer, supplies that final chord, the final lyric. Or, to mix a metaphor, once all the plates are spinning, at the right speeds and at the right angles, there is a moment in which the work is as alive as it will ever get. On those rare but blessed occasions when that moment occurs in our writing, we need to get our writer's self out of the scene as quickly as possible. Cut, print. Get out while the getting's good.

❖ ❖ ❖

Author's Note

This essay began as a brief contribution to "Playing for Keeps: Intensity and Creativity in the Lyric Essay," a panel presented at the 2011 AWP Conference in Washington, D.C. I invite readers who wish more in-depth discussion of the structural concepts mentioned in this essay to consult *Word Painting: A Guide to Writing More Descriptively* (Rebecca McClanahan, Writers Digest Books, 1999) or the following craft essays and interviews:

"Frelection: the Transformative Power of Reflection in Nonfiction." <http://www.creativenonfiction.org/brevity/craft/craft_frelection.htm>.

The following interviews are accessible through <www.mcclanmuse.com>:

"On Voice Prints, Ghost Thoughts, and Plates Set Spinning: An Interview with Rebecca McClanahan," conducted by Gretchen Clark and first published in *River Teeth: A Journal of Nonfiction Narrative.*

"An Interview with Rebecca McClanahan" conducted by William H. Coles for *Story in Literary Fiction* online magazine.

"A Conversation with Rebecca McClanahan," conducted by Nancy Zafris for *The Kenyon Review Online.*

I also highly recommend *Creative Writing: Four Genres in Brief*, edited by David Starkey, which includes in-depth commentary on the craft of brief nonfiction.

Works Cited

Barnes, Kim, "Balancing Music and Meaning: An Interview with Kim Barnes," *Brevity: A Journal of Concise Literary Nonfiction.* <http://www.creativenonfiction.org/brevity/>.

Brox, Jane. "Bread," reprinted in *In Brief: Short Takes on the Personal*, ed. by Judith Kitchen and Mary Paumier Jones, Norton, 1999.

Capote, Truman. *In Cold Blood*, Random House, 1965.

Chesterton, G. K. "A Piece of Chalk," reprinted in *The Art of the Personal Essay*, ed. by Phillip Lopate, Doubleday, 1994.

Hersey, John. *Hiroshima*, Alfred A. Knopf, 1946.

Datcher, Michael. "the spinners" from *Raising Fences: A Black Man's Love Story*, Riverhead Books, 2001.

Daum, Ann. "Calving Heifers in a March Blizzard," reprinted in *In Brief*, Norton, 1999.

Gilman, Charlotte Perkins. "On Advertising for Marriage," reprinted in quotidiana.org <http://essays.quotidiana.org/>

Harvey, Steven. Quoted from panel presentation "Playing for Keeps: Intensity and Creativity in the Lyric Essay," AWP Conference 2011.

Hearne, Vicki, "What's Wrong with Animal Rights,"

reprinted in *The Best American Essays Fourth College Edition*, ed. by Robert Atwan, Houghton Mifflin, 2004.

Hurd, Barbara. "Moon Snail," *Short Takes: Brief Encounters With Contemporary Nonfiction*, ed. by Judith Kitchen, Norton, 2005.

Kitchen, Judith. "Blue," *Distance & Direction*, Coffee House Press, 2001.

Kooser, Ted. "In Nebraska," *Local Wonders: Seasons in the Bohemian Alps*, Nebraska, 2002.

Kupfer, Fran. "Everything But the Truth," reprinted in *The Fourth Genre: Contemporary Writers Of/On Creative Nonfiction*, ed. by Robert L. Root, Jr. and Michael Steinberg, Allyn and Bacon, 1999.

Kuusisto, Stephen, "Night Song" reprinted in *Short Takes*, Norton, 2005.

Lynch, Thomas, "The Golfatorium," *The Undertaking: Life Studies from the Dismal Trade*, Norton, 1997.

Mallonee, Barbara. "Semi-Colon," *Short Takes*, Norton, 2005.

Miller, Brenda. "Artifacts," reprinted in *In Brief*, Norton, 1999.

Milne, A. A., "A Word for Autumn," reprinted in quotidiana.org <http://essays.quotidiana.org/>

Moore, Dinty W. "Son of Mr. Green Jeans," *Between Panic & Desire*, Nebraska, 2008.

Oliver, Mary. "At Herring Cove," *Blue Pastures*, Harcourt Brace, 1995.

Panning, Anne. "Remembering, I Was Not There," *In Brief*, Norton, 1999.

Purpura, Lia. "On Miniatures," *Brevity: A Journal of Concise Literary Nonfiction* <http://www.creativenonfiction.org/brevity/>

Saner, Reg, "Late July, 4:40 A.M.," reprinted in *In Brief*, Norton, 1999.

Saner, Reg. "Pliny and the Mountain Mouse," *The Four-Cornered Falcon*, Johns Hopkins University Press, 1993.

Schaeffer, Susan Fromberg. *The Madness of a Seduced Woman*, Hamish Hamilton Ltd, 1984.

Singer, Peter. "The Singer Solution to World Poverty," reprinted in *The Best American Essays Fourth College Edition*, ed. by Robert Atwan, Houghton Mifflin, 2004.

Talese, Gay and Barbara Lounsberry. *Writing Creative Nonfiction: The Literature of Reality*, Longman, 1997.

Wilkerson, Isabel. The *Warmth of Other Suns: The Epic Story of America's Great Migration*, Random House, 2010.

Woolf, Virgina. "The Death of the Moth," *The Death of the Moth and Other Essays*, Harcourt Brace, 1942.

❖ ❖ ❖

Terri Garland. *Hoop, Lower Ninth Ward, New Orleans, La.* 2006. Archival pigment print. 16 x 16 inches. Courtesy of Alan Klotz Gallery, New York.

Herons

April was forty-eight. Ryan was sixteen. I was twenty-seven, closer to his age than I was to his mother's, so it was surprising how gracefully he handled the situation. He was a kid I might have smoked a joint with behind the carwash if I hadn't been sleeping with his mother. And he was a kid I might have punched, had the situation been reversed—had he been twenty-seven and sleeping with my mother when I was sixteen—but he acted like I was any other guy she brought around, which is to say that he looked at me with scorn, but, for the most part, said nothing. I was grateful for that.

I could never have imagined how he felt, of course, because my mother was still married to my father, which probably bothered me almost as much as I bothered him, albeit for a whole different set of reasons. The thing with my parents was that, in spite of an almost desperate craving for his approval, I'd never really liked my father very much, and I sort of hated my mother for staying with him.

When I was a freshman in high school, he'd encouraged me to get involved with sports. "Sid," he said. "You ought to get involved with sports. You ought to play football. You ought to join the wrestling team." So I joined the wrestling team. I wore yellow tights that made me look like a banana with matchstick arms, and when my father came to my first meet, he saw me pinned in six seconds. We drove home in silence. I kept looking over at him, wanting to say something, but he wouldn't take his eyes off the road. He had a thick, gray beard and a red splotch on the right side of his face, spreading out over his cheek like a spider web of capillaries, and every time I looked at him, the red splotch was looking at me.

That night he told my mother that she'd overcooked the roast, then left his plate on the table and went up to his room with a glass of vodka. I watched her do the dishes in silence, imagining that she felt terribly oppressed, wondering how she put up with it, feeling guilty for being a part of it, but I didn't get up to help. I just sat there.

Aside from the differences in our family histories, I figured Ryan was probably a little like I'd been. He wasn't athletic at all, and he was kind of a strange kid in other respects, not the kind of kid who fit in, his face covered with pimples, his head shaved, in spite of the wispy pubescent mustache he was trying to grow. He wore baggy jeans, and he had a black t-shirt that said, "Hillary Sucks. Monica Blows." I didn't know what to make of that. Was it supposed to be rebellious? What did his mother think? I'd never asked.

April and I didn't talk politics. Maybe we should have. It might have been nice to know what she thought about life outside the bar. We'd met in the bar, and we spent most of our time in the bar, unless we were in bed, in her trailer, Ryan in the next room, playing video games, watching MTV.

❖ ❖ ❖

One weekend, when Ryan was staying with his father, April and I got out of bed late at night and went outside to have a cigarette. It was nice, April in her pale green bathrobe, sitting on the cinderblock steps up to her front door, me standing there listening to the crickets, looking at her bare feet in the dirt, thinking we had a good thing going.

"Remember the night we met?" she asked. "At the bar? You were still going out with that young thing. What was her name?"

"Deirdre," I said, and when she shook her head, I thought we were headed for trouble.

Deirdre was eighteen when I met her at the local dive. I got her drinks all night long, brought them to her at a table in a dark corner, away from the bartender, away from the bar. I didn't know she was under twenty-one until the next morning. I just thought I was doing really well with her. I couldn't believe it, because she was so beautiful. The long red hair. The angular jaw. Green eyes. Perfect complexion. She wore a red v-neck t-shirt that showed so much cleavage I thought I was going to die.

When April brought it up that night on the front step, I thought she was about to get jealous. I thought she was going to ask me if it was better, being with a woman so young. I thought I was going to have to reassure her, maybe even lie, tell her that the sex wasn't that great. I was already practicing it in my head; she didn't know what she was doing, I'd say. A girl that age.

But April said, "Ryan dated her, too."

My face must have dropped pretty hard. It felt like she was making fun of me. I was a joke. "A couple years ago," she went on. "When he was fourteen. She was sixteen, I think. Just a couple years ahead of him in school. She kept calling and calling. It was pathetic."

"Does he know I went out with her?" I asked.

She nodded, laughing out loud, now. "I told him," she said. "Oh, Sid. You should have seen his face. I'd have given anything if you could have seen his face."

I thought it was going to be impossible to show my face around there again, I was so embarrassed, but April kept inviting me over, and I wanted to see her, so I kept going, surprised by how normal it seemed, how everything went on, as if nothing was out of place. The way Ryan treated me. It didn't change.

I'd get up before work, and he'd be at the kitchen table, eating a bowl of cereal, and I'd say, "Good morning," and he'd look up without saying anything, and every time I left I felt like I should have apologized, like I'd done him some horrible injustice. Not because of Deirdre. Because of his mother. But as I walked out to my car in the morning, she'd be standing in the doorway in her bathrobe, smiling, her short brown hair a mess, a cup of coffee in her hand, and I'd think "this is my life," and I was happy, because—whether I'd admit it or not—I kind of imagined that when I was growing up, when my father went off to work in the morning, if he had looked back at the door, he would have seen something the same.

❖ ❖ ❖

Part of the reason Ryan tolerated me to the extent that he did was no doubt that he'd hated

Romulus, the guy who'd been with his mother immediately before me. Her older brother, Dan, didn't mind that I was 27 at all, for precisely the same reason: in his view, I was an improvement over Romulus. He was the one who told me not to worry about Ryan. He was the one who told me what Romulus had done.

One afternoon, when April was working at the hospital, Dan and I were at a bar called Skipper's, on James Island, near Charleston. It looked like a big white boat from the outside, but inside it was an ordinary dive. The only exceptions were the wooden rafters, the walls that curved upwards and out, like we were really below deck, in the hull of a ship. The bartenders kept the lights low, and they sold glasses of Icehouse Beer for 50¢ at happy hour. It was happy hour when I saw Dan at the bar. He'd finished a job early, and he was there with a pitcher of Icehouse, sawdust on his t-shirt and jeans. He'd been cutting two-by-fours all day, building a bungalow in some rich guy's backyard, and he was very drunk by the time I ran into him, by the time he told me that I was okay. "You're okay," he said. "I like you."

"Thanks. I just wish Ryan felt the same way."

"He likes you alright. I mean, you could only be a step up from Romulus. That's not saying much, but it counts for something. He was a weirdo. I mean, he was into some weird shit."

❖ ❖ ❖

A couple weeks later, Dan invited Ryan, April, and me to watch the Superbowl at his place on James Island. I'd been there a few times before, and I liked it a lot. He had a townhouse with a deck out back that looked out over the marshlands, and the herons would land there, sometimes, disappearing into the tall yellow grass, the marsh grass, and no matter how many times I saw it, I was always surprised by the way they would burst out again, lifting off into the sky and gliding overhead, over the row of townhouses, off to wherever they went, whatever they did.

But we didn't go out to the deck that day. We sat in the living room, which was small and cluttered, a couch and a love seat with clunky wooden coffee tables in front of them. An old TV, complete with antennae and knobs for UHF and VHF, sitting on a milk crate against the opposite wall. I hadn't seen a TV like that in years.

It buzzed like a fluorescent light off the ballast, and every once in a while the picture would fragment into narrow lines and static over, and Dan would curse, get up and hit the top of the set with the flat of his hand to make the picture come in again. It was like my parents' living room. It was like we'd traveled back in time.

Dan sat on the couch. April and I sat on the love seat. Ryan was on the floor, watching the game, more interested than I'd expected him to be. Like I said, I hadn't taken him for a kid who would care about sports.

Dan kept offering me things. "Can I get you a sandwich?" he asked.

"I'm okay," I said.

"Another beer?"

"Thanks, but I'm set."

I wanted to tell him to relax, to stop fussing over me, but I didn't want to be rude, so I finally said yes to chips and salsa. He got up quickly, stumbling on his way to the kitchen. He was drunk again. April looked at me, and I shrugged. When Dan came back with the dip, she asked him if he was alright. "I'm fine," he said, and set the chips and salsa down on the coffee table in front of me.

Ryan was quick to sit up and grab a chip. When I grabbed my first, he looked at me suspiciously. "Don't double dip," he said.

I ate the chip without salsa, then got up to use the bathroom. Dan pointed. "In the hall," he said.

It was nasty in there, walls papered yellow, linoleum grungy and pale green. It was clear that Dan didn't clean much. When I finished up and came out, Ryan was standing against the wall. We stood there looking at each other for a second.

"Are you a drunk?" he asked.

"No."

"My mother's a drunk," he said.

"She seems alright to me."

"Romulus was a drunk, too."

"He probably still is," I said. "It's just that you can think of his drinking in the past tense, now, because he's not with your mother anymore."

Ryan paused a second, then said, "That's an interesting point."

"I know a lot about grammar," I told him. "I used to be an English teacher."

I'd taken an intensive, four-week course to get a certification to teach English as a Foreign Language. It was a quick and easy alternative to college, and I'd thought it would give me the opportunity to travel the world. As it happened, I went to Milwaukee. I taught Mexican immigrants. I wasn't a very good teacher, and even if I'd taught them to speak perfect English, they'd have been lucky to get jobs as busboys back then, in the early '90s.

Eventually I ditched it, moved to South Carolina to start a new life at the carwash. Washing cars wasn't nearly as disheartening. The work was inconsequential, but at least I could see the results; the cars came in dirty and left clean, and I had the sense that I'd accomplished something, no matter how irrelevant, no matter how small.

It seemed important, this revelation I'd had, like stuff I should have told Ryan, but while I was standing in the hallway, lost in thought outside the bathroom at Dan's place, Ryan was having thoughts of his own, and he wasn't afraid to tell me what they were.

"You don't care about football," he said.

"No," I told him. "Not really."

"Isn't it a tad duplicitous, then, on your part, coming over here for Superbowl Sunday?"

"The alternative was to be rude."

He looked at me with what could only have been the utmost sincerity and said, "Don't think you can eat chips and salsa with impunity."

I was about to say that he might have been misusing the word impunity, but there was a crash from the living room, then a short scream, stifled immediately. It sounded like Dan. "Oh, Fuck," he said. "It hurts."

April said, "Are you okay?" and he said, "No, I'm not okay, you fucking moron. Obviously I'm not okay," and she said, "I think it's broken." Although I wasn't sure, at that point, what she was referring to—it could have been one of the coffee tables, for all I knew—April was a registered nurse, so I figured if it was an arm or a leg, she was qualified to make a diagnosis.

I couldn't see what was going on from where I was standing, in the hall with Ryan, but when he started for the living room, I grabbed his arm and said, "Don't."

"I could help," he said.

"They'll take care of it," I told him. "You'll just embarrass him."

I felt wise and grown up, for a second, but then April shouted, "Ryan, Sid, get in here," like we should have been there already, and the feeling was gone.

In the living room, Dan had tripped over the coffee table. His leg was broken, alright. Very broken. Broken in a way that seemed disproportionate with what you would expect, when someone had only tripped over a coffee table. April had rolled up his pant leg, though, and it looked like if his shin had been any more broken, it would have torn through the skin, like Stevie's shin, in *The Deer Hunter*, or Joe Theisman's, when he got tackled that time, maybe in the '80s. I remembered it abruptly, how my father had been so satisfied, how I'd thought there was something sick about him for that.

We had moved to Washington, D.C., from Chicago, and my father didn't like living in D.C., didn't like his new job or our new neighbors. He missed Chicago and his Chicago friends. He missed Chicago food, Chicago sports teams.

With Dan there on the floor, his leg broken almost like Joe Theisman's, it became suddenly clear to me that my father's hatred of the Washington Redskins and his resentment of their success were rooted not in a general negativity, but in his longing for Chicago, and at once the satisfaction he took in Joe Theisman's broken leg was not mean-spiritedness, but profound sadness.

Joe Theisman, by the way, was the quarterback for the Washington Redskins in their heyday. Stevie was the guy in *The Deer Hunter* who said, "Do as your heart tells you."

❖ ❖ ❖

In the waiting room at the hospital, April stood by the reception desk, talking with the woman behind the counter, while Ryan and I watched the rest of the game on a television they had on a ceiling mount in the corner. It seemed to me we hadn't missed much since Dan's fall, but it was clear that Ryan's team was losing, and that Ryan was losing hope.

He sighed and said, "I don't care about this game, anymore."

I didn't say anything, and he leaned forward, elbows on his knees, hands folded in a triangle, fingertips to his chin, almost meditative. "Why did you say Dan would be embarrassed if I saw him?" he asked.

"He's drunk," I said. "And he's your uncle. He probably thinks he's setting a bad example."

"If anything, it makes me want to stay away from that shit."

"He probably doesn't want to look weak in front of you either," I said.

A fat woman stood with a doctor at the other end of the room. She wore a pink t-shirt and cried out loudly: "My baby," she said. "My poor baby." The doctor was a young guy. He looked like he didn't know what to do, like maybe *he* was her baby, or at least her baby's age, and when he touched her shoulder, she shoved his hand away. "Don't you touch me," she seethed. Her t-shirt said, "I kissed Justin."

"The drinking shit isn't news to me," Ryan said. "I've seen my mom plenty wasted."

The fat woman was crying into the doctor's chest, now. He had his arms around her. He looked pretty uncomfortable, patting her back, like the whole world was upside down.

"My mom says you're a good guy," Ryan said.

"I'm not a bad guy."

"Didn't you work with starving children in Mexico or something?"

"Milwaukee," I said. "And they weren't children. They were Mexican."

"But you worked with starving kids and shit."

"Most of these guys were older than me."

"So why did my Mom act like you were some kind of philanthropist?"

"I think you're misusing the word philanthropist," I said.

"What's a philanthropist?"

"A guy who gives money away."

"What were you?"

"I told you," I said. "I was an English teacher."

❖ ❖ ❖

After a few minutes, April came over to us. "You guys don't have to hang around here if you don't want to," she said.

Ryan said, "Good, let's get out of here," and I said, "Um."

I said "um" because I felt like I was being thrust into a parental role, like I'd be responsible for Ryan for two hours, and one of the things I liked about working at the carwash was that I didn't have to be responsible for anything. Not really. I mean, I was responsible for washing cars, but I wasn't responsible for telescopic antennas, power antennas, loose chrome or mirrors, bug shields, luggage racks, sun visors, running boards, non factory-installed equipment, or valuables left in cars, and I certainly wasn't responsible for sixteen-year-olds.

But April said, "Go get something to eat," and Ryan said, "Let's go to that diner on Savannah Highway," so what could I do?

"Don't you want to watch the rest of the game?" I asked.

"It doesn't matter, anymore," he said. "We're doomed."

I decided that I was hungry, anyway, and that any emotions I felt about being responsible for Ryan could be attributed solely to that, so I agreed. It seemed like the rational thing to do, and since I was a rational man, I figured I was capable of looking after a sixteen-year-old for a couple hours. It didn't occur to me until much later that at sixteen, Ryan didn't need a lot of looking after. He might have needed discipline and school and advice, but he didn't need it from me, and he certainly didn't need help going to the diner.

❖ ❖ ❖

Outside, the night was like the inside of a cloud. Inside, the diner was bright and ugly, green and white spotted Formica tables, seats so squishy you could feel the springs pressing into your ass. I'd been there before, because it was one of the only places in town that was open late night, but I'd forgotten that, before midnight, it was a teen hangout, too.

There were high school kids all over the place.

I figured that was why Ryan wanted to go, that he was probably hoping to hook up with some of his friends, but—while he nodded to a couple guys when we walked in—he didn't make any effort to talk to them. He didn't talk to them. He didn't go over to their tables. He acted like they weren't there, the same way I would have, if we'd run into someone from the bar.

"Have you played Delta Force?" he asked.

"What's Delta Force?"

"Never mind."

I found out later that Delta Force was a video game about shooting people—terrorists, I think—but at the time I had no idea, so I really didn't know what to say to him. I just looked around. There were little wooden signs on the walls, engraved with sayings like, "No pants,

no service." I'd never thought they were funny before, and I didn't really think they were funny now, but I pretended to, just to make conversation.

When I tried to joke about them, Ryan said, "I hate these signs."

"Why?" I asked.

"They give the place personality," he said. "I hate personality."

"I know what you mean," I told him, but it felt dumb and insincere, and I didn't want to say anything else. Ryan was way ahead of me.

"The first polygraph," he said, "was tested in a sorority house. I heard about it on NPR. The man who invented it married the first woman he tested it on."

"She must have been honest," I said.

"She was ten years younger than him," Ryan said. "He was in his thirties."

"I didn't think about that."

"All the people who've tried to perfect the polygraph have been men," he said.

"Is that so?"

The waiter came over. He was crazy good-looking, in his early twenties if not younger, with a blond mop of hair and thick, full lips. His skin was perfect. His eyes were blank. He was like a pretty robot. He looked from me to Ryan and back to me as he recited the blue plate specials. "Chicken fried steak," he said. "Chicken fried chicken."

"Do you go out with older women?" Ryan asked.

"Not generally," he said.

Ryan ordered a hamburger. I ordered Huevos Rancheros. Once the waiter had gone, Ryan said, "Women don't need to use polygraphs. They can tell you're lying from the look on your face."

"My face?" I asked.

"Anyone's," he said. "That's why it's always men who do the research."

"Does it bother you that I'm with your mother?" I asked.

"It bothers me that she goes through a lot of men. I'm just taking it out on you for now. I'll take it out on the next guy, when he comes along."

"Okay."

"And, in some ways," he said, "I'm glad she's with you. She used to get hammered with Romulus."

That's when I looked to my left and saw Deirdre. It was an unlucky coincidence, but not that surprising. As big as Charleston was, we were in West Ashley, which was basically a suburb, and the diner was the only place that was open all night. Every one ended up there, eventually.

Deirdre was exactly the way I remembered her—stunning—the red hair braided on either side of her young face, and everything in my chest sank, everything in my stomach tightened, because even though April and Ryan knew that she was a girl we had in common, they didn't know what had happened between us; that she'd been the one to get bored with me.

Ryan was startled when he saw her. Even more startled than I was. Almost afraid. "Deirdre," he said. "I didn't see you come in."

"What are you doing with Sid?" she asked.

"Having a hamburger."

"I don't see any hamburger."

Just then the robot brought his hamburger, and Ryan was vindicated. Deirdre walked away. "Nice to see you, too," I mumbled. My Huevos Rancheros looked a little green.

"I used to date her," Ryan said, explaining as if he didn't know his mother had told me.

I couldn't let it slide. I wanted to confess. I didn't know why, exactly. It could have been that I didn't want him to pity me. It could have been that I wanted him to know it was okay. Maybe I just wanted to get it all out in the open, clear out any bullshit that might have been between us. So I told him: "So did I."

"Isn't she a little young for you?" he asked.

"Isn't she a little old for you?"

"I have a thing for older women," he said.

"I think we're on the same page, there." I thought that would get a laugh out of him, but he wasn't listening. He nodded in Deirdre's direction. "Check it out."

Another young woman had walked in and taken a seat beside Deirdre. Her hair was curly brown. She had a button nose and a full figure. A low-cut shirt that left little to the imagination.

"I like her nose," Ryan said.

But I was thinking about those nights months ago, in the bar, when Deirdre and I would sit kissing in the corner, and how I'd thought it was because we had some passionate thing going, because she couldn't keep her hands off me. I'd

bring her a beer and she'd bite my earlobe. It wasn't until we bagged it that I figured out that was just how she was. She liked public displays of affection. April wasn't much into that sort of thing. I kind of missed it.

"I broke up with her," Ryan said.

"Deirdre?" I asked. "Oh. She broke up with me."

❖ ❖ ❖

I wanted to make love to his mother that night. I kissed her mouth, then her breasts. She pulled me on top, and soon I was inside her. We moved slowly at first, and she moaned and moaned and told me to do it harder, and when she sounded like she was about to come, she just quit, pushed me off and rolled away; gave me her back.

A minute later, her voice was soft when she said, "It's okay, baby. Just forget about it. Just go to sleep."

I couldn't forget about it, though, and I couldn't go to sleep, because I kept thinking that in the end I didn't really know that much about her. I knew she had a son, and I knew she was a nurse. I knew she made me feel good, brought me sandwiches at the carwash, won every game of backgammon we ever played, but that was all textbook shit—shit that anybody could have known—and it didn't really tell me anything about her, what she liked, what she didn't like, what she wanted or needed. Not just in bed, but in general. I didn't know what she thought about the world, and it made me wonder why she kept me around.

After me, there'd be a guy named Theodore, or maybe Calvin, and he'd be big and dopey looking, but he'd be an accountant, so he wouldn't actually be dopey, he'd just look dopey, and I'd wonder why she kept him around, too, because he'd be nothing like Romulus and nothing like me, and he would never really know her, either; the only thing he'd know would be her favorite song. It was the one that goes, "The only one who could ever reach me was the son of a preacher man," and she would dance around her trailer listening to it, and Ryan would say, "Mom, please stop," but she would just ignore him, spinning and spinning like an angel while Theodore or Calvin sat there and stared, wondering what was coming next.

❖ ❖ ❖

Cynthia Atkins

Shelf-Life

I followed the invisible keeper
of the shelf—Languishing, dated
as dried ink-wells in the lofty residuals
of antique malls. The past was a skin,
a trinket lined in satin, like an old school
Valentine someone finds in a drawer.
       All the morticians
have thumbed their noses
at mortality—then pinched us into
distinction. *"No pearls before*
swine, and Madam, please move
to the back of the line." My pages
were immured like sacred parchment
in exotic rain forests—The sloppy words
went damp as motel towels, scrimmed
under a door.
       One time I slammed that door
on my finger and sent the bats flapping
to higher ground—All my former thoughts
resembled smudged chalk or dead insects.
       No harm done. I was the first
of my kind. These are the thousand reasons
we are inconvenienced on a dark planet
       to be exiled from home—then stranded
at the corner pay-phone of the last century.
When I slipped on the ice at the rink
of the page, it was a sucker's sacrifice.
So tooth and jowl, you ask,
Now what? What now?

Taylor Deupree. *Swingset Bermuda*. 2004. Photograph.

John Holman

Cannon

The boy, seven years old, gripped the chains and pumped his legs until he rode the rubber seat of the swing to the heights of tree limbs. The backswing took him into the shade of the woods behind his house, and the forward thrust raised him into the afternoon sunlight of the yard. Pumping, he rode the curve of air like a pendulum. Into the sun he could see his father's head through the kitchen window, fluoresene glinting on his father's scalp. Into the shade he was a bullet in the barrel of a gun ready to fire. Into the sun he saw his father's face look out at him and smile, his father's soapy hand wave. Into the shade he was an intake of breath, then a comet. Into the sun he saw the slope of yard, the grass waving like the wind he rode. Into the shade his back brushed the bark of a pine tree, sunlight slid along the pine needles. Into the sun he saw his father's back which blocked his view of the pots on the kitchen stove, and the ground moved under him like a wave. Into the shade he was a high diver atop a platform. Into the sun he let go of the chains and flipped backward while sailing forward, a cannonball spinning for no other purpose than flight.

When the ground came, it was hard. Pain shot through his arm and shoulder and soaked into his back and skull. He couldn't breathe, and that terrified him. Air was in the sky. He wanted desperately to breathe before his father got to him. This pain, this emptiness of air, was a mistake. He didn't want to be helpless. He heard the back door slam, footfalls in the grass. His father's voice, calling "Ray," unusually high-pitched. His father's face was above him. His father's face blocked the sky, and air was in his mouth. Sweat slicked his father's forehead. His father's mouth was large and firm. His father's mustache brushed Ray's nose. His father pinched Ray's nostrils and blew air into his mouth. Ray gasped and gulped air. His father turned him on his side and lifted him. Pain shot through his shoulder and swallowed his arm. Tears squeezed from Ray's eyes. He held onto his father's shirt with one hand, but not the other. He thought his other arm was still on the ground, but he couldn't see it as his father carried him out of the yard.

❖ ❖ ❖

That's what I wrote for the continuing education writing class I took. I was twenty-nine, finally dedicated to doing something with my life. I had stories to tell. On the first day of class, we were told to write a true sentence using first person, then to write one using third person. First I wrote, "I didn't make up my bed this morning." The teacher, a very short, white-haired woman, nodded, frowned, and said nothing. Then I wrote, "He deliberately wrecked the powder-blue Pinto his father gave him for his birthday." The teacher said, "You seem to tell more significant truths in third person." I nodded, frowned, and said nothing. Then we were told to go home and write about an early frightening event. So I wrote about hurting myself in that fall. I had to revise it about three times before the teacher said to stop. I did it in first person, then in third person; then I added some lyrical touches.

My dad also used to tell the story of when I broke my arm. Dad had mixed or changing motives when he told it, depending on who was listening. Basically, it was to make fun of me, good-naturedly, and I guess I good-naturedly endured it. He would tell it at the barbershop when men were talking loudly about dumbness. He would tell it to my high school friends as a weekend warning for us not to go "cannonballing" all over town, don't get into trouble, you know. Or he would bring it up when he thought I was embarking on some dangerous idea, like the time I wanted to buy a Volkswagen bus that was incredibly cheap because the brakes were bad, the shocks were shot, and the exhaust leaked up through the floor into the cab. That was just before he surprised me with the Pinto, which I did not deliberately wreck. He told it to Marie and her parents the night they came over for dinner to discuss our desire to be married. I was eighteen years old, and Marie had just turned twenty. We were about to be high school graduates.

In part, I allowed, he was giving them some of our family lore, a gesture to ease them into the family, or to show them what kind of family they would be joining if the wedding were to happen. I thought, too, it was to point out my shortcomings when it came to foresight, a hint that my wish to be married might be poorly considered. Never mind that when I was seven years old I was unlikely to give much forethought to anything other than Halloween and Christmas. "He believed," Dad explained, "that he could launch from the upswing, flip as many times as he wanted, and land on his feet, I guess." That great plan still tickled Dad, eleven years later. The swing set was made of timber and bolts and chains. It had two swing seats and a see-saw. Dad and his brother, Uncle Lee, had built it for me. An hour before my launch, I had been in my bedroom trying to predict which card would turn up from a deck Dad shuffled. It was one of our after-school games, me trying to make myself special with the discovery that I had ESP. Dad had been telling the Hargroves that, too. "Anyway," he said now, "he might get lucky and guess the two of clubs, but he couldn't predict that he might break his neck or leg or arm if he cannonballed onto hard ground." Ha-ha.

We all laughed at my idiocy. It broke—Ha!—some of the tension, as neither my parents nor Marie's seemed enthusiastic about our plans. So our laughing together, even at me, was a good sign. My mother seemed happy right then, party-red lipstick brightening her pretty smile. Marie's mother chuckled deeply, her large hoop earrings swinging against her cheeks. Plus, the food was tasty, and they were drinking wine. Marie and I were hopeful that if the parents hit it off, then we might get their cheerful consent.

Unlike other times Dad told the story, that night he didn't stop at what was funny to him. He told about taking me to hospital, about how frightened he was about my arm. Both forearm bones were broken, the ulna and the radius.

"When I held it," he said, "the arm bent in the middle like a cooked noodle." He worried about severed nerves, muscle tear, blood blockage. He couldn't remember the proper first aid, so when he should have made a splint he tried to use a scarf from Mom's drawer for a sling. Maybe the mouth-to-mouth was appropriate, maybe not. I'd knocked the breath out of myself. He stretched me out on the back seat of the car and drove me to the emergency room, when he should have called for an ambulance. "I'm telling you," he said, "I cursed stop lights and pot holes and everything responsible for them, including the mayor, the board of aldermen, and rain. I was mad at Beverly" (Mom) "for being out of town at a conference. Mad at myself for not being out back with Ray instead of in the kitchen trying to get dinner on." Driving, he remembered turning off the burners on the stove top, but he couldn't remember turning off the oven. He kept telling me, "We're almost there, we're almost there." If it wasn't for this or that damned traffic light, that damned blocked lane, that damned slowpoke in the exhaust-spewing pickup truck pulling out in front of us, we'd have been there already.

He said, "When I hustled Ray into the emergency room I saw how wrong that silk scarf sling was. The triage nurse gently removed it and had him lie on a gurney, Ray's wobbly little arm across his stomach. I stuffed the scarf into my pocket and debated with myself about when to call Beverly."

While Dad debated, I lay silent in the emergency area hallway and held my throbbing wrist with my good hand. All of the treatment rooms were occupied. Other people waited on gurneys, too. My throat was dry and I couldn't work up enough moisture to swallow. I said I was thirsty, and when Dad snagged a nurse going by she told us I couldn't have anything to eat or drink before a doctor said it was okay. "Why, for God's sake?" Dad asked. "Either get a doctor out here to see him or get him some water, please."

"I'm sorry, sir. Just please be patient."

"Just be patient," he said to me, smiling. "Funny, huh?" He touched my forehead, as if to check for a fever. "Does your arm hurt bad?"

I was slow to answer. "I don't know."

That sent another wave of panic through him. If my arm was numb, maybe it was dead. But when he looked at me I was obviously in pain, and afraid, tears wetting my lashes.

I felt a terrific ache all through me. I didn't know what really hurt and what didn't. I didn't know if the pain was extraordinary or not. I said, "Is my arm going to fall off?"

"No," he said, chuckling. "We're going to get it fixed. You're going to get an x-ray, but that won't hurt."

He still didn't know why I couldn't have anything to drink. It was absurd. There I was, not even complaining, asking only for water, and I couldn't even get that in a hospital. "He needed his mom," Dad said to Marie, who sat next to me, across from her mother and father at the dining table. My parents sat at the ends. I felt as if Marie and I were like a Little David couple confronting two couples of Goliaths. Dad's talking about my childhood was undermining my hope to seem a grownup. It was odd enough that we were eating in the dining room, that I was sharing the table with both my parents at the same time, that the table was set with the good china and heavy silver and gold-rimmed wine and water glasses. "He needed someone more skilled at confrontation, more skilled at comforting him." Tears filled Dad's eyes, now as well as then. He said, "I looked at his little face, at how brave he was being. It hurt me that I couldn't help him. I felt guilty, helpless, like he deserved a better dad."

"You're getting all sentimental, now, Melvin," Mom said.

"Yeah, I know," Dad said.

"Looks to me like you're a great dad," Mr. Hargrove said.

"Anyway, I stopped a different nurse going by and asked for water. 'He didn't get his dinner. He's been playing outside. All he wants is some water.'"

"Hang in there, dude," she said. She must have noticed my teary eyes. "I'll check on something for his thirst."

Dad told us, "I wished I had a deck of cards, so that we could play ESP. Ray, you hardly ever guessed a card right. Sometimes you'd stare at the back of a card for minutes before guessing wrong. You would touch it, close your eyes in what looked like painful concentration. You were stubborn. And as prescient as a brick." He looked around at the rest of us at the table. He said, "I looked around at the other patients.

I wondered what their problems were. If any were life-threatening. But would they still be waiting in the hall if so? Who could say that Ray's injury wasn't? A bone sliver in the bloodstream finding the heart or the brain?"

The Hargroves, Marie included, wore a slight smile, in sympathy for Dad's fear, but aware that it was for nothing. There I was sitting among them, my arm intact.

"Down the hall," he said, "a kid about Ray's age was in a wheelchair, his dark scrawny leg home-bandaged with a blood-stained yellow washcloth and tape. The triage nurse hadn't removed that. His grandmother stood beside him. She kept telling everyone who would listen, 'He got bited by a dog. My little grandboy. I don't know what kind, but that dog don't belong to nobody.' She had gray, too-tight cornrows that started near the top of her head. Looked like they ought to hurt. Woven in were red threads. The boy was whimpering. For some reason, that grandma made me mad.

"An old white man was on a gurney on the other side of the hall. He was by himself, a sheet up to his neck, his eyes closed the whole time. I'd stare to see if he was breathing. He had white scruff on his pasty face, and white hair filled his nostrils like cotton batting. He could have been dead."

Marie said, "Healthcare in this country needs a lot of work. Sometimes I think about going into hospital administration after med school."

"One thing at a time," Mr. Hargrove said. "First college. People change their minds a lot in college, sometimes." He looked at her unsmiling, as if waiting for her to change her mind now, about marrying me, I feared. "Anyway, it's the insurance industry that needs an overhaul."

Dad sucked his teeth, a habit that both Mom and I found annoying. He shrugged. "Yeah, I guess." He picked something off his tongue with his napkin. "So this old guy is lying there. People in blue scrubs and funky rubber clogs scurried by pushing blood pressure carts and carrying clipboards. I got to wondering if some of them were sick, too. If they had deep worries that you couldn't tell just by looking at them."

He said he remembered a time when he waited for Mom at the airport when she was returning from a different conference. She had been in Colorado, and, as he said, "Ray was with me at the gate, five then, concentrating hard on a plastic dinosaur he wobbled across the blue plastic seat beside him. People moved to their gates, deplaned, their faces searching, happy with reunion, or blank. And then, coming off the plane your mama was on—Do you remember this Ray?—was a woman with torrential tears, helped along through the crowds by another woman."

I knew that story, all right. I didn't remember it happening, but Dad had told about it enough times before that I knew the moral he drew from it. "Dad," I said, "how about a more cheerful subject."

Mr. Hargrove looked like he was ready for a smoke break. He was fiddling with a pack of matches on the table in the space where his dinner plate had been, since Mom and I had cleared the table of everything but dessert plates and forks and glasses. Mr. Hargrove nodded patiently and said, "Let's hear it, Mel. I'll bet we can take it."

"The one crying," Dad said, "was so distraught that no amount of public scrutiny could stop her. Her face was awful, twisted, lifted to the ceiling, emitting deep heart-wrenching grunts. She had on some kind of orange fur coat. Beverly came through the jetway door looking grim. Everybody looked grim. They had traveled hours on that plane with that woman. Her husband had died during their vacation, see— suffocated from an allergic reaction to eating shrimp. Her sister, the lady who helped her along, had flown to Denver to fetch her."

Mom said, "Weeping and wailing had come from their row near the middle of the plane for the whole other-worldly flight. It was horrible. Poor thing." She drew in her lips, dimples appearing in her thin cheeks.

Dad said, "You expect misery in a hospital, but who can tell, other places, who is hurting, what dreaded mission someone is on, what suffering goes on in public? We don't always see it."

"You're so right," Mr. Hargrove said.

"Anyway," Dad said, "in the hospital, I massaged Ray's little legs to distract him from his arm. I didn't want to wait any longer to call Beverly, but I didn't want to leave him to find a phone. Then I thought, Why worry her with incomplete news? She was in Miami this time, probably not in the hotel anyway. I hoped she wouldn't have to endure another grim flight,

this time with her own grief, maybe coming home to a boy who would have his arm amputated or something."

Dad had put me in a glum mood. Yet it seemed to charm Marie and the mothers. This dinner was supposed to be about my future, with Marie. And what was Dad doing? Talking about pain and misery, basically being a downer.

I said, "Dad, do you think there are places where people are secretly happy?"

He sort of smirked, and squinted an eye at me.

Mom said, "Jail?"

"Hmn," Marie said. "And camp."

"Dad," I said, "here's the difference between you and me. You thought that when we played the card game that I was trying to guess, or predict, the next card. But I was trying to change it. I wanted to influence what it would be. And I wasn't mindlessly cannonballing off the swing set, or wishing that I would land ok. I was suggesting to the ground that it accept me. I was willing that there was no difference between me and the ground."

He just looked at me, his eyes wide this time. I can guess now what he must have been thinking—that that was the dumbest thing he'd heard yet. He said, "Well, you're about as stubborn as the ground." Everybody laughed.

I hadn't intended to be laughed at again. Sitting there amongst our parents, I couldn't muster the feeling of being adult. Dad was acting as if nobody before him had discovered that people suffer in private, in public. He didn't know about all the days and nights I had agonized over Marie before she agreed to live the rest of her life with me, afraid she didn't really love me, afraid that I wasn't good enough for her, afraid that someone else would attract her, afraid that I might never for some reason even see her or speak to her again. During the day I'm sure I maintained a placid demeanor, but at night I sobbed prayers into my pillow. If I could, I would have whisked her away, but I didn't have the means. I worked as a waiter at a country club. Besides, we weren't the type of kids who would elope. She certainly wasn't. We respected our parents. We hoped to please them. We would depend on college loans and scholarships and part-time work. Love for her was my only strength. Sometimes it felt like a very weak strength. Hence the desperate prayers.

"Are you going to let me tell this story, or not? Let me at least get to the point."

"I thought you had," Mom said, smiling.

Marie took my hand under the table and put it on her thigh. Soft under the creamy Nylon skirt she wore. "How did they save his arm, Mr. Fielding?" she asked.

"Oh, an orthopedic surgeon on duty ordered some x-rays. They got him prepped for surgery, but found a way to manipulate the bones in his sleep without having to cut. He got to stay in the hospital overnight. The possibility of his getting the anesthesia was why he couldn't have any water, but a nurse did come by with a crinkled cup of chipped ice. By the time Beverly got home, he was in a cast and happy. Seemed like a miracle after all my worry."

"Show your arms," Dad told me. I slipped my hand from Marie's and placed my arms on the table. My forearms were long and lean and almost equally straight, soft black hairs shading the muscle.

Dad said, "How'd you get here, shot through time into the body of this handsome young man? When I dream about you, you are still four or five years old. And how can you be so in love? How can you know you want to get married? I myself never knew. Who are you?"

Mom got up and walked around the table, then play-slapped Dad on the back of the head. "You knew," she said.

"Well, maybe after you told me," he said, ducking in case she took another whack at him.

But she went into the kitchen. From there, she said, "And your point is?"

"It's not obvious?" Dad asked.

"It's not too obvious," Mr. Hargrove said. "You mean that life's serious business, right?"

Dad shrugged with one shoulder, leaned his head to that side. "Yeah. I guess."

Really, I couldn't believe all this moroseness about my broken arm, which was nothing compared to what Marie and her parents had gone through. During dinner, her mother had already recounted the story of Marie's survival of ovarian cancer. Marie had had a hysterectomy. She was out of school for two years. That is why she was older than me but in my graduating class. Her illness is what firmed her desire to be a doctor. Talk about serious business.

We already knew the broad facts. But Mom and Dad were, I think, just tonight realizing

that they might never be grandparents if I married Marie, and they weren't anxious for me to get married in the first place. But I wasn't thinking about wanting children; Marie still had check-ups to confirm that she was in remission.

First though, her mother had also told us about a dream she'd had before she knew she was pregnant with Marie. She saw herself raking leaves in their yard, and a smiling woman in a pale green dress approached her with a wrapped present, the name "Marie" on the raspberry ribbon.

Dad must have been thinking about that now. He said, "Marie is the real miracle, huh? A real dream girl. You folks are a strong family."

That softened me toward Dad some. I supposed that by telling about my broken arm, he'd been trying to tell her parents that I was special, too. That he loved me as they loved her. Maybe he'd been trying to soften her parents toward me, show me as resilient, determined, so they would accept me—as I had wished of the ground during my flight off the swing.

Mom brought in a banana cream pie, cut into it, and served the ivory colored plates.

Mr. Hargrove tasted a bite. He said, "Well, we certainly hadn't counted on an early marriage for Marie. And it has nothing to do with you, Ray. But if you can cook like your mother, that would be one less thing to worry about."

"Thank you, thank you," Mom said, chuckling. "He hangs around the kitchen sometimes."

I wasn't sure what was happening. Were they giving us their blessings? If I could cook?

Dad said, "It's good to know what you want. And it's good to have a partner through life. Marriage is life-long, you know. Supposed to be. I have some wishes and I have some hopes. I know you two don't know what you're doing, but I hope it works out."

"Hopes and wishes," Mrs. Hargrove sighed. She frowned at her pie.

Dad said, "Look, obviously, we would prefer you two to wait. Marie, you're ambitious. Planning to go to medical school and all. Ray, by golly, you've already achieved a truly ambitious goal. Somehow, you've caused a girl as pretty and smart as Marie to want to marry you. But," he turned to her parents, "I know you don't want anymore handicaps and obstacles for her."

He stopped then, leaving that statement hanging. He bowed his head toward his wedge of pie, as if he were about to say the grace again before eating it. The light from our brass chandelier shone on his scalp. Surely we understood that I was the handicap and obstacle he meant. This angered me. While I waited for someone to speak in my defense, I held Marie's hand again. She dug into my palm a little, as if to urge me to speak up. The parents all looked lost in thought. I had the feeling all of a sudden that they weren't thinking about me. Or that maybe all this talk had them remembering their youth, when they were ambitious, and musing about whatever handicaps and obstacles they'd had to endure. Mom had managed to get her Master's degree when I was a baby, but never her PhD. Dad had to have wanted to do something besides be a modern-day butler in a rich white man's house. As far as I knew, Mrs. Hargrove had never worked outside of their home. And her husband, who did own a gas station, maybe he wished for a life that didn't have him wearing overalls every day. He'd been a football star in high school. But he'd dropped out of college when he discovered that he needed to know how to read, which he learned to do, Marie told me, by taking classes at the Y after she was born. What misery and tears had they been hiding in public? Plus, there were Marie and I, possibly drags on our parents' lives. We had to be. The money we cost them. The worry. It was the first time I'd considered myself that way. I sat there a minute and really wondered how I seemed to Dad, to all of them, but to Dad especially. Stubborn, shortsighted, foolish, young. Selfish? While I was on the other side of the table, having that out-of-body moment, I saw my thinness made narrower by both arms under the table now, my hands grasping Marie's. I saw a bright-eyed young dude with the slender frame from his mother, a boy with his mother's light-brown complexion. He had his mother's "forest creature eyes," as Dad said when he teased her. Tea-colored, narrow. I saw something in those eyes. Confusion and fear. Determination, desperation, and guilt. I was desperate to establish my life. I was determined to have Marie.

So even then I could see myself in third person, as I was instructed to do years later on the first day of writing class. For my sixteenth birthday, Dad had bought me the Pinto that I wrote the sentence about. But no, I never wrecked it. It was slow and boring and embarrassingly new, though used. Within a year, the engine just seized up one day, leaving me frustrated and angry. Cheap piece of crap, smoke pouring from under the hood.

Marie said, "Mr. Fielding, I don't consider Ray a handicap to me. I consider him as much my future as every next day's sunrise."

He reared back in his chair. He had a barrel chest and a high round stomach, which he rubbed through the fabric of his tan knit shirt. He had a big, shiny bald head. When I was little I used to imagine he was a genie. "That's not exactly what I meant," he said. "You kids are launching yourselves too soon, throwing yourselves out there with no sure place to land—like Ray from that damn swing set. You don't know how frightening that is for us."

Marie said, "We do know how scary it is, Mr. Fielding. We are aware that you can never really know what will happen. Who would have predicted that Ray and I would fall in love? But we'll work jobs. We'll go to college. We'll still have you. We'll be helping each other, not handicapping."

"Why don't you just wait?"

"But why?" she asked.

The parents looked at each other. Mr. Hargrove struck a match and then blew it out. "Sorry," he said. They looked helpless and lost. Marie had that glow about her that I found so mysterious and irresistible.

Dad smiled and ruffled his mustache. Then he grinned. "Cannonball!" he called her in a booming voice that startled me. "You really knock me out!"

"Good heavens, Mel," Mom said.

I like ending this here, with Dad's long-winded echo of my old cannonball adventure. That was when he cleared the way—for me to be whoever I could think of to be.

❖ ❖ ❖

Thomas Reiter

Ownway

they call the sea off Lava Rocks
on the Atlantic coast of St. Kitts.
No fishermen launch from here.
An hour ago, the waves
barely tending toward shore,
you could skim from off the bay
ash blown two hundred miles from Montserrat.
But now swerves of deep current, surges
from vents in the sea floor
give themselves over to breakers,
and suddenly one taller than his father
sends a boy tumbling
among the shells and fragments of reef
he's gathering in an old pillow case.
He's ten and won't let go.
These coral fans, plumes, and tubes,
these ark shells, cockles, and cones—
his mother sells them at market
to builders of time-share units
who stucco them onto privacy
walls. Down in the riprap between waves
because Ownway is calming again,
he finds a length of the coral
they call dead man's bones.
He twirls it like a baton at Carnival
and marches out of the sea.

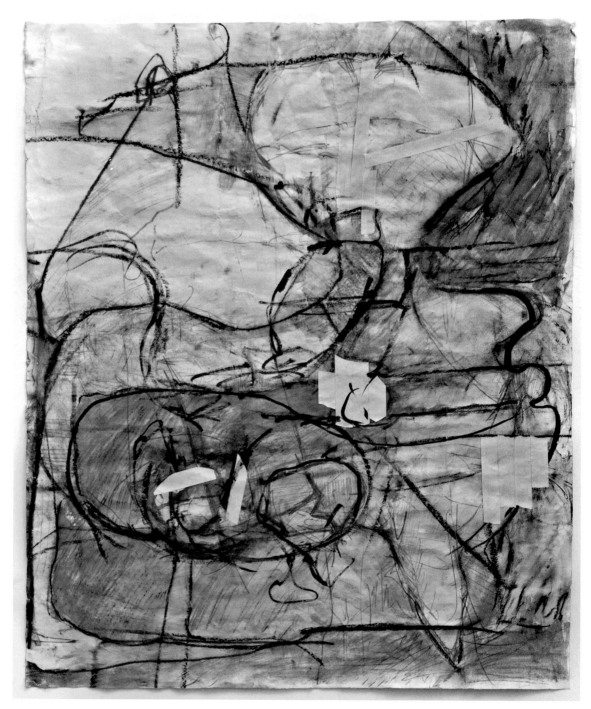

J. Parker Valentine. *Untitled*. 2012. Graphite , ink, and tape on paper. 36 x 24 inches.

Karen Stefano

Five

My mother sleeps in spurts, twitching in her dreams, while I slouch at her bedside watching *Jeopardy!* The contestant I've named Science Dork is creaming the competition.

"This substance is attached to its shell by a pair of strands called chalazae."

Science Dork hits his buzzer. "What is an egg yolk?"

"That is correct!" Alex Trebek is jubilant.

It was recently pointed out that one of my problems is that I think I am smarter than I really am. So now I make it a habit to watch *Jeopardy!* to remind myself of all I do not know. The pre-packaged twenty-three-minute dose of humbling holds the added benefit of drowning out the silence in this box of a room, a terrifying stillness interrupted only by the drone and hiss of an oxygen machine and my mother's ragged breathing.

❖ ❖ ❖

A nurse called last month and informed me that my mother had been upgraded to Five. I interrupted mid-sentence. "Shouldn't it be called *downgraded*? My mother's been *downgraded* to Five?" The nurse ignored me and explained that a bed in Five had become available and my mother would be moved there immediately. The nurse didn't mention what event had caused a bed to become available.

At Mayfair Retirement Village, life has three levels. "Independent" living, "Assisted" living, and "Skilled Nursing," the last stop at the end of the road, known at Mayfair by it's building number, Five. When my mother moved to Mayfair two years ago, she started in Assisted Living and gave me unsolicited daily reports on her neighbors.

"Remember that woman Sonya? She sat at my table for meals?" My mother released a sigh and shook her head. "They had to put her in Five."

I had learned to brace myself whenever my mother prefaced a statement with, "Remember that man . . . ?" Or "Remember that woman . . . ?" Our last phone call had been, "Remember that nice young man Robert? The crippled one?"

"Yeah . . ." I held my breath.

"He died." Her voice was like a bullet to the chest.

This was the downside of living in a place like Mayfair. You built affections for the inhabitants of your little village, but then they died, departing with a punch to the stomach, another reminder of what lurked around the next curve. I had met some of the Mayfair residents at events choreographed for the families. There was Lilian, who had just turned one hundred and one and seemed more aware of her surroundings than I was; Edith, a former stage actress who thought Harry Truman was still President; and Robert, who was only sixty-six but looked a hundred because of the psoriatic arthritis that had attacked his spine and feet, leaving him, in my mother's words, "crippled." The word made me cringe. I thought about correcting her, educating her on politically correct terminology, but what was the point? You could say impaired, handicapped, vertically challenged, but when it came right down to it, they all meant the same thing. Words had different meanings at Mayfair Village anyway. When my mother called to report that her neighbor Jon was in rehab, I knew it was not the same kind of rehab I had just come from.

❖ ❖ ❖

When the doctors pronounced my mother "very sick," I had shifted to a daily on our phone calls. I was still locked up in my own invented community of misfits then and couldn't leave for another sixteen days. But since my release back into the world, it had become more difficult to perform on those calls each night, nights when I only felt like curling into a fetal ball, maybe lifting my head to slurp from a glass of gin or wash down a pill, instead putting on a chipper voice to say, "Hi, Mom!" a voice that sounded so contrived to my own ears, I wondered why she couldn't hear it too.

❖ ❖ ❖

I snap to attention now as my mother bolts upright in bed. "What's that goddamn cat doing here?" she screams.

"What?" I scan the shadows of the room like a fool. "There's no cat, Mom."

"You didn't bring Nader?"

"No, Mom. Nader's not here."

She squints at the corners of the gray-green room, unsure whether to believe me, then falls back against her pillow. After a moment, she seems to relax again, then closes her eyes. Nader was the Himalayan Siamese I had to put down last year when his kidneys failed, a cat mourned as deeply by my mother as by me. These outbursts set my heart racing, though I know it's just the Prednisone talking, the drug doctors prescribe when they don't know what else to prescribe, the drug my mother's been taking for weeks.

I tilt my face back toward the television where Alex Trebek is still going strong, and so is Science Dork.

"This four-letter chemical abbreviation refers to the rave drug, Ecstasy."

Now this one I happen to know.

"What is MDMA?" I whisper, and Science Dork echoes me onscreen.

Science Dork is tall and lean, and I catch myself wondering what he has tucked inside those Dockers and whether he knows how to use it. My mind wanders like this sometimes, because I haven't had sex in a year and there are parts of it that I miss. A year ago I was still married, still hanging by a thread to a life that didn't feel like mine, but a life nonetheless. One night my husband sat on the couch in his boxers watching *Jerry McGuire* on TV. I looked up from my book at the scene in the elevator where Renee Zellweger sees a deaf man sign to his girlfriend, "You complete me." I couldn't stop myself from saying out loud that if it were a movie about my life, and I had been the one signing in the elevator, the line would be, "You deplete me." The next morning my husband packed up and left, calling me "pathologically insensitive" as he walked out the door.

"Pathologically insensitive? That doesn't even make sense!" I had shouted after him. But later, staring at the empty space of rumpled sheets next to me, I worried whether it was better to be with the wrong man than no man at all. Some months later, after gliding down the slippery slope of self-medicating against my lopsided existence, I sat on a straight-backed metal chair in an antiseptic room two hundred miles from home. Across from me, a counselor sipped tea and asked, "Do you want to be right, or do you want to be in love?"

"I want to be right," I said, and the counselor winced.

❖ ❖ ❖

Now I sit staring at the woman who is my mother and wonder how long it will be. When I think of her dying, both my parents gone, it seems important to remember my childhood, the only pure form of our time together. I think that if I can remember, I might understand how I got here, maybe even know what to do next. But when I try to remember, I can't. I only have pieces and don't even know if those pieces are real or imagined. My only memories spring from yellow tinted snapshots of a joy staged and impermanent, a Polaroid past that provides few clues for deciphering the present, except for the certainty that there was never a time when I felt comfortable inside my own skin.

The photos are a montage of birthday parties, pink frosted cakes, candles for wishes, and Barbie dolls with the price tags left on. There are Christmas trees, Easter eggs, and the uncle my mother warned me about each holiday, "Be careful; I think Uncle Ed touches little girls where he's not supposed to."

In an overexposed snapshot labeled by my mother's crooked handwriting, "Katy's B-Day —1969," I stand rigid in our living room, a stiff blue taffeta dress confining me like a straitjacket. My hands are clasped behind my back in a pose manufactured by my mother, who had bent over me in irritation, manipulating my limbs like a mannequin while her burning cigarette bobbed between her clamped lips. "Say Cheese!" she sang, but in the photo my round face wears a deer-in-the-headlights expression. I knew that if I moved, even breathed, the picture could be ruined, and flashbulbs were expensive. My lips form a straight line, not the broad smile that would serve as an exhibit, a piece of evidence establishing definitive proof of a happy childhood. "Why can't you just smile, for Chrissakes?" she had complained later, tossing the photo into a pile.

In the next photo it's summer at the beach, but instead of a bathing suit she has me dressed in a white t-shirt and navy blue polyester shorts that itched my crotch. Because the ocean was loaded with deadly creatures and riptides that sucked little girls out to sea, I couldn't go in. I posed at the shoreline, squinting into the sun, watching the other kids from the corner of my eye as they shrieked with laughter, slapping the water as they jumped over tiny waves. But I knew better than to question my mother. It was like this everywhere. We didn't go to the snow—there might be an avalanche. After dark we stayed inside because the roads swarmed with drunk drivers then. At the mall, there were purse snatchers and perverts. Everywhere, danger lurked, and my mother wore herself out guarding against it. She was teacher; I was student. I paid attention and learned the lessons she taught so well.

In the photo labeled "Easter, 1970" my mother is forty-six, a year older than I am now. She stands at the kitchen counter, pressing cloves into a ham. Next to the ham is the blender in which she chopped cabbage for the cole slaw, the same blender she would later slip her hand inside when it didn't look like the blades were moving. But those blades moved fine, and she wrapped her hand in a paper towel that soaked to crimson as she screamed at me to go to my room and stay there. My father took her to get stitched up and when she returned, she berated me like I had told her to put her hand in the blender in the first place. "I could have lost my fingers!"

"Yeah, but you didn't," I said and her good hand sent me reeling with the sting of a slap.

"Bad things happen everywhere, so you have to be careful all the time. You can't let your guard down—not even for a minute." She shoved gauze-covered fingers in my face in case I'd missed her point. Sometimes, my mother's avoidance stemmed from sheer paranoia, a black abyss of neurotic fear. Other times, her instincts seemed spot on. Bad things could happen anywhere. Now it seemed even home wasn't safe.

"My job is to protect you. Understand?" That was her mantra, the words I heard when I wasn't allowed to attend sleepovers or go to sixth-grade camp. She did have lapses, inexplicable contradictions, like letting a five-year-old play with a stapler, or the night she disintegrated into a crazy woman after a fight with my father. She had mutated into an unrecognizable stranger, snapping, "Stop hanging on me, for Chrissakes!" when I wouldn't let go of her hand, then "Don't call me that!" when I looked up through eyes puddled with tears to whine, "Why, Mommy?"

I never forgot the flash of sheer hatred in her eyes, the eyes of a woman at the end of her rope. She taught me how to feel, how to fear, then recoiled, disgusted that I could be so high strung when she had sacrificed everything to give me the perfect life, a life painstakingly constructed out of safety and avoidance.

❖ ❖ ❖

Photos of my mother showed her pensive, tense, a cigarette burning by her side, clenched between two slender fingers. In the only photo of us together, my mother stands next to me, one arm resting stiffly on my shoulder, the skin around her lips stretched back into a tight smile. I was responsible for her happiness and I was failing miserably. As I grew older, I had trouble talking to people, strained to make friends. What I lacked in personality, I made up for in smarts, but that got me into trouble too. "No one likes a smarty-pants," my eighth grade teacher scolded. So I learned to keep my mouth shut—most of the time. By high school, something dawned on me: my mother had no friends, and neither did I. We were wholly dependent upon each other for companionship. We played cards, watched TV movies, gave each other manicures, and baked the cookies, pies, and cakes that I devoured. I lived this way for years, straining between the comfort of insulating myself from the world, yet yearning for its gifts—even gifts that might bring pain. My mother guarded against the dangers I set in motion through my misguided desire to create something more. "Don't count your chickens, missy." "You can't win for losing." "Pride comes before a fall." The words hit with a thud. *She doesn't mean it, She doesn't mean it,* I whispered to myself over and over. I knew she didn't want me to get my hopes up, because that way I couldn't feel the burn of disappointment, the pain of loss. Her motivations were good, yet I hated her for those words and the thousands just like them, for instilling her doubts as my doubts, for making her fear my fear. Still, I counted no chickens, stayed out of the game, abandoned all aspirations for pride.

❖ ❖ ❖

"I have to go to the bathroom," my mother announces.

This takes a long time. I help her sit up fully in bed, and we pause for a minute so she doesn't get too dizzy. Then, slowly, carefully, she puts her weight on the floor one foot at a time. She inches forward with her walker, me shuffling behind, grabbing at the air around her, thinking I can catch her if she falls.

At the toilet, she shifts her grasp from the walker, to me, to metal bars bolted to the walls. Her arms occupied, she looks at me and without a word I know to pull the white cotton underwear down her stick-like thighs, past her knees, all the way to her ankles. I try not to stare at the shriveled folds of thin skin covering her belly or the fireworks display of varicose veins creeping up her calves. Even with the photos in mind, it's hard to think of my mother as once having been young. So close to the body in which I grew, a body used and failing, I feel an awkward intimacy that makes me shy. I had shared that body, then clutched that belly and clung to those thighs. I step back to give her privacy and catch my reflection in the mirror. I will never be called beautiful, but sometimes when I glimpse my crooked nose, I pretend that I am. That nose is my mother's. It's the feature that tells the world I am her daughter. It's also the feature that once prompted my ex-husband to ask, had I ever broken my nose? I wondered now what my mother saw when she looked at me and if she ever searched my face and saw herself. Or did the person I had become, broken and biting, make that impossible?

❖ ❖ ❖

We get her back into bed and she blows out another sigh.

"Kate?"

"Yes?"

"What is HD?"

"What is what?"

"HD! HD! What is it?" She is half screaming again, her voice pitched with irritation at my thick-witted response to a simple question. She seems to catch herself and asks again, softly this time, "What is it?"

I pause before answering, still uncertain. "It stands for High Definition. It's a TV broadcasting system. It's supposed to make the picture more clear."

"Oh." She settles back into the pillow and inhales deeply from the oxygen tube.

❖ ❖ ❖

A week earlier, my mother's head turned on that pillow, and she looked at me, the lines of her face seeming to etch more deeply under the weak overhead light.

"I'm scared," she whispered, and she didn't have to say of what.

I want to save her from past and present both, erase her fear for good, but I don't know how. I want to go back in time and give her a new life, one without fear that the floor beneath her will collapse, fear that, in her case, may have been justified. It seems important now to finally understand the roots of the terror that had shadowed her for a lifetime, the doubt that made her search for the worst until she found it everywhere, the apprehension she had passed to me like a birthright. But in all my life, I never discovered more about her than bits and pieces. The first thing I had learned was that she couldn't swim.

"Really?" I had laughed at her. I thought she was joking, then realized by the shamed look on her face that she was telling the truth. But how could that be? Who didn't know how to swim? Next, I learned she couldn't ride a bike either. And then there was the matter of her teeth. I watched her soak the dentures she had worn since before she met my father, her lips curling in on her toothless gums as she scooped the dentures from a fizzy liquid and scrubbed them hard.

"What happened to your real teeth?" I had asked.

She gave me one of her standard shrugs, popped the dentures in place with two clicks, rinsed and spit and said to the bathroom mirror, "I guess they fell out."

As a child, I tried to break her past into manageable chunks, categorize it, force it into a sensible chronology, but I never could. My mother never detailed the excuses she made for her own mother, a woman who dumped her infant daughter at an unsuspecting neighbor's house in 1925 and disappeared, resurfacing five years later, standing on the porch with a new husband and a lipsticked mouth brimming with promises. From the fragments, I gathered that my grandmother liked men and liked to wear them out. She repeated her vanishing act four times before my mother turned thirteen, showing up out of the blue every few years with a new husband on her arm.

"It wasn't her fault," my mother coughed, saying all she would ever say about the worst thing you can do to a child. All evidence to the contrary, my mother swore her childhood was happy. Maybe it was, once she finally gave up waiting for her mother to be a mother.

❖ ❖ ❖

"Kate." Her face tilts toward me on the pillow, her brown eyes flat and empty.

"Yes?"

"Whatever happened to that cute John Kennedy boy? They never talk about him anymore."

There's no easy way to say this, so I just say it. "He's dead, mom. Plane crash. Remember?"

"Oh."

❖ ❖ ❖

Time and her place in it fluctuate now. Back in Assisted Living days, there were events to help mark the passage of time in a sunshine city where seasons are no help. I accompanied her to the Valentine's Day Ice Cream Social, Memorial Day Barbecue, Fourth of July Picnic and in those long months before the holidays, formulated events like Country Western Day, where the more ambulatory residents could line dance to "Achy Breaky Heart." In Assisted Living days, I took her on outings. We went to the mall with her walker and portable oxygen tank for sales at J.C. Penney and lettuce wraps at P.F. Chang's. We went to the yarn store, sometimes out for Sunday breakfast. Our roles had reversed completely by then, with me strapping her in under a seatbelt that her own hands were too shaky to operate, cautioning her to watch

her fingers as I closed the passenger door and walked around to climb into the driver's seat.

My mother did not get the newspaper during the week, only Sundays. On one of our breakfast mornings, I fed a machine quarters and carried the heavy lump of newsprint back to our table. I slurped my coffee and watched my mother flip through the sections.

"What's new in the world?" I had been on a self-imposed news detox then, shielding myself, living by the creed that ignorance really was bliss.

"Oh, I don't know." She paused and her brown eyes rolled up to look at me from a face bowed in a familiar pose of shame. "I don't read the news."

I gave her a dubious smile. "Then what do you read?"

"I read the obituaries, sometimes the anniversary notices." Her shoulders gave a tiny shrug. "I just like to read about people and the lives they had together."

My throat tightened, and I busied myself with the laminated menu, pretending to be intrigued by so many choices. I wondered what my mother thought about her own life. What would she change? What moments would she live over and over again? Did she wonder at how even through all the pain, it had still been beautiful and gone by so fast? What would she want the paper to say about her life, for the world to read about over breakfast with their daughters? Tears burned my eyes as I thought about how empty her life would sound, eighty-four years of living crushed into a two-inch column. No one reading it would understand what her life had been. That would be left up to me alone. But even I didn't know a goddam thing.

Before my nose formed the lopsided bump of physical proof, I had tortured myself with conspiracy theories. In 1964, the year I was born, no one had babies past the age of forty. My parents had been married sixteen years before I came along, and yet I had no siblings. Something had to be off, I was sure of it.

"Am I really your daughter?" I asked my mother when I was twelve, as I leaned over the kitchen counter that still held the faded stain of her blood.

My mother had looked into my face and smiled, a real smile, and her voice almost purred, filled with a fleeting wholeness, as she reached out to stroke my cheek. "You're all mine, baby girl. All mine."

❖ ❖ ❖

But if I am yours, then you are mine. What happens when you are gone?

Science Dork? Science Dork, I lived inside her shell. What is the name of the strands that attached me to her? I floated warm and happy inside a womb percolating with anxiety, then she labored to push me out into a world I learned to fight and fear. I was once inside her, but now she's inside me.

❖ ❖ ❖

"Kate?" My mother's voice is a croak.

I lean over her. "Yes?"

"Turn off the TV."

I click the remote and the picture dissolves. In the darkness of the screen, my reflection appears, filmy and ghostlike, but I can still make out our nose. The silence bears down like a weight on my chest, like it is my lungs that are failing.

"Mom?" I whisper.

But she is already asleep.

❖ ❖ ❖

William Miller

A Suicide at Gettysburg

The man who shot himself,
 on a slope of the battlefield,
had no name.

It was night; the park
was closed, except for
three tourists looking
for ghosts.

They found the body
in the rocky grass,
their flashlight
pinning it there.

And the gun still
pointed at his chest,
a blue-black pistol
in his right hand.

The rangers came,
the police with questions
for a dead man
sunk into himself.

But he didn't speak,
tell why he stumbled
through the dark
for this piece
of broken ground.

Puzzled, they lifted
him from shadows,
like a soldier
where others died,
his face and lonely war
unknown.

Scott Roberts. *Low-Poly Chili. 2003.* Digital print sculpture. 17 x 11 x 21 inches. Courtesy of the artist.

Dog Days

The Chihuahua, perched six inches behind the property line, had been yapping, every three seconds, for the past half hour. My wife and I were finishing our Sunday brunch on the deck. From behind her big sunglasses she muttered, "How do you say shut the fuck up in Spanish?"

Our new neighbor is a young Hispanic woman who does the weather for a local TV station. "*Silencio,*" I said. "More or less."

"*Silencio!*" she shouted, more or less toward the dog.

But instead of retreating, it crossed the line and stood next to our garden shed. "Her electric fence isn't working," I explained. "The battery on the receiving collar must be dead."

The tiny dog kept barking, thirty feet from us. It couldn't have been bigger than a good-sized squirrel.

"*Silencio,* you son of a bitch!"

"I think it's a female dog," I said.

That was a mistake. A big mistake. "How would you know?" My wife took off her sunglasses, glared at me, and slipped her bare feet into her Crocs. Then she limped across the back lawn and turned on the spigot to the garden hose that she uses to water her perennial beds.

"Bitch of a bitch!" she screamed, and, with the full force of the water, pinned the dog to the side of the shed. When it fell onto its back, she came closer with the nozzle and zeroed in on its nose. "Bitch of a bitch!"

Now she adjusted the nozzle to Jet Stream and started pushing the little dog back toward the property line, still aiming toward its head. She didn't have to touch it, not even with her waterproof sandals. When she got it past the red training flags for the electric fence, she finally turned off the hose. The dog wasn't moving.

"The premises are secure," she smiled, baring the dentures she's worn ever since her teeth were knocked out and her knees broken, in our own home. Our former home. Then she returned our dishes and silverware to the bamboo serving tray and brought them back into the house we've been living in for the past ten years.

The dog still wasn't moving. But when I raised my eyes to our neighbor's master bedroom, I could have sworn the curtains parted. Of course, that was impossible, since our neighbor lived alone and she'd been double-shifting on Weekend Weather after her new job in Atlanta didn't work out last year, after she'd slunk back to her old one in South Carolina. Her salary couldn't amount to much, especially now. I wondered how she'd been able to buy into Belladonna, even one of the patio homes. When she'd introduced herself to the neighborhood at the poolside picnic on the Fourth of July, she'd said she'd gotten a Chihuahua for protection. They were *pequeñas*, but they were good watch dogs. She'd used the feminine adjective, *pequeñas*, while she'd laughed and tossed back her long, glossy hair. Nobody had said anything. I remembered thinking she was the kind of woman who makes grown men speechless and grown wives just as speechless, but for a very different reason. Then I saw those rippling curtains again, across her sliding glass door, and I figured the air conditioning must be coming up through her floor vent.

❖ ❖ ❖

I was hoping the whole afternoon that the dog was just unconscious. That it would get up and trot, or at least stagger, back to its miniature igloo beneath the pyracantha. But it didn't.

We'd had a pet once, right after we'd moved to Belladonna—an orange tabby named Peaches. During the winter it liked to snuggle up with me, right between my chin and the fringe of the comforter. One night, after my wife had gotten up to use the bathroom, it nested on her pillow before she could get back to bed. So she picked up the pillow, cat and all, and put it into the laundry room, inside the dryer. She didn't turn on the machine, of course, but she'd latched the metal door, just to teach it a good lesson.

When she came back in the morning, the cat had made a mess of everything. Number One and Number Two. I didn't know any of this at the time. I'd slept through the night, and I'd left for my office while it was still dark outside. I figured Peaches had gone out through the cat door. But when I got home that evening, my head spinning from corporate tax returns, my wife told me about the dryer and the cat. After I wondered aloud where Peaches was hiding, she said, "Peaches is no longer with us." I hoped she'd just taken her to the animal shelter, but I didn't ask for details. It was only a couple of months after her own accident, and I'd already figured out that Martha now regarded her own domestic tranquility as a divine right, or at least a minor form of divine justice.

But when I heard our neighbor's automatic garage door opening, I thought I owed the woman an explanation. I found an old blanket in the bedroom closet, went into the back yard, and wrapped up the dog. It was so little, so *pequeña*, that my arms could hardly tell the difference in weight. Then I brought it around to the front of her house, where I was planning to ring the doorbell. But instead I found my neighbor in a midriff-knotted blouse and denim cutoffs, getting ready to wash her Mini-Cooper in her driveway. The car must've been in her garage all day long.

I didn't know what to say, so I handed her her dog. Despite my wife, it didn't even look bruised. "I'm sorry," I finally stammered. "I found her outside. I'm sorry." That, I thought, was just true enough. As a tax accountant, I'm well aware of the difference between avoidance and evasion.

She put the dog down inside the garage, picked a few blades of grass out of its front paws, and covered its muzzle with the blanket. Then she went back outside to pick up her hose. I almost ducked, but I caught myself in time. She smiled her TV smile at me and said, "You are good to bring her home."

Although the woman didn't seem to have an accent on WFOP, she sounded different in person. More ethnic. "It was no trouble."

"Your wife, she is the only one Maria would bark at. *Otro lado*."

The other side. I took three years of Spanish in high school.

"Dogs, they know."

I was afraid to ask her what they knew, so I merely nodded.

"But she was only a dog," the woman continued. "I can get another."

"I can pay—"

She shook her head and picked up a big sponge, squeezing its suds over the hood of her Mini-Cooper. "It must be hard. It must be very hard." She shrugged her dark hair behind her shoulders, so it wouldn't get wet while she leaned over. "Living with that *loca*." I watched her hips move, behind her denim cutoffs, while I listened to the squish and squeak of the sponge. I couldn't help myself.

❖ ❖ ❖

Loca. She hadn't always been *loca*.

We'd married late, and we both had plenty of money, and we both loved to garden. So we bought a big house, a McMansion built long before they called them McMansions, with three acres of land for us to play with. Out in the middle of nowhere. We landscaped the hell out of that place—me with my lawn tractors and line trimmers, Martha with her tea roses and giant peonies and more annuals than I could name, or even count. We had underground irrigation, fieldstone terraces. A poolside cabana. For protection, I installed a security system, and I bought a gun. Our nearest neighbors were more than half a mile away.

One night, near the April 15 deadline, I was working late. Too late. By the time I got home from my office, the cop cars had turned our circular driveway into a light show, and Martha was already on her way the hospital.

She'd given up on me and gone to bed, and she'd forgotten to set the alarm system, which was usually my job. When she'd heard the commotion downstairs—and the women's voices—she'd grabbed my gun and called the county police.

That's when one of them came into the bedroom, while she was still on the phone, and blinded her with a flashlight. Martha pointed the gun, and tried to pull the trigger.

Nothing happened. The safety was still on.

Martha doesn't remember much after that. Only the nylon stocking over the burglar's face, only the gun being pulled out of her fingers. And the laugh—a woman's laugh—as the flashlight beat down on her own face, again and again and again. Her knees must have come later.

The burglars figured the cops were on their way, so they didn't have time to grab much. Just the jewelry in plain sight, including the big diamond solitaire and the wedding band on Martha's fingers. And the gun.

We never got anything back—although the insurance covered all of it, of course—and I never bought another gun. While Martha was still in the hospital, I put the house up for sale because I couldn't bear to take her back there. I never wanted her alone in that place again. Hell, I didn't want to be alone in that place again. Anywhere else, I told her. Anywhere else. Her choice. So we moved to Belladonna, the safest gated community on the planet, or at least in Greenville County, South Carolina. I wouldn't need my tractors anymore, so I sold them along with the house. But we'd still have a quarter-acre for Martha to putter around in, once she was back on her feet.

❖ ❖ ❖

August came and went. It's a slow month for me, so I do a lot of swimming. It keeps me in pretty good shape for a guy who's pushing fifty. On Labor Day, on my way to Belladonna's community pool, I met our neighbor, going in the opposite direction. Barefoot, in a bikini, she was walking a little dog that looked identical to her old one.

"Where is your wife?"

Even before her accident, Martha wouldn't be caught dead in a bathing suit. "She doesn't swim," I said.

"*Yo tambien*. Not today."

"They're pretty strict about the rules around here," I said. "You can't bring pets to the pool." I bent my knees to scratch behind the dog's ears. "Even this wittle baby. What's your name, wittle baby?"

She jerked the dog's choke collar, lifting its four feet clear from the sidewalk. It looked like it was treading water, twisting and whimpering, trying to get back to my extended hand. "She will be just like my first Maria." When I backed away, the woman returned the dog to the ground, to the same spot where I'd been scratching it. "*Pequeña*. But fierce."

❖ ❖ ❖

When I returned home, after twenty laps in the big pool, Martha was sobbing in the sunroom. She was still in her gardening clothes. Speechless, she led me to the answering machine and played the message she'd found after she'd finished dead-heading her flowers.

Someone was thanking me. Thanking me for making her feel alive. For feeling her pain. For making her feel like a woman. "Who is it?" Martha finally said. "Who is it?"

What could I say? I'd just walked down the street in my bathing trunks. "Martha, just take a deep breath, okay? You can smell the chlorine." I hugged her, to make my point. Her sobbing slowed down to a teary moan.

"Who is it, for God's sake?"

"I don't know, Martha." My chin was perched on her trembling shoulder, and I looked out the sunroom window into the back yard. "I don't know." And I didn't know. But I had a pretty damn good idea.

❖ ❖ ❖

That September, whenever I was late from work, there'd be a call. If Martha answered, the phone would go dead. But if she let it ring, there'd be a message, for me, for Clayton, always similar, but never the same. Thanking me, hinting at intimacy but never saying anything specific about times, or places, or means of gratification. I tried not to be late, but in my business that's not easy. Clients will walk in at quarter to five, on their own way home from work, with letters from their investment brokers or the IRS, and they'll want their answers right away. They're worried. We're in the middle of The Great Recession. You can't blame them.

We thought about disconnecting the machine, or changing the number, but clients call me at home, too. We reprogrammed the message with Martha's voice instead of my own, but it didn't make any difference. The woman kept calling.

One Saturday evening, I was watching Notre Dame football on TV when Martha came home from the supermarket, from her weekly shop. "How could you, Clayton!" she screamed. "How could you?" She was holding the blanket that I'd used when I'd taken back the first Chihuahua. That's when I remembered it was the one we'd used for picnics, before we were married.

"That's it," I said. I didn't even bother to grab a coat, even though it was damn close to freezing, and I ran straight over to our neighbor's house. When I rang the bell, the new dog started barking. It wouldn't stop, and I wouldn't stop. After five minutes, the woman finally answered the door, and I walked inside.

No furniture anywhere, a bare room with nothing but drapes.

"I hope you're moving out," I said. "That would be a good idea."

"You've been talking with your *loca*," she said. She was holding the dog in her arms, against her red bathrobe. "It shows."

"What did you tell her?"

"*La verdad*," she said. "That is about to happen." She tossed the dog, underhand, in my direction. Without thinking, I caught it, then lowered it to the hardwood floor. It seemed unsurprised, as if it had been rehearsing for this all afternoon, and even licked my hand. When the dog followed the woman toward the back of the house, I followed the dog.

We both stopped at the end of the hallway. The woman was standing at her bedroom window, with her robe puddled on the floor behind her. The curtains on the sliding glass door were fully open, and she was facing outside. Toward my house. I could see Martha at our kitchen window, her hand over her mouth.

Now the woman turned off the overhead light, and she walked toward me. "Your *loca* killed my dog." She held her open palms toward me, the red running down from her wrists, then sank to her knees.

I ran for the robe, to get something to stop the bleeding. That's when she turned the light back on, and I looked at Martha, and then at my own two hands.

❖ ❖ ❖

She hadn't slashed her wrists. She'd used nail polish, which I hadn't seen in the living room, since the robe was red and had oversized sleeves. She laughed when I bent over to help her, and she even kissed her lipstick onto the front of my shirt.

"What the hell are you, anyway?" I said.

"A *loca*. Just like your wife." Now she broke into Broadcaster's English. "But I can speak Anglo for you, Clayton. I'll just pretend my nose is in my mouth. Do you like that better?"

I wasn't looking at her nose, or her mouth. Her breasts were poised and perfect, staring straight at me. She was still naked, the most beautiful woman I'd ever seen that way. In the flesh. I was still holding her robe. So I wrapped up the dog, and I walked, backwards, very slowly, back down the hallway.

"Take it home!" she shouted. "For your *loca*!"

And I would. I'd tell Martha I'd rescued it. I'd explain everything. I'd show her the nail polish that had passed for blood in that dark hallway, nail polish that she could peel with her own fingers off the nubs of that terrycloth robe. I'd tell her we'd keep the dog, and we'd name it together, and we'd build a fence, a real one, out back, and when she asked me how high, I'd tell her, "Whatever it takes." She'd believe me. I knew she'd believe me. We've been through worse than this. But just to be sure, I took the little dog's rear end and rubbed it into that red blotch on my shirt, until it was the dull, ugly color of the truth.

❖ ❖ ❖

Notes on Contributors

Lavonne J. Adams is the author of *Through the Glorieta Pass* (Pearl Editions, 2009), and two award-winning chapbooks, *In the Shadow of the Mountain* and *Everyday Still Life*. Her work appears in journals including *Prairie Schooner, Missouri Review, Cincinati Review,* and *Crab Orchard Review*. She has completed residencies at the Vermont Studio Center; the Helene Wurlitzer Foundation, Taos; and the Harwood Museum of Art, University of New Mexico-Taos. She teaches at the University of North Carolina Wilmington.

Gilbert Allen is the Bennette E. Geer Professor of Literature at Furman University. He is the author of five collections of verse, including *Driving to Distraction*, which was featured on Garrison Keillor's *The Writer's Almanac*. He received the 2007 Robert Penn Warren Prize in Poetry from *The Southern Review*. Some of his newest poems and stories have appeared in *Able Muse, Measure, Sewanee Theological Review, Shenandoah,* and *The Southern Review*. He lives in South Carolina, on the western slope of Paris Mountain, with his wife, Barbara.

Sheri Allen's poetry has previously appeared in *Best New Poets 2010, Birmingham Poetry Review, Boulevard, Poetry Southeast,* and *The Sagarin Review*. "From the Capitol" is from her first full-length manuscript, *American Alefbeit*, a collection organized around a series of poems about Hebrew letters. Sheri has also published short fiction in *Image* and translated several medieval and renaissance-era poems from Hebrew to contemporary English, one of which has been published in *Subtropics*. She received her MA from Washington University in St. Louis, her MFA from the University of Florida, and is currently a PhD candidate at the University of Cincinnati.

Cynthia Atkins is the author of *Psyche's Weathers*. Her second collection of poems, *In the Event of Full Disclosure*, is forthcoming in July 2013 from WordTech. Her poems have recently appeared or are forthcoming in *Alaska Quarterly Review, Del Sol Review, Harpur Palate, Hawaii Review, In Other Words, Inertia, The Journal, North American Review,* and *Thema*. She lives on the Maury River in Rockbridge County, Virginia, with her family.

Robert Bense is the author of a collection of poems, *Readings in Ordinary Time*, published by The Backwaters Press. His poems recently appeared in *The Sewanee Review* and *Salmagundi*.

Lorna Knowles Blake's first collection of poems, *Permanent Address*, won the Richard Snyder Memorial Prize from the Ashland Poetry Press. Poems have appeared recently or are forthcoming in *The Hudson Review, Literary Imagination, The Raintown Review,* and *Tampa Review*. She has been the recipient of a residency from the Virginia Center for the Creative Arts and a Walter E. Dakin Fellowship from the Sewanee Writers Conference. Currently she teaches creative writing at the 92nd Street Y and serves on the editorial board of *Barrow Street*. She lives in New York City, New Orleans and Cape Cod.

Paul Crenshaw has received the Thomas H. Carter Prize in Nonfiction from *Shenandoah*, the Editor's Prize from *Southern Humanities Review*, and a 2011 North Carolina Arts Council Fellowship in Fiction Writing. His stories and essays have appeared or are forthcoming in *Best American Essays* (2005 and 2011), *Shenandoah, North American Review,* and *Southern Humanities Review*, among others. "Essay in Five Photographs" is one of a collection of essays about the author's time in the military.

Jessica Cuello teaches French in Central New York. Her first chapbook, *Curie*, a biographic poem cycle about scientist Marie Curie, came out in 2011 from Kattywompus Press. Her poems have appeared in *Copper Nickel, RHINO, The Dos Passos Review, Conte, Harpur Palate,* and other journals. She won the 2010 Vivienne Haigh-Wood Poetry Prize and recently received a "Best of the Net 2010" nomination.

Ron De Maris has work forthcoming in a number of journals, including *Paris Review, Southern Review, Atlanta Review,* and *Ploughshares*, and his poems have previously appeared in publications like *Poetry, The New Republic, The Nation, Southern Review, Salmagundi,* and *Tampa Review*. His new manuscript, *36 Elegant Diversions*, is looking for a publisher.

Taylor Deupree is a sound artist, graphic designer, and photographer residing in New York. In 1997, he founded 12k, a small record label respected worldwide that focuses on minimalism and contemporary electronic and acoustic hybrids. Deupree has been working as a freelance graphic designer in New York for sixteen years. His photography and design can be seen on hundreds of CD covers and have been featured in international design publications from the U.S., U.K., and Japan. His work is pervaded by themes of minimalism, stillness, atmosphere, nature, imperfection, and an intense passion for the working process.

James Doyle was born in New York City and grew up in the Bronx. He is the author of *Einstein Considers a Sand Dune* (2004), winner of the 2003 Steel Toe Books Poetry Prize, and *Bending Under the Yellow Police Tapes* (2007). His poems have been published in *Chelsea, Green Mountains Review, Iowa Review, Massachusetts Review, Poetry, Prairie Schooner, Tampa Review,* and *Puerto del Sol* and featured by Ted Kooser in his "American Life in Poetry" column. He lives in Fort Collins, Colorado, with this wife, poet Sharon Doyle.

Kerry James Evans is the author of *Bangalore* (Copper Canyon, 2013). His poems appear in *Agni, Narrative, New England Review, Ploughshares,* and elsewhere. He lives in Tallahassee and is currently a PhD candidate in Creative Writing at Florida State University.

Jen Fawkes holds a BA from Columbia University, an MFA from Hollins University, and will soon enter the doctoral program in fiction writing at the University of Cincinnati. Her work has appeared or is forthcoming in *Michigan Quarterly Review, The Massachusetts Review, Mid-American Review, Shenandoah, The Southeast Review,* and other journals, and has been nominated for a Pushcart Prize.

Gary Fincke won the Stephen F. Austin Poetry Prize for his latest book, *The History of Permanence*, published in 2011. His memoir, *The Canals of Mars*, was published by Michigan State in 2010. His next book will be a collection of short stories, *The Proper Names for Sin*, from West Virginia University Press. He is the Charles Degenstein Professor of Creative Writing at Susquehanna University.

Terri Garland is an artist who specializes in photographing the social fabric of the American South. As a graduate student at the San Francisco Art Institute, Garland began an examination of white supremacist culture that has spanned over two decades, photographing individuals within the Ku Klux Klan, Aryan Nations, American Nazi Party, and the Christian Identity Movement. Since 2005, she has divided her time between Louisiana and Mississippi. Her photographs are included in the collections of The Center for Creative

Photography in Tucson, Arizona; The Art Institute of Chicago; The di Rosa Preserve in Napa, California; The Cleveland Museum of Art; Saint Elizabeth College in Morristown, New Jersey; the Bibliothèque Nationale, Paris; and Special Collections at the University of California at Santa Cruz. Among her awards are a WESTAF/NEA Fellowship, Silicon Valley Arts Council Grant, and a Rydell Visual Arts Fellowship. She teaches photography at San José City College.

Chris Gavaler earned an MFA from the University of Virginia and teaches at Washington & Lee University in Lexington, Virginia. His novel *School for Tricksters* was published by Southern Methodist University Press (2011). His short fiction appears in over two dozen national journals, including *Prairie Schooner, Shenandoah, Hudson Review,* and *Best American Fantasy.*

Dan Graham lives and works in New York City. He has had retrospective exhibitions at The Museum of Contemporary Art, Los Angeles (2009), The Renaissance Society, University of Chicago (1981); Kunsthalle Berne (1983); the Art Gallery of Western Australia, Perth (1985), Van Abbemuseum, Eindhoven (1993); and Museum of Modern Art, Oxford (1997). In 2001, a major retrospective, "Dan Graham, Works 1965-2000," opened at the Museu Serralves, Porto, Portugal, and traveled to the ARC/Musée d'Art Moderne de la Ville de Paris in Paris; the Kröller-Müller Museum, Otterlo; and the Kunsthalle Düsseldorf. His work is in major collections throughout the world, including the Museum of Modern Art, New York; Chicago Art Institute; Tate Gallery, London; Gallery Shimada, Tokyo; Musée National d'Art Moderne, Centre Georges Pompidou, Paris; Tel Aviv Museum of Art, Israel; Arken Museum of Modern Art, Ishoj, Denmark; Moderna Museet, Stockholm, Sweden; and many others.

Juliana Gray's second poetry collection, *Roleplay*, was the winner of the 2010 Orphic Prize, and is forthcoming from Dream Horse Press. Recent poems have appeared in or are forthcoming from *Barrow Street, Measure, 32 Poems, Waccamaw,* and elsewhere. An Alabama native, she lives in western New York and is an associate professor of English at Alfred University.

Roger Hart lives in Storm Lake, Iowa, with his wife, Gwen. His stories and essays have appeared in *Inkwell, Natural Bridge, Passages North, Runner's World* and other literary magazines. His story collection, *Erratics,* won the George Garrett contest and was published by Texas Review Press. When he's not writing, he's riding his bike, playing the sax, or walking his hundred and fifty pound Newfoundland, Buster.

Rebecca L. Huntman is a writer, photographer, visual artist, Latin dancer, choreographer, and teacher. She is the founding director of Chicago's award-winning Danza Viva Center for World Dance, Art & Music, and One World Dance Theater; her producing credits include Dance Chicago's *Dance Everywhere* series, *What Moves You?* and *Deep Draw,* all performed at Chicago's Athenaeum Theatre. Her work in the arts has been featured in *Latina Magazine, Chicago Magazine,* the *Chicago Tribune,* Metromix the TV show, Fox News, ABC News, Borders Books, Transitions Bookplace, and the Chicago Women's Entrepreneurial Conference. She is the recipient of grants and awards from the Illinois and Oak Park Area Arts Councils. Rebecca studied journalism, creative writing, history and art at Northwestern University and the School of the Art Institute of Chicago, and received a master's degree from Columbia College. She has recently joined the MFA program in creative writing at the Ohio State University in Columbus, Ohio.

Steven Husby is an artist who lives and works in Chicago. He received his MFA from the School of the Art Institute of Chicago. Recent solo exhibitions include "RUBICON" at

Julius Caesar Gallery, Chicago, and "we speak the way we breathe" at Peregrine Program, Chicago. His work can be seen online at stevenhusby.com.

Julie Iromuanya is Assistant Professor at Northeastern Illinois University. Her short stories and novel excerpts appear in *The Kenyon Review, Passages North, KRO: Kenyon Review Online,* and the *Cream City Review,* among other journals. She was a finalist for the *Glimmer Train* Family Matters and Very Short Fiction prizes, and the *Kenyon Review* Short Fiction Contest. A scholarly essay appears in *Charles Chesnutt Reappraised* and another is forthcoming in *Converging Identities.* Iromuanya earned her PhD at the University of Nebraska-Lincoln and was the inaugural Herbert W. Martin Fellow at the University of Dayton. "Only in America" is an excerpt of her novel manuscript, *Mr. and Mrs. Doctor.*

Valerie Jaudon was born in Greenville, Mississippi, and studied at the Mississippi University for Women, Columbus; Memphis Academy of Art, Tennessee; University of the Americas, Mexico City; and St. Martins School of Art, London. She has exhibited her work nationally and internationally since the mid-1970s, becoming influential in the development of Post-minimal Abstraction and in the Pattern and Decoration movement. Her work is found in numerous private and public collections in the United States and Europe, including the Albright-Knox Art Gallery, Buffalo, New York; the Fogg Art Museum, Cambridge, Massachusetts; the Hirshhorn Museum and Sculpture Garden, Washington D.C.; the Indiana University Art Museum, Bloomington; the Ludwig Museum, Aachen, Germany; the Ludwig Museum, Budapest; the Mississippi Museum of Art, Jackson; the Museum of Modern Art, New York; the Museum Moderner Kunst Stiftung Ludwig, Vienna, Austria; the Museu de Arte Moderna, Lisbon; the National Museum of Women in the Arts, Washington, D.C.; the Stadel Museum, Frankfurt; the St. Louis Art Museum, Missouri; and the Whitney Museum of American Art. In 2011 she was elected to membership in the National Academy of Design. She is Professor of Art at Hunter College.

Stephen Kampa received the 2011 Florida Book Awards' Gold Medal in poetry for his first collection, *Cracks in the Invisible.* He works as a musician in Daytona Beach, Florida.

Margarite Landry holds an MFA from Vermont College of Fine Arts, and a PhD in Victorian Literature from Columbia University. Her fiction has appeared in *Nimrod, Vermont Literary Review, Pisgah Review, Bellingham Review,* and *Provincetown Arts.* Her novel-in-progress won the James Jones First Novel Fellowship in 2008 and is currently completing a collection of short stories.

Lance Larsen was recently named Poet Laureate of Utah. He is the author of three poetry collections: *Erasable Walls, In All Their Animal Brilliance* (winner of the Tampa Review Prize for Poetry) and *Backyard Alchemy,* both from University of Tampa Press, which will also publish a new collection, *Genius Loci,* in fall of 2012. His poems have appeared in *New York Review of Books, Paris Review, Grand Street, New England Review, Times Literary Supplement, Kenyon Review, New Republic, The Pushcart Book of Poetry: the Best Poems from the First 30 Years,* and elsewhere. In 2005, he co-directed a semester-long study abroad program in London and taught creative nonfiction. A professor of English at BYU, he currently serves as associate chair. Former poetry editor at *Gulf Coast,* he has received grants and awards from The Cultural Arts Council of Houston, the Joseph Campbell Society, the Utah Arts Council, Sewanee, and Writers at Work. He is married to Jacqui Larsen, a painter and mixed-media artist.

Michael Lauchlan poems have been published in many journals, including *New England Review, Virginia Quarterly*

Review, The North American Review, Ninth Letter, Natural Bridge, Innisfree, Crab Creek, The Tower Journal, Nimrod, and *The Cortland Review,* and have been included in *Abandon Automobile* (WSU Press) and in *A Mind Apart* (Oxford). He has recently been awarded the *Consequence* Prize in Poetry.

J. M. Lennon is an award-winning writer, editor, and photographer whose photographic work appears regularly in national and regional publications and is part of the permanent collections of the University of South Florida's Marshall Center and the University of Tampa's Scarfone/Hartley Gallery. "Passo Doble" comes from his ongoing series *On Stage,* which documents live performances of dance, music, theatre, and visual art.

Alex Maclean is a pilot and photographer who has flown his plane over much of the United States documenting the landscape. Trained as an architect, he has portrayed the history and evolution of the land from vast agricultural patterns to city grids. His photographs have been widely exhibited in the U.S., Canada, Eurpoe, and Asia. He is the author of eleven books, including *Up on the Roof: New York's Hidden Skyline Spaces* (Princeton Architectural Press, 2012) and *Over: The American Landscape at the Tipping Point* (Abrams, 2008). Among his many awards are the 2009 CORINE International Book Award, The American Academy of Rome's Prix de Rome in Landscape Architecture, and grants from foundations such as the NEA and Graham Foundation. He maintains a studio and lives in Lincoln, Massachusetts.

Malerie Marder was born in Philadelphia and grew up in Rochester, New York. She received her BA from Bard, where she studied photography with Stephen Shore, and attended Yale's MFA program, winning both the Schickle-Collingwood Prize and the John Ferguson Weir Award. She now lives and works in Los Angeles. Her photographs have appeared in magazines including *Artforum, The New Yorker* and *Purple,* and her work is included in the permanent collections of The Solomon R. Guggenheim Museum, New York; The Metropolitan Museum of Modern Art, New York; The National Gallery of Victoria, Melbourne, Australia; The National Gallery of Art, Washington, D.C., and others. Her first monograph, *Carnal Knowledge,* was published in April 2011 by Violette Editions.

Rebecca McClanahan's tenth book, *The Tribal Knot,* a multi-generatious memoir, will be published by Indiana University Press in 2013. Other books include *The Riddle Song and Other Rememberings* (winner of the Glasgow prize in nonfiction) and *Deep Light: New and Selected Poems.* Her work has appeared in *Best American Essays, Best American Poetry, The Kenyon Review, The Gettysburg Review, The Sun,* and numerous other journals as well as in anthologies published by Norton, Doubleday, Putnam, and Beacon Press. McClanahan teaches in the MFA programs of Queens University and Rainier Writers Workshop.

Peter Meinke has published fifteen books of poetry, seven in the prestigious Pitt Poetry Series, the most recent being *The Contracted World* (2006). He is also the author of two books of short stories, *Unheard Music* (2007), and *The Piano Tuner,* which won the 1986 Flannery O'Connor Award. His latest book is the new and revised edition of *The Shape of Poetry: A Practical Guide to Reading and Writing Poems.* He was appointed as the first Poet Laureate of the City of St. Petersburg, Florida, in 2009.

Travis Mossotti is currently the Poet-in-Residence at the Endangered Wolf Center in St. Louis, Missouri. He was awarded the 2011 May Swenson Poetry Award by contest judge Garrison Keillor for his first collection of poems, *About*

the Dead (USU Press, 2011), and his work has appeared in such places as the *Antioch Review, Prairie Schooner, Southwest Review,* and many others.

Colin Chan Redemer teaches at Saint Mary's College of California, writes whenever and wherever he can find the time, and lives in Oakland, California, in community with his beautiful wife and fellow church members.

Mary Hutchings Reed is the author of a novel, *Courting Kathleen Hannigan* (Ampersand, 2007), based on her experience as one of the first wave of women lawyers to join a large, virtually all-male law firm in Chicago in the mid 1970s. "This Change Not Come from Sky" grows out of the Dalai Llama's actual appearance on the *Today* show in 2010 and the author's imagination. For the past eighteen years, Mary has combined the practice of intellectual property law at Winston & Strawn with writing, and is the author of the musical, *Fairways,* about golf, honest, and love. Her additional novels are represented by April Eberhardt, San Francisco.

Thomas Reiter is the author of *Catchment,* his most recent collection of poems, published in 2009 by LSU Press. His poems have appeared or are forthcoming in *Poetry, The Georgia Review, The Sewanee Review, The Hudson Review, The New England Review, The Southern Review,* and *The Caribbean Writer.* He has received fellowships from the NEA and the New Jersey State Council on the Arts.

Scott Roberts earned a BFA from the Milwaukee Institute of Art and Design and both an MA and MFA from the University of Wisconsin–Madison. His sculptures, video installations and animations have been exhibited internationally, including solo exhibitions in New York City, San Francisco, and Chicago, and screenings in Spike and Mike's Sick and Twisted Animation Festival. He also has over ten years of professional experience in television art direction, post-production, animation and 3D game art, and was the production designer for the independent film *Making Revolution.* He lives in Evanston, Illinois, with his wife, daughter and dog and is an Associate Professor in Animation at DePaul University's School of Cinema & Interactive Media in Chicago, where, along with Josh Jones, he co-founded the Animation program.

Martin Rock is a poet, editor, and educator living in Brooklyn. His poetry appears or is forthcoming in *Black Warrior Review, Conduit, Salamander, Mississippi Review Online,* and others. He edits for *Epiphany, a Literary Journal* and the new online journal, *Loaded Bicycle.*

J. Allyn Rosser's most recent collection of poems is *Foiled Again,* which won the New Criterion Poetry Prize. Her two previous books are *Misery Prefigured* and *Bright Moves.* She has received awards and fellowships from the Guggenheim Foundation, the Poetry Foundation, the Lannan Foundation, and the NEA. She teaches in the creative writing program at Ohio University, where she edits *New Ohio Review.*

Sam Ruddick is a Henfield Prize-winning fiction writer whose work has most recently appeared in the 2012 PEN/O. Henry Prize Winners Anthology. His previous work has appeared in publications including *Glimmer Train, Prairie Fire,* and *The Threepenny Review.* He has just finished his first novel, and hopes that someone will buy it soon.

Martin Sheehan, Assistant Professor of German at Tennessee Tech University, earned his PhD in Germanic Literatures and Languages from the University of Virginia, a program internationally recognized for its contributions to the criticism of German Expressionism. He has written on the dramatic language of Carl Sternheim, translated in the field of musicology, and taught German studies and comparative literature seminars at universities in both Germany and America. His latest manuscript *On Radical Comedy* investigates the social significance and performative boundaries of comedy on television and the German stage.

Ernst Stadler (1883-1914) was a German Expressionist poet, born in Colmar, Alsace-Lorraine, and educated in Strasbourg and Oxford. In 1906 he was awarded a Rhodes Scholarship to study at Magdalen College, Oxford. His early verse was influenced by Stefan George and Charles Péguy, but after 1911, Stadler began developing a different style, and his most important volume of poetry, *Der Aufbruch* (1914), is regarded as a major work of early Expressionism. Stadler was killed in battle in the early months of World War I.

Karen Stefano has had short fiction published in *The South Carolina Review, The Santa Fe Literary Review,* and other journals. Her nonfiction pieces have appeared in *California Lawyer, Georgia REALTOR,* and elsewhere. She is the co-author of *Before Hitting Send: Power Writing Skills for Real Estate Agents,* a how-to business writing guide targeting the unique needs of real estate agents, published in 2011. She is currently at work on a novel.

Marjorie Stelmach received the Marianne Moore Poetry Prize for his first book, *Night Drawings* (Helicon Nine Editions, 1995), and has two other books in print, *A History of Disappearance* (2006) and *Bent upon Light* (2009), both from the University of Tampa Press. Her work has appeared in *Epoch, Gettysburg Review, Image, Kenyon Review Online, Lullwater Review, Mid-American Review, New Letters, New Orleans Review, Notre Dame Review, Poetry Daily, Prairie Schooner, Quiddity, River Styx,* and *Tampa Review.*

Ellen Sullins is the author of the chapbook *Elsewhere,* and is a past winner of the New Millennium Writings Prize for Poetry. Her work has appeared in *South Carolina Review, descant, Nimrod, Calyx,* and *Red Wheelbarrow,* among others. She lives in Tucson, Arizona .

Hanssie Trainor is a professional photographer based in California. She has enjoyed a variety of clients from "glamorous everyday people" to celebrity portraits, fashion photography, and weddings. Her commission to travel to Dallas to photograph Australian actor Daniel Goddard, who is featured on television in *The Young and the Restless,* was commissioned by a fan group, Official Goddard Family of Fans. Her website is <www.hanssietrainorphotography.com>.

Wayne Thiebaud was born at Mesa, Arizona, in 1920. He spent ten years in New York and Hollywood as a cartoonist and ad designer, interrupted by four years serving with the U.S. Army Air Force from 1942 to 1946. He graduated from Sacramento State College in 1951 and began teaching in the Art Department of Sacramento City College where he remained for eight years, after which he joined the University of California, Davis, as professor of art. He is best known for his paintings of production line objects found in diners and cafeterias—including pies, pastries, and scoops. His work is found in major collections around the world, including the Art Institute of Chicago, Hirshhorn Museum, National Gallery of Art, National Gallery of Australia, and the Tate Gallery. Among his many awards is the National Medal of Arts presented by President Clinton in 1994

Scott Treleaven was born in Toronto, studied at York University, Ontario College of Art and Design, and the University of Toronto, and today lives and works in Paris and Toronto. He is a filmmaker, collagist, and multidisciplinary artist. A press release for his 2011 solo exhibition at Invisible-Exports, New York, describes him as "an ardent advocate for the socially transformative power of marginalized cultures (occultism, esoterica, collage, punk aesthetics)." His drawings were included in the popular Mapplethorpe group exhibition, *Night Work,* at Alison Jacques Gallery, London, and the Weatherspoon Art Museum *Art on Paper Biennial,* North Carolina. Other exhibitions of note include: *Male,* Maureen Paley, London (2010); *Cimitero Drawings,* Marc Selwyn Fine Art, Los Angeles (2010); *Silver Make-Up,* The Breeder, Athens (2009); *Where He Was Going,* John Connelley Presents, New York (2008); and the *Biennale de Montreal* (2007). A program of his films was presented at the Museum of Modern Art in New York, and his work has been featured in *Artforum, Frieze, The New York Times,* and *Interview Magazine,* among others

J. Parker Valentine was born in Austin, Texas, and completed her BFA from the University of Texas at Austin and her MFA from the San Francisco Art Institute. Her recent solo shows include Peep-Hole Gallery, Milan, Italy; Supportico Lopez in Berlin, Taka Ishii Gallery in Kyoto, and two solo exhibitions at Lisa Cooley Gallery in New York. Among her many group shows are: *Organic Relationships,* The Center for Cosmic Wonder, Tokyo (2010); *Substance Abuse,* Leo Koenig Inc., New York (2010); *Christopher Orr & J. Parker Valentine & Rezi van Lankveld,* Front Room, Contemporary Arts Museum, St. Louis, Missouri (2009); *If the Dogs are Barking,* Artists Space, New York (2009); and *Creswell Crags,* Lisa Cooley Gallery, New York (2008). She lives and works in New York City and Austin.

Jesse Wallis has had poetry published or forthcoming in *CutBank, Inkwell, Poet Lore, Poetry East, The Southern Review* and *Southwestern American Literature.* He studied art at Syracuse University and the California Institute of the Arts and writing and film at the University of Iowa. After living in Japan for nine years, he returned to his hometown of Phoenix, where he currently works in human resources for a public school district.

Max Warsh received his MFA from the University of Illinois at Chicago in 2004 and has exhibited his work in New York, Los Angeles, and Chicago. He is a co-curator at Regina Rex in New York.

Charles Harper Webb is the recipient of grants from the Whiting and Guggenheim Foundations. His latest book is *Shadow Ball: New & Selected Poems,* published by the University of Pittsburgh Press. *What Things Are Made Of,* also from Pitt, is forthcoming in 2013. Webb teaches in the MFA Program in Creative Writing at California State University, Long Beach.

Will Wells is the author, most recently, of *Unsettled Accounts,* a book of poems that won the 2009 Hollis Summers Poetry Prize and was published in 2010 by Ohio University/Swallow Press. On its basis, he was chosen as a Walter E. Dakin Fellow in Poetry for the 2010 Sewanee Writers' Conference and as 2010 Ohio Poet of the Year. He has previously won an Individual Artist Fellowship from the Ohio Arts Council (1996), an NEA Fellowship, and four fellowships from the NEH, most of which have involved translation of various Italian poets. His previous volume of poems, *Conversing with the Light,* was awarded the 1987 Anhinga Prize and published by Anhinga Press. He is Professor of English at Rhodes State College in Ohio.

William Wright is author of five collections of poetry, most recently *Bledsoe* (Texas Review Press, 2011) and *Night Field Anecdote* (Louisiana Literature Press, 2011). He is Series Editor of the multi-volume *Southern Poetry Anthology* and Founding Editor of *Town Creek Poetry.* His work has appeared in many journals.

❖ ❖ ❖

Announcing the Anita Claire Scharf Awards

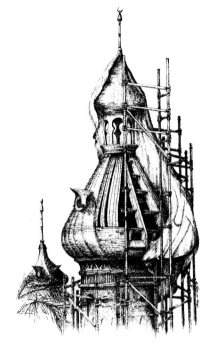

In tribute and recognition of

Anita Claire Scharf

1928-2010

Literary & Artistic Visionary

Founding Editorial Assistant of *Tampa Review*

whose dedicated service, aesthetic judgment,
and creative imagination unveiled new possibilities
for literary publishing at the University of Tampa.

The Anita Claire Scharf Awards will support the mission of *Tampa Review* as a literary journal that celebrates the creative interplay of contemporary literature and visual art, emphasizing links between the Tampa Bay region and the international cultural community. Anita was founding Editorial Assistant of *Tampa Review,* beginning in 1987. She later became Associate Editor and Contributing and Consulting Editor, serving through 2004 and the publication of *Tampa Review* 27. During seventeen years of leadership, she helped define the aesthetic and global values the journal continues to espouse and aspire to today.

THE FIRST ANITA CLAIRE SCHARF AWARD will be given to support publication of a book of poetry submitted to the annual Tampa Review Prize competition that significantly exemplifies the interrelatedness of visual and verbal art and the interconnections of global culture. The first award is presented to

Ira Sukrungruang for *In Thailand It Is Night*

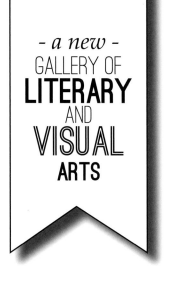

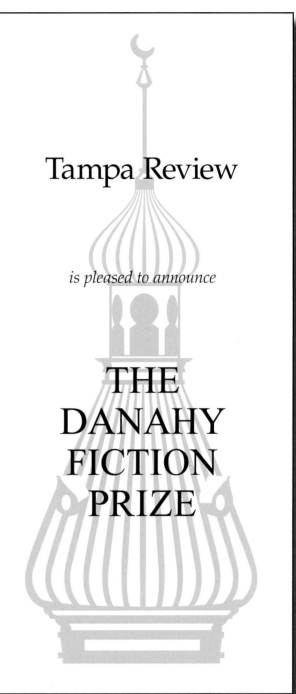

The Danahy Fiction Prize is an award of $1,000 and publication in *Tampa Review* given annually for a previously unpublished work of short fiction. Submissions between 500 and 5,000 words are preferred; manuscripts falling slightly outside this range will also be considered. *Tampa Review* editors will judge, and all entries will be considered for publication.

Manuscripts should be double-spaced and include a cover page with author's name, mailing address, and other contact information, plus a total word count for the manuscript. Enclose a $20 entry fee payable to "Tampa Review." All entrants receive a one-year subscription to *Tampa Review*. Entries must be postmarked by November 1 and mailed to:

Tampa Review
Danahy Fiction Prize
The University of Tampa
401 West Kennedy Blvd.
Tampa, FL 33606-1490

Or submit online at
www.ut.edu/tampareview

Tampa Review

is pleased to announce

THE DANAHY FICTION PRIZE

Congratulations to Mark Krieger
Winner of the 2012 Danahy Fiction Prize

"Scar" by Mark Krieger of West Bend, Wisconsin, has been selected by the editors of *Tampa Review* as winner of the sixth annual Danahy Fiction Prize. His story will appear in the next issue. Entries are invited for next year's award and submissions can now be made online. All contestants receive a one-year subscription to *Tampa Review*.

The Friends of Tampa Review

TAMPA Review gratefully acknowledges
the financial support of the corporate and individual donors
who help make the publication of this magazine possible.

LITERARY BENEFACTORS

Tammis Day
Judge & Mrs. Paul Danahy
Leland M. Hawes Jr.
Tim and Robin Kennedy
Michael and Tiba Mendelsohn

IN MEMORIAM
Michael J. Mendelsohn
1931–2012
Distinguished University Professor
Professor of English Emeritus, 1972–2012

LITERARY PATRONS

Claire and Alan Downes
Dorothy and Lee Hill
Les and Anita Scharf
Jim and Linda Taggart
James R. Wiley
Alexandra Frye

LITERARY SUPPORTERS

Julienne H. Empric
Shelley Manes
Dona Rosu
Laura Tierney
Ellen White
Anonymous